# MURDER ON BANK STREET

**Center Point
Large Print**

# MURDER ON BANK STREET

## *A Gaslight Mystery*

## Victoria Thompson

## CENTER POINT PUBLISHING
## THORNDIKE, MAINE

This Center Point Large Print edition
is published in the year 2009 by arrangement with
The Berkley Publishing Group,
a member of Penguin Group (USA) Inc.

Copyright © 2008 by Victoria Thompson.

All rights reserved.

The text of this Large Print edition is unabridged.
In other aspects, this book
may vary from the original edition.
Printed in the United States of America.
Set in 16-point Times New Roman type.

ISBN: 978-1-60285-568-7

Library of Congress Cataloging-in-Publication Data

Thompson, Victoria (Victoria E.)
  Murder on Bank Street : a gaslight mystery / Victoria Thompson.
    p. cm.
  ISBN 978-1-60285-568-7 (library binding : alk. paper)
1.  Brandt, Sarah (Fictitious character)--Fiction.
  2.  Malloy, Frank (Fictitious character)--Fiction.
  3.  Women detectives--New York (State)--New York--Fiction.
  4.  Midwives--Fiction. 5.  Spouses--Crimes against--Fiction.
  6.  Police--New York (State)--New York--Fiction. 7.  New York (N.Y.)--Fiction.
  8.  Large type books.  I. Title.

PS3570.H6442M866 2009
813'.54--dc22

2009018406

*To my husband, Jim,*
*for always supporting me!*

# Prologue

DANNY DIDN'T LIKE LYING TO THE DOC. Everybody knew he wasn't like the rest of them. Most doctors were drunken bums, at least the ones who'd come into the Lower East Side. They didn't have no pity neither, no matter how sick somebody was. They wouldn't come unless you could pay. They'd want to see the money first, too, before they'd even look to see what was wrong. Like as not, they couldn't help even if you *could* pay them, though, so Danny never did understand why anybody'd send for one in the first place.

Doc Brandt was different, though. He was never drunk, and he'd always come if somebody was in a bad way. Didn't seem to care much if he got paid or not, which was why everybody gave him as much as they could. That was why Danny didn't like lying to him.

"How much farther is it?" Doc Brandt asked. He was panting a little, trying to keep up with Danny. Maybe because he had to carry that big black bag.

"Not far now," Danny replied, not looking the doc in the eye.

Of course, he wasn't really lying. He was just playing a trick on him. That was what the swell had said it was, a trick. He wanted to meet Doc Brandt

7

someplace where nobody'd see them together. That was all, just a private meeting. The swell, the rich fellow with the silk top hat and silver walking stick, he was afraid Doc Brandt wouldn't meet with him, so he'd hired Danny to fetch him. All he wanted to do was talk, though, so what harm could it do?

Danny could live for two weeks on the five dollars the man had paid him, too. Or buy a pair of shoes. With winter coming, he could do with a pair. He'd sure never be able to sell enough newspapers to fund such a purchase. On a good day, he might earn fifty cents, but that was rare, and he had one of the best corners in the city, right beside one of the Sixth Avenue Elevated Train steps. At least half his pay went to the Newsboys' Lodging House for his bed and board, though, and most of the rest went to Nick, the older boy who protected him and let him use that corner to sell his papers. Yeah, when would he ever see five dollars all together again?

"It's just up here a ways," Danny said when they turned the corner.

Doc Brandt was frowning. They'd crossed over into the warehouse district, down by the river. The huge buildings, silent at this time of night, loomed over them, their dark windows like dead, empty eyes. The stench from the water hung thick in the air, and traces of fog swirled around them like a living thing. Nobody lived down here, or at least there weren't any tenements. Street Arabs, the abandoned children like Danny who hadn't come to the lodging houses yet, might find a hidey-hole here, or a drunk who'd lost his way. But nobody who could afford even five cents for a lodging house bed would be in this neighborhood at this hour.

"Are you sure you're not lost?" the doc asked.

"We're almost there," Danny insisted.

The doc sighed, but he followed Danny down the alley.

The alley was wider than most and not completely dark because the gaslight on the corner cast a feeble glow into its opening, but Danny stuck to the middle, where there was less chance of encountering a pile of moldering garbage or a dead cat or even a dead person. Danny heard the doc drawing a breath to question him again, but before he could, another voice broke the silence.

"Hello, Brandt."

The swell was waiting for them, just like he'd said he would be. He struck a match, and in its flickering light, Danny saw that the doc recognized him.

"You," he said. He didn't sound happy to see him, but he didn't sound scared or anything either. It was like the swell had said. They was just going to talk.

"Danny," the other man said. "You can go now. Here's a little something extra for your trouble."

He flipped a coin into the air, and Danny caught it in the instant before the match went out. A silver dollar. He recognized it by the size and weight of it in his hand.

9

Every instinct told him to run, but he hesitated. "Doc, I—" he began, but the swell interrupted him.

"Go on now," he said. He no longer sounded friendly.

"It's all right, Danny," Doc said.

That was all he needed to hear. Danny turned and loped back down the alley until he reached the street. He should've kept going. Wasn't none of his business what the swell wanted with Doc Brandt. He stopped, though. Maybe he was just curious, or maybe . . . Well, no matter. He stopped and listened. Didn't hear anything at first, though. They was just talking, like the swell had said. Just talking, that was all. He started down the street, but then he heard the swell shouting. He stopped dead in his tracks. Wasn't none of his business, but he crept back to the opening of the alley to listen.

Doc was shouting now, too. They was both plenty mad. Danny had heard a lot of angry words in his short life, and he knew what anger sounded like.

"You ruined my daughter!" the swell was saying.

"I was trying to save her!" Doc said back.

More arguing, but he couldn't make out the words. Then one of them, it sounded like Doc, said, "Decker?" like he was surprised.

The swell said something Danny couldn't understand, and then the doc hollered, "No!"

The next sound made Danny wince. He'd heard it a lot of times before, too. The sound of something hard hitting living flesh and bone. Someone was

10

coming down the alley now, moving fast, his shoes slapping against the damp cobblestones. The gaslight illuminated the street, so Danny ducked back into a shadowed doorway just as the man emerged into the street. He looked left and right, checking to see if anyone was around, and Danny held his breath. He wanted it to be the doc. He wanted that mighty bad, but when the man turned and moved past him, near enough that Danny could've reached out and grabbed his sleeve, he saw the flash of gaslight reflected off the silver the man held in his hand. The big silver knob of his cane.

In a few more seconds, the swell was gone, vanished into the shadows. Danny let out his breath in a rush, and then he listened again. He waited for the sound of staggering steps that would tell him Doc was hurt and looking for help. Danny would help him. That was the least he could do. So he waited, but he heard nothing. Nothing at all.

After what seemed an hour, Danny crept back into the alley. "Doc?" he called, but no one answered. All he could hear was the sound of rats scurrying across the cobblestones and water dripping someplace far away. "Doc?" he tried again, and then he saw the darker shadow on the ground that hadn't been there before.

"Doc!" he cried in alarm, but the figure didn't move. Danny knelt down on the filthy cobbles and tried to shake him awake. "Come on, Doc," he pleaded. "Get up. I'll help you!"

No response.

Danny leaned in closer, listening to see if he was breathing, but he heard nothing. He reached out his hand to see if he could feel any breath, and when his fingers touched Doc's face, they came away wet. Wet and warm and sticky, and Danny knew from the smell that it was blood.

"Doc, please," he begged frantically. "I didn't mean it!"

But he knew it was too late. The doc was dead.

# 1

*New York City, 1897*

SARAH BRANDT OPENED HER FRONT DOOR AND stepped inside, grateful beyond words to have arrived home again after a long and exhausting night. As a midwife, she had spent many such nights helping babies into the world. Usually, morning found her instructing the new mother on how to care for her infant, but this morning had been different. The baby had come much too soon and had never even taken a breath. Sarah had spent her time consoling the young parents and assuring them that they had done nothing wrong to cause their child's death. They hadn't believed her. They never did. Parents always blamed themselves, and Sarah had never figured out how to lift that burden of guilt from them.

At least she no longer had to return to an empty house to brood alone after a night like that. Her lips curved into a smile as the sound of running feet echoed through the house. In another instant, Catherine appeared, her small face alight with joy.

"Mama!" she cried as she raced through the front room that Sarah used as her office. Catherine's "cry" was little more than a whisper, but Sarah had to fight the sting of tears. She could not have been happier to hear a choir of angels. The child had been mute when they'd found her abandoned on the steps of the Prodigal Son Mission months ago, but in the safety of Sarah's house and surrounded by people who loved her, she had begun to speak again.

Sarah set down her heavy black bag so she would have both hands free to catch the child when she ran into Sarah's arms. "What have you been doing this morning?" she asked, lifting the girl up until they were eye to eye.

Catherine squinched her face into a comic grimace as she pretended to consider the question. "Cooking," she finally decided to reply. Sarah could have guessed that, since Catherine wore a child-sized apron tied over her gingham dress and had a smudge of flour on her cheek.

"Cooking something delicious," Sarah guessed, sniffing the air appreciatively.

"We're making hot cross buns," Maeve announced as she emerged from the rear of the

13

house at a much more dignified pace than Catherine. Maeve was the girl Sarah had hired to be Catherine's nursemaid. Prior to coming to live with Sarah a few months ago, both girls had resided at the Prodigal Son Mission on the Lower East Side.

"What a nice surprise," Sarah said. "I hope they're ready, because I'm starving."

"Mrs. Ellsworth is getting them out of the oven right now," Maeve reported. "She said you'd probably like to come home to something sweet."

"Mrs. Ellsworth was right," Sarah confirmed happily.

Mrs. Ellsworth was the elderly lady who lived next door. She'd once filled her lonely life with gossip about her neighbors. Now she spent her time teaching Maeve and Catherine the joys of home-making, although she still managed to keep track of her neighbors' comings and goings, too.

Catherine wiggled down, out of Sarah's arms, and grabbed her hand to lead her back to the kitchen. Sarah managed to shrug out of her cape before Catherine had pulled her too far. Maeve took it from her and hung it up as Sarah and Catherine disappeared into the back hall.

"Welcome home, Mrs. Brandt," Mrs. Ellsworth greeted her in the kitchen, wiping her hands on her apron. "You're just in time."

"So I heard," Sarah confirmed, letting Catherine push her into one of the kitchen chairs. "Or rather smelled. Can't remember the last time I had fresh hot cross buns. Oh, coffee! Thank you!" she added in gratitude as Mrs. Ellsworth set a steaming cup in front of her.

For the next few minutes, Sarah ate and exclaimed in delight over the buns while Catherine gazed at her adoringly and Maeve blushed modestly at the praise. "You girls are getting to be such good cooks, maybe we should open a bakery," Sarah suggested as she licked the last of the gooey frosting from her fingers.

"Mrs. Ellsworth says we need to know how to cook so we can catch husbands," Maeve informed her with mock seriousness.

Sarah exchanged a glance with Mrs. Ellsworth, who apparently didn't realize Maeve was teasing. "A man doesn't want a wife who can't keep a house or fix his meals," she agreed.

"Maybe you should be teaching Mrs. Brandt how to cook, then," Maeve said, her eyes gleaming with devilish delight.

"Mrs. Brandt?" Mrs. Ellsworth echoed in surprise.

"Yes, so Mr. Malloy will marry her," Maeve said slyly.

Catherine giggled in delight, and Sarah gasped in feigned outrage.

"Oh, I don't know," Mrs. Ellsworth said, still serious, although Sarah could see now that she was in on the game. "I don't think Mr. Malloy cares whether she can cook or not."

This time Sarah's gasp of outrage wasn't feigned,

but all three of her companions burst out laughing at her chagrin.

Sarah howled in mock fury and pretended to lunge at Catherine, who squealed and raced from the room with Maeve at her heels. Sarah took off after them but let them escape, laughing uproariously, up the stairs to the second floor. "I'll get you later!" she called after them, grinning broadly at their shenanigans.

Her smile faded, however, when she thought of the reality of her situation. Frank Malloy was a detective sergeant with the New York City Police Department. Over the course of the past year, they'd worked together to solve several murders, and their relationship had evolved during that time from outright dislike to something more than friendship. How *much* more, Sarah didn't like to consider, because there was little hope that anything permanent could come of it, the girls' teasing notwithstanding.

As she turned to go back to the kitchen, she saw that she had left her medical bag sitting in the hallway. Memories of the night before came flooding back at the sight of it, and the sadness of the baby's loss weighed heavily on her shoulders. Wearily, she went over and picked the bag up. She needed to empty it out to wash the sheets she took with her to deliveries and to replenish her supplies. She carried it over to the desk where she sometimes saw patients.

The desk where her husband, Dr. Tom Brandt, had seen his patients when he was alive.

She set the bag on the desk and looked at it, really looked at it, for the first time in a long time, even though she carried it with her on every call. The leather was starting to show its age, scuffing on the corners. The tarnished brass plate near the handle was engraved with Tom's name. She ran her fingers over the delicate ridges that formed the letters and tried to remember his face.

"Everything all right?" Mrs. Ellsworth asked.

Sarah looked over to where her neighbor stood in the hall doorway. "I guess I'm just tired."

"Difficult night, I expect. I can always tell when things didn't go well. I hope the teasing didn't bother you," she added with a worried frown.

"Oh, no," Sarah lied, opening the bag so she didn't have to meet Mrs. Ellsworth's eye. She pulled out the soiled sheet.

"Here, I'll take that. Come on back and have another cup of coffee." She took the sheet from Sarah's unresisting hands and led her back to the kitchen.

Sarah sat down and allowed herself to be served. Mrs. Ellsworth poured herself some coffee, too, and took a chair opposite her.

"Mr. Malloy is in love with you, you know," Mrs. Ellsworth said after a moment.

Sarah didn't know what to say to that, so she said nothing.

"I think you have feelings for him, too," she tried again.

Sarah bit her lip. "He's Catholic, and I'm not."

"I thought he'd turned his back on his church."

"He's a policeman," Sarah reminded her. She didn't have to add that most people considered the police no better than the criminals they arrested, and in most cases they weren't. Graft and corruption were rampant in the force, and Malloy's hands were far from clean. He simply couldn't be honest in that environment.

"Yes, and he's poor and you're rich, or at least your family is," Mrs. Ellsworth said. "That didn't bother you the first time you married."

"You're right," Sarah agreed, idly stirring her coffee. "I married beneath myself when I married Tom, or at least that's what my family and everyone else thought. But Tom was worth a hundred of those *suitable* young men my mother wanted me to choose."

"So is Mr. Malloy."

Sarah sighed. "Did you know he's trying to find out who killed my husband?"

"Mr. Malloy is? After all this time?" Mrs. Ellsworth exclaimed in surprise. "How long has it been now, three years?"

"A little more than four."

"Good gracious! How does he expect to solve that murder now when they couldn't do it back then?"

"Apparently, no one even tried to solve it back then," Sarah said, the frustration of it welling up, as if it had happened just yesterday. "My father should have offered a reward, but he didn't, so no one cared about finding the killer." Their association with Malloy had taught them much about the police. No one on the force bothered to investigate a crime unless a "reward" was offered. Everyone understood the reward was simply a bribe paid to get good service.

"Wouldn't your father have known that?" Mrs. Ellsworth asked.

Sarah had wondered herself. "Maybe he did. Maybe he just didn't want Tom's murder solved."

"I don't believe it. Why wouldn't he?"

"My father doesn't like scandal. His daughters had already brought him enough of it. Perhaps he thought it best to let Tom rest in peace."

"But Mr. Malloy doesn't think so."

"No," Sarah said. "He wants justice."

"He wants justice for you," Mrs. Ellsworth guessed. "Do you want it, too?"

Sarah stirred her coffee again. "I want the man who killed Tom to be punished, but that won't bring justice. Tom will still be dead."

This time Mrs. Ellsworth sighed. "That's too true. But how can he hope to find the killer now? Where would he even start to look?"

"He's been investigating," Sarah explained. "He found some new information that made him think

Tom was killed because of one of his patients."

"One of his patients? Why would someone kill him for being a doctor?"

"People get angry at doctors all the time," Sarah reminded her. "Many people die no matter how hard the doctor tries to save them. It happens every day."

"Does Mr. Malloy think Dr. Brandt was killed because he let someone die?"

"Oddly enough, no, it's not that at all. Actually, he thinks someone killed Tom because one of his patients fell in love with him."

"*What?*" Mrs. Ellsworth exclaimed in outrage. "Why would that make somebody want to kill him?"

"I know, it doesn't make sense, but Malloy has found some information that makes him think it's possible. He still may not be able to find Tom's killer, but he's determined to try."

"Of course he is," Mrs. Ellsworth said. "I think that man would walk through fire for you."

Sarah was very much afraid she was right.

"I know your parents wouldn't approve of Mr. Malloy," Mrs. Ellsworth was saying, "but you didn't let that stop you the first time you married. His mother is a problem, too, but she'll come around if she doesn't have any choice, and that dear little boy of his—"

"Mrs. Ellsworth, please . . ." Sarah felt the sting of tears. She was just too tired for this conversation.

"You know I'm right," she went on, undaunted. "You're so perfect for each other. You can't let what other people think stop you."

Sarah smiled sadly and shook her head. "I'm not the one you should be trying to convince."

"What do you mean?"

"I mean," Sarah said wearily, "that Frank Malloy is every bit the man you think he is, and that means he's much too honorable to ever ask me to take a man he thinks is so far beneath me."

FRANK MALLOY DIDN'T LIKE THIS. USUALLY, when he investigated a murder, someone was at least a little interested in solving it. But four years after Tom Brandt's death, no one even remembered his name. Frank had been trying to find out information about the crime for months now. He'd succeeded in finding a witness, the boy Danny who'd lured Brandt to the meeting with his killer, and learned some details about the killer. Sarah's father, Felix Decker, had provided additional information and hired a crew of Pinkerton detectives to find out as much as they could about Brandt and the circumstances of his death. Now Frank had file folders full of information and at least three good suspects. All he had to do was get a bunch of people who had no interest in solving a four-year-old murder to cooperate with him.

He knocked on the front door of the imposing residence. He'd have to mind his manners here.

Luckily, he'd learned some since meeting up with Sarah Brandt.

A maid answered the door. She was a pock-marked girl in her early twenties, and she knew immediately that Frank was trouble. "What will you be wanting, then?" she asked rudely.

"Is that how your betters taught you to treat their visitors?" he chided her.

She looked him over head to foot dismissively. "Tradesmen are to use the back door," she sniffed and started to slam the door in his face. He'd had this door slammed in his face the last time he'd been here. Back then, he'd had no real authority. This time he did.

Frank raised his arm and slapped the door with the flat of his hand, pushing it just forcefully enough to send the girl staggering back into the front hallway. He stepped inside before she could gather her wits. "I want to see your master," he said. "Tell him it's Detective Sergeant Frank Malloy of the New York City Police."

Her already surprised expression grew shocked. "The police! But they said you wasn't going to arrest her!"

"Arrest who?"

"Why, Miss Or —" But she caught herself. "Wait a minute. What did you want to see the master about?" she asked warily.

"None of your business. Just tell him I'm here. I want to talk to him about Miss Ordella." Knowing the woman's name convinced her he was serious. She didn't have to know he'd gotten the name from the Pinkertons' report.

"Mr. Werner ain't . . . isn't in. Only Mrs. Rossmann."

"I'll see her, then."

"If she's home," the girl said in warning. Ladies of society could instruct their servants to tell visitors they were not at home even when they were, a polite way of avoiding company if they didn't want any.

"She's at home," Frank said in a warning of his own.

The girl left him standing in the hall as she scurried away in search of her mistress. From the Pinkertons' report, he knew that Mrs. Rossmann was Ordella Werner's aunt. She would probably be easier to intimidate than the girl's father anyway.

Frank used his wait to look around. The hallway was furnished with a few heavily carved chairs that looked as if they had come from a castle somewhere. A richly figured carpet covered the floor, and portraits of sour-looking ancestors hung on the ornately wallpapered walls.

After a few minutes Frank heard a sound and looked up to see a middle-aged woman descending the stairs. She was tall and straight, and her face still held traces of the beauty she had been in her youth. She moved with stately grace, her expression betraying none of the anxiety she must feel to find a police detective on her doorstep.

When she reached the bottom of the steps, she stopped and studied Frank for a long moment. "Meg said you're from the police."

She was a cool one, but her voice had cracked ever so slightly over the word *police*.

"That's right. Detective Sergeant Frank Malloy. Is there someplace we can talk in private?"

She seemed to shake herself a bit. "Of course. This way." She led him into one of the rooms that opened off the front hall, pushing the double doors open to reveal an elaborately furnished and immaculate parlor that was probably used only for formal occasions. She stood aside for Frank to enter, then carefully closed the doors behind her.

"You're here about Ordella," she said. It wasn't a question.

"That's right, Mrs. Rossmann. You're her aunt, I believe."

"Yes." She wasn't going to offer anything else.

"Have you always lived with the family?"

"Just for the past ten years, since my husband died."

"But you've known Ordella all her life."

"Of course I have. She's my brother's child."

"When did you first notice that she wasn't quite right?"

Mrs. Rossmann's shoulders rose ever so slightly, as if Frank's question threatened her in some way. "Is this necessary?" she asked, her composure slipping just a bit. "We've sent Ordella to an asylum upstate already. I thought you people weren't going to press charges against her."

Frank mentally cursed the Pinkertons. Something had happened with Miss Ordella Werner, something violent, and they hadn't had a thing about it in their report.

"We aren't," Frank bluffed, "but we still need to make a full report. Maybe we could sit down," he suggested. "I know this isn't easy for you."

Mrs. Rossmann drew a deep breath, as if to fortify herself. "I'm sorry. I should have offered you a seat." She walked over to where two overstuffed chairs sat beside the cold fireplace and lowered herself onto one of them carefully, as if afraid she might break. She indicated Frank should take the other one, and he did.

"So, let's start again. When did you first notice she wasn't right?" he repeated.

"About six years ago, I think," she said. "Ordella had always enjoyed good health, but she had a serious fever that summer. For a while, we thought she might even die."

"That's when she met Dr. Leiter."

She seemed surprised he knew the doctor's name. "No, she'd known him for years, but as I said, she'd never been sickly, so she'd had little contact with him until then."

"But she had a lot of contact with him when she was sick."

"Of course. He was here daily at first, until the

crisis passed. Then he would come by regularly to check on her."

"And she fell in love with him."

The color rose in Mrs. Rossmann's cheeks. Frank couldn't tell if it was anger or embarrassment, but he could see she hated discussing this. "She developed an . . . *attachment* for him," she allowed.

"When did you first realize she had this *attachment* for him?"

She tried to remember. "I don't know exactly. She was . . . At first she seemed to have a relapse, so of course we called the doctor in. It happened several times, and we hated to bother him so often, but Ordella would insist. She'd become hysterical if we even hesitated to summon him. Finally, we began to understand that she was only pretending to be ill so he would come. So she could . . . see him," she added reluctantly.

"How did he react to this?"

"He was patient at first. Lots of females develop a certain affection for their doctors, so this wasn't the first time he'd been the object of admiration."

"But this was different," Frank guessed.

Again she seemed surprised at his understanding of the situation. "Yes, it was. Dr. Leiter is married. He has three children. He's not a young man or even very . . . Well, quite frankly, he's rather plain looking. Not at all the kind of person to inspire a young woman's devotion."

"But he inspired your niece's devotion."

"Yes, and the more we tried to reason with her, to explain how foolishly she was behaving, the more devoted she became. She even . . . Well, she even began to insist that Dr. Leiter loved her in return."

"You're sure he wasn't encouraging her?"

"Absolutely not! He was appalled by her attentions. She would go to his office and to his home. She would leave gifts for him and love notes. She even . . ." Her voice broke, and she lifted a hand to rub her forehead. Plainly, she didn't want to tell the rest of this story.

Frank waited, knowing that if he said nothing, she would continue, almost as if she'd forgotten he was there.

"She went missing," Mrs. Rossmann said after a few moments, filling the silence he had allowed to stretch. "We searched everywhere, but we couldn't find her. She was gone for two days. We were frantic. Dr. Leiter had taken his family away for a holiday, although we didn't know it at the time. While they were gone, Ordella . . . she had gone to their house and . . . and lived there. She ate in their kitchen and even slept in . . . in Dr. Leiter's bed. They found her when they returned home. Poor Mrs. Leiter, she was beside herself. Dr. Leiter was quite upset, too, as you can imagine. We had to . . . to use force to bring Ordella home."

Only his years of training enabled Frank to keep his expression blank. None of this had been in the Pinkertons' report, just the bare fact that Ordella

27

Werner had become obsessed with her doctor.

When Mrs. Rossmann looked up, Frank could see she had tears in her eyes, and he felt a pang of guilt for putting her through this. "Do you have enough for your report yet, Mr. Malloy?" she asked bitterly. "Or should I continue?"

Frank hated himself for continuing to browbeat the poor woman, but he needed a little more information. "How did Dr. Tom Brandt get involved in Miss Werner's case?"

"Dr. Brandt?" she asked in surprise. "How did you know about him? I'd almost forgotten myself!"

Frank didn't reply. He didn't need to. All he had to do was wait. Wait and stare at her with his implacable glare, the one that had broken those much tougher than she.

Mrs. Rossmann sighed in defeat. "I never did know how he heard about Ordella. He just knocked on our door one day with a letter of introduction from Dr. Leiter."

"What did he want?"

She frowned. "He said he was studying cases like Ordella's," she recalled after a moment. "He said she wasn't the only female to have developed an irrational attachment to a man who had no interest in her. He was . . . he was trying to find a way to help these women, I think."

"What did your brother think of Dr. Brandt?" Frank asked, not allowing any emotion into his voice.

"My brother?"

28

"Yes, did he approve of Dr. Brandt trying to help your niece?"

Plainly, she thought this an odd question. "We . . . I think we were all willing for him to try, at least at first . . ."

"But later?" Frank prodded.

"He upset Ordella. He was trying to reason with her, but we'd already tried that. We'd already explained to her that Dr. Leiter was not in love with her, that he had a wife and family and had no interest in leaving them for her."

"But she didn't believe you," he guessed.

"She said he only stayed with them because he didn't want to hurt his children. She claimed his wife had threatened to ruin him if he left her, and he wouldn't be able to earn a living. She had all sorts of excuses for why he pretended not to care for her, even though none of them made sense to anyone but her."

"But Dr. Brandt still tried to reason with her."

"Yes, and he wasn't any more successful than we had been. In fact . . ."

"In fact what, Mrs. Rossmann?" His tone made her shoulders tense.

"I never blamed him. Dr. Brandt, that is. I never believed his visit had set her off, but shortly afterwards, Ordella managed to get away again. This time we knew where to look for her, though."

"She'd gone to Dr. Leiter's house again?" Frank guessed.

"They found her hiding in the cellar. She . . . she had a knife."

Frank's blood seemed to freeze in his veins. "What did she intend to do with it?"

Mrs. Rossmann's eyes glittered like glass. "Knowing what's happened since, I'm sure you can guess, Mr. Malloy. She never admitted to anything, though. Not then. We took her home and we kept a much closer watch on her after that."

Frank's mind was racing. He didn't want her to know he had no idea what Ordella had done recently. He'd have to find that out from another source. He also had to leave a door open so he could return and question her again. "Mrs. Rossmann, you said that *you* never believed Dr. Brandt was responsible for what happened, but what about your brother? What did he think?"

Mrs. Rossmann lifted her chin. "My brother will blame Dr. Brandt until the day he dies."

# 2

FRANK SPENT MOST OF THE AFTERNOON trying to locate the person he needed to see next. A trip to the local precinct house had sent him wandering through the neighborhood in search of the right saloon. By the time Frank found it, Detective Sergeant Sean O'Cork was a little worse for wear. At least he was a pleasant drunk, unlike too many Frank had encountered in his life.

Frank identified himself as a detective assigned to Police Headquarters.

"Pleased to meet you, Detective Sergeant Malloy," he said a bit too cheerfully. O'Cork was a portly man of middle years, his bulbous nose an indication that he had spent far too many afternoons in saloons just like this one. "Have a seat. Peter, me boy," he called to the bartender, "bring a glass for my new friend here."

The bartender complied, and Frank obligingly took a sip of the beer.

"What brings you all the way uptown?" O'Cork inquired without a trace of concern. As a "ward detective" assigned to a local precinct, he might well be suspicious of a visit from Headquarters. Traditionally, the ward detectives had been the ones who, in addition to their crime-solving duties, had collected the bribes and distributed them to the rest of the men in the precinct, giving them considerable power and influence. In his early days as police commissioner, Theodore Roosevelt had abolished the position and centralized all detectives at the Headquarters building in an attempt to stem corruption, but his edict hadn't stood for long. He'd quickly discovered that sending detectives out from Headquarters to investigate crimes all over the city cost valuable time that allowed the criminals several hours' head start. So now the ward detectives were back, collecting bribes and chasing criminals.

"I need some information from you, O'Cork,

about a woman named Miss Ordella Werner."

"Miss Ordella?" he echoed in amazement. "Who's she stabbed this time?"

"She stabbed somebody?" Frank asked, dismayed that his worst suspicions had been correct.

"She most certainly did," O'Cork reported, tipping up his glass and leaning his head back to get the last drop of beer from the bottom.

Frank gestured to the bartender to get O'Cork a refill. O'Cork accepted it gratefully.

"You're a good egg, Malloy. What can I do for you again?"

"Tell me about Miss Ordella."

"Oh, yes, Miss Ordella. What do you want to know?"

"Everything."

"Have you met her yet?"

"Not yet."

O'Cork pretended to shudder. "She's a bird, all right. Plain as a foot and mean into the bargain. She's got a high opinion of herself, though. Thinks her priest is in love with her."

"Her *priest*?" Frank echoed, recalling what Mrs. Rossmann had said about the doctor. "Are you sure it was her priest?"

"Well, not a *priest*," O'Cork allowed. "She's Protestant. Lutheran, maybe. Something like that. What do they call their priests?"

"Ministers," Frank said.

"Yeah, that's right. Anyway, he's married to a

perfectly nice lady, but Miss Ordella thinks he's in love with her. Now, if you could see her, you'd know just how crazy this is, but that's what she thinks. Seems she's had these spells before where she thinks some poor fellow is in love with her when he's not. Like I said, she's crazy. But nobody can talk her out of it, and she decided that if the priest's wife were dead, he'd be free to marry her or something like that."

"She stabbed the wife?" Frank asked in surprise.

"Tried to. Even drew some blood. Lucky thing, the wife's got on a corset and all that other stuff ladies wear, so the knife skids off a corset stay and just slices her chest. Not very deep, but she starts screaming like a banshee, and since they're in the church and it's Sunday morning, lots of people come running. Her dress is all cut and bloody, but she ain't hurt too bad."

Frank rubbed the bridge of his nose, trying to ward off the headache forming behind his eyes. This was worse than he could have imagined. "Do you know this isn't the first time she's tried to kill somebody?"

*"What?"* O'Cork cried in dismay. "They never told me that! How'd you find out?"

"Her aunt told me."

"Mrs. Rossmann?" O'Cork asked, outraged now. "She never said a thing to *me*. Such a nice lady, too. Butter wouldn't melt in her mouth."

"Like you said, this minister isn't the first man

33

Miss Ordella has taken a fancy to, either. First time, it was her doctor."

O'Cork downed the last of his beer, tipping his glass straight up again, as if he needed fortification to hear the rest of this story. He wiped his mouth with the back of his hand and motioned to the bartender for another. While he waited, he turned to Frank again. "Who did she stab that time?"

"Nobody, thank God. They found her hiding in her doctor's house before she could do any harm, but she had a knife with her. The doctor was married, too, so I'm guessing she wanted to kill *his* wife."

O'Cork scratched his head. "That makes sense. Or as much sense as any of this makes. I couldn't figure out why the priest . . . I mean, the minister didn't just tell her he didn't want anything to do with her, but he said he already did, more than once. She wouldn't believe him, though. She said she knew he really loved her, no matter what he said. Her family told her the same thing, too. Wouldn't listen to reason, no matter who told her."

The bartender set his refilled glass in front of him. O'Cork glanced at Frank's glass. "Drink up, Malloy. You'll need it if you're going to be talking to Miss Ordella."

That was the last thing Frank wanted to do, but he took a polite sip of the beer anyway. "So what happened with the minister's wife?"

"She wanted Miss Ordella locked up. Can't

blame her for that. The minister did, too, but the family has money. You seen their house?"

Frank nodded.

"Then you know what I mean. They wouldn't want her down in the Tombs," he said, naming the city lockup. "Or in the crazy house neither. People like that, they keep their troubles private."

Frank did know about people like that. Sarah Brandt's family was the same way. "Did they pay off the minister?"

"Nobody told me so, but they must've. The minister, he decides he don't want to cause any trouble. He sends his wife to stay with her folks for a while. They live in Albany or somewhere. Then he packs up his stuff and leaves town. Don't say where he's going either. Guess he don't want Miss Ordella to find them."

"Can't blame him for that," Frank said.

"No, you can't. I figure Old Man Werner greased his palm to help him with the move. Maybe even helped him find a church somewhere else."

"What kind of a man is this Werner?"

Even drunk, O'Cork knew this wasn't a casual question. He peered at Frank as if trying to bring him into focus. *"Rich,"* he said, giving the word a wealth of meaning.

Frank knew every one of those meanings—arrogant, powerful, proud. The rich were above the law, and they knew it.

"Now I get to ask a question," O'Cork said.

35

"Why the hell do you care about Miss Ordella and her rich pa?"

"I'm investigating a murder."

"Whose?" he asked with great interest.

"A doctor's."

O'Cork's bloodshot eyes widened. "Miss Ordella's doctor? The one whose wife she tried to kill?"

"No, a different one. This one tried to help cure her."

"And you think she killed him?" he asked doubtfully.

"No, the killer was a man, a man who was mad at the doc for trying to help his *daughter*."

"You think it was Werner?" O'Cork's expression was only mildly interested.

"I don't know yet. I haven't even met him. Do you think it could be him?"

O'Cork shook his head drunkenly. "Don't matter if it is. Like I said, he's rich."

CATHERINE HAD BEEN TUCKED INTO BED, AND Sarah was settling in for a quiet evening when someone knocked on her front door. Her heart sank. So much for catching up on her rest after the delivery last night. She shouldn't resent being called out, no matter what the hour. This was how she made her living, after all.

She met Maeve in the front hall. The girl was coming down from upstairs, where she'd been getting ready for bed herself.

"I'll get it," Sarah said, but Maeve waited to see who it was, in case she was needed. "Who's there?" Sarah called through the door, since it was too dark to see.

"Malloy," he replied, and Sarah's disappointment instantly evaporated.

She threw open the door. "Malloy," she said, feeling absurdly happy to see him. How long had it been since he was here last? Just days, but she'd missed him more than she cared to admit, even to herself.

He stepped inside and saw Maeve standing at the foot of the steps. Sarah noticed she was smiling, too. All the females on Bank Street adored him, apparently. Too bad Catherine was asleep. She would have thrown herself into his arms.

"Good evening, Miss Maeve," he said, making her blush.

"Nice to see you, Mr. Malloy," she replied. "Can I take your coat?"

When he'd been relieved of his coat and hat and offered food, which he refused, they ushered him into the warmth of the kitchen and convinced him to try the remains of the hot cross buns from that morning.

He looked tired, but that wasn't unusual at this hour of the night. More importantly, he wasn't teasing Maeve. Something was on his mind. When he'd finished the bun, Sarah said, "Maeve, you can go on to bed now."

The girl nodded, understanding that Malloy must have something private to discuss with Sarah, but he surprised her by saying, "Don't go just yet, Maeve. I think you should hear what I have to tell Mrs. Brandt."

Her eyes wide with surprise and her cheeks flushed with pleasure at being allowed to hear the adult conversation, Maeve took a seat at the table beside Sarah and across from Malloy.

Sarah waited, not sure she really wanted to hear what he had to say.

"Maeve, do you know that I'm investigating Dr. Brandt's murder?"

She glanced at Sarah, who had been about to say that Maeve knew nothing about it, and Sarah realized she had been wrong about Maeve's ignorance. "I . . . I've heard you talking about it," she admitted. "I couldn't help it," she added, pointing to the ceiling, where a grate let heat escape into the upper floor.

Malloy rubbed a hand over his mouth to hide a smile, and Sarah made a mental note to discuss truly private things somewhere else from now on.

"Well, then," Malloy said, regaining his composure. "I'll tell you both what I've found out so far. The man who killed Dr. Brandt was wealthy and middle-aged. He probably struck Dr. Brandt with a cane that had a large silver head on it. He'd hired a boy, a street Arab, to bring Dr. Brandt to an alley down near the docks on the pretense of taking him to see somebody who was sick. The boy doesn't know the rich man's name or anything else about him except that he heard the man accuse Dr. Brandt of harming his daughter in some way."

Both Maeve and Sarah waited, giving Malloy a chance to say more. When he didn't, Maeve said, "Is that all?"

He hesitated. He didn't want to tell them this part, and Sarah felt her body tense, bracing for whatever he would say. "The boy heard one of them say the name *Decker.*"

Sarah gasped. Decker was her maiden name. Could her family have been involved in Tom's death?

"Mr. Decker had received a letter from someone accusing Dr. Brandt of seducing young women who were his patients," Malloy hastened to explain.

"What!" Sarah cried in outrage. She felt as if someone had punched her. "You never told me that! And neither did my father!"

"The letter came just a day or two before Dr. Brandt was killed, so your father didn't see any point in doing anything about it. He . . . he didn't want to hurt you," he added a bit self-consciously.

Sarah knew immediately Malloy was lying about that. Felix Decker would not have hesitated to hurt her if he thought it was for the best. Her father's reasons for not telling her about the letter had nothing to do with her feelings, but she felt an overwhelming sense of tenderness toward Malloy for wanting to shield her from that knowledge.

Maeve was more focused on the case. "Who sent the letter?"

"We don't know. He didn't sign it, but it sounded like his daughter was one of the young women."

"So . . ." Sarah mused, forcing her mind back to the real issue. "That's why you were looking in Tom's old files," she remembered. "You were looking for patients who were young women and who might have been the ones this person who wrote the letter was talking about."

"Was it true?" Maeve asked, with an apologetic glace at Sarah. "Was Dr. Brandt really doing those things?"

Malloy frowned, and for a moment, Sarah held her breath, terrified at what he would say. After what seemed an eternity, he said, "I don't think so."

"What do you mean, you don't *think* so?" Sarah demanded.

He leaned back in his seat and drew a deep breath, letting it out in a gusty sigh. "I've found four women so far that I think are the ones the letter writer was referring to. I haven't investigated all of them yet, just the first two, but both of them are . . . crazy."

"Crazy?" Sarah echoed. "You mean they aren't in their right minds?"

"You know about one of them already," he reminded her. "Edna White."

Sarah needed a moment, but then she remembered the conversation she'd had with Malloy a few weeks ago. "Oh, yes."

"Who's this Edna White?" Maeve asked. "What did she do?"

"She was one of Dr. Brandt's patients," Malloy told her. "She's a spinster who lives with her brother. Dr. Brandt treated her when she was sick, and she . . . I guess you could say she fell in love with him, but it was a lot more than that. She thought he was in love with her, too."

"She started coming by his office," Sarah recalled. "She'd bring him presents and things that she'd baked for him. She even gave him her father's gold watch."

"That's not very ladylike," Maeve informed them, and this time Sarah had to fight a smile. She and Mrs. Ellsworth had been diligently teaching Maeve how a lady should conduct herself. Pursuing a man was something no lady would ever do.

"Remember, I said she was crazy," Malloy reminded her. "She thought Dr. Brandt loved her, too."

"Why didn't he just tell her he didn't?" Maeve asked.

"He did tell her," Malloy said. "He asked her to stop coming to his office and to stop giving him gifts, but she thought he was just being gallant because he was married. She honestly thought he loved her, and that if he wasn't married, he would marry her."

"Why wouldn't she believe him?" Maeve asked, her brow creased in confusion. "Why would she want to keep making a fool of herself?"

"I told you, she's—"

"Crazy," Maeve supplied in disgust. "I know."

"In fact," Malloy went on, "she's so crazy, she told me that she still meets Dr. Brandt at a flat in Chinatown where they carry on an affair because he can't get a divorce."

"What?" Sarah exclaimed in horror.

"But he's dead!" Maeve cried, then turned to Sarah in instant contrition. "I'm sorry, Mrs. Brandt, but he is. He's been dead for years! Why would she say something like that?"

"Because she thinks it's true," Malloy said.

"Didn't anyone tell her he died?" Sarah asked, nearly overwhelmed with revulsion at the macabre tale.

"Of course they did. Her brother thought that would be the end of it, but she just decided everyone was lying to her. She thought they were just saying he was dead so she'd forget about him. From what I could tell, it only made her more determined than ever."

"You said she goes out to Chinatown to . . . to meet Tom," Sarah said, the words nearly sticking in her throat. "Where does she really go?"

"No place. She never goes out at all. Her brother hired a companion to watch her. It's all in her imagination."

Maeve gave a little shudder. She looked at Sarah. "I used to call some of the girls at the Mission crazy. I'll never do that again."

Sarah reached over and patted Maeve's hands where they lay folded on the table. Then she looked at Malloy. He had told her a bit about Edna White, but none of the details. "I had no idea she was that bad. Did Tom know?"

"He must have. Remember, you told me he was trying to learn more about this . . . this disease Miss White had. It's called Old Maid's Disease, and he was trying to find a way to cure her. He found some other women who have it, too."

"Oh, yes, those three other women we talked about before," Sarah recalled.

"Other women fell in love with him like that?" Maeve asked in amazement.

"No, they'd fallen in love with other men, or at least other doctors. Maybe because the doctor was nice to them when they were sick, like Dr. Brandt was with Miss White. Whatever it was, he found three other women who were like this with their doctors."

"And you think all of this has something to do with Tom being murdered," Sarah said.

"I think it's possible," Malloy hedged. "The killer thought Dr. Brandt had harmed his daughter in some way, and the letter your father got accused him of seducing young women. From what I've been able to find out, women who suffer from this disease sometimes imagine seductions, like Miss White did. She spoke frankly about her imaginary affair with Dr. Brandt to me, a strange man she'd known only a few minutes. If I didn't know Dr. Brandt was dead, I would've believed her."

"And if a woman told her family a man had seduced her, they would believe her, too," Sarah said.

"That's terrible!" Maeve decided.

"Of course it is," Sarah said. "But many terrible things happen in this world, as we all know," she added gently.

She watched as Maeve absorbed the meaning of her words and remembered all the terrible things that had happened to her in her short life. Sarah would probably never know about most of them, and she didn't really want to.

After a moment, as if to distract herself from her own memories, Maeve turned back to Malloy. "How are you going to find out who killed Dr. Brandt?"

"I'm going to investigate the families of the three women."

"You said there were *four* women," Maeve reminded him.

"Edna White's father was dead when Dr. Brandt was murdered. The other three women all have fathers who are still alive."

"But what will you do?" Sarah asked in frustration. "You can't just go up to these three men and ask them if they killed Tom."

Malloy's lips twitched in the briefest of smiles. "I thought you'd have a little more confidence in my abilities than that."

"You know I do," she snapped, too angry to be teased. "But four years have passed. How can you even begin to investigate? What would you ask and whom would you ask it of? No one will tell the truth, even if they remember anything after all this time."

"Four years is a long time to carry the guilt of a murder, especially for a respectable man who never did anything violent before. If I can figure out who the most likely suspect is, I can probably get him to admit it."

This time Sarah sighed. She'd helped him investigate murders before, and she knew it was never so easy as that. A long moment passed while each of them considered the situation, and then Sarah had an unsettling thought.

"Why did you come here tonight to tell us all this, Malloy?" He'd told her before, in no uncertain terms, that he didn't want her involved in this investigation. She hadn't expected to see him again until he'd finished.

Only because she knew him so well did she catch the flicker of regret in his dark eyes. "I found out something today that you need to know."

"What?" Maeve asked, enthralled now by the mystery of the tale.

"One of these women, Miss Ordella Werner, she

. . . Well, first she was in love with her doctor, and then later, she turned her affection to her minister. Both times, she . . . The first time, they found her hiding in the doctor's house with a knife."

"A knife?" Sarah echoed. "What was she planning to do?"

"They didn't know then, but just recently, a few weeks ago, she stabbed her minister's wife."

"Oh, no!" Sarah cried, and Maeve gasped in surprise.

"She didn't do much damage. Just cut the poor woman, but that wasn't what she intended. She intended to kill her. She thought that if the wife was dead, the minister would be free to marry her."

"How awful!" Sarah said. "How could she imagine the man would marry her if she'd killed his wife?"

Malloy gave her a look. "Didn't I mention that she's crazy?"

"What happened to her? Miss Werner, I mean," Maeve asked. "Did they put her in the Tombs?"

"Nothing happened to her," Malloy admitted bitterly. "Her father paid the minister to move away and forget about everything."

"But shouldn't they lock her up?" Sarah asked. "She might try to harm someone else."

"The detective who investigated the case told me her father promised to keep her confined from now on."

"I should hope so," Sarah said. Then she noticed

Malloy was staring at her, his eyes hard and cold. He had more to say. "What is it?"

"This is what I had to tell you, Mrs. Brandt. These women, sometimes they get violent, and this one wanted to kill the wife of the man she loved. At least one of these women loved Tom Brandt, and you're Tom Brandt's wife."

"You can't think I'm in any danger from poor Edna White," Sarah scoffed, instinctively refusing to believe it.

"Nobody thought Ordella Werner would stab the minister's wife, but she did," he reminded her grimly. "I don't know anything about these other two women yet. They might be dangerous, too."

"My pap, he used to say when you turn over a rock, you never know what will crawl out," Maeve said, surprising Sarah. The girl had never spoken of her family before.

"And I'm going to be turning over a lot of rocks," Malloy said. "You just need to be on your guard."

"I KNEW SOMETHING WAS WRONG," MRS. Ellsworth said the next morning when Sarah told her what Malloy had said the night before. "I dropped an egg this morning, and it didn't break. That always means bad luck."

"We haven't had any bad luck yet," Sarah reminded her a bit sharply. They were in the kitchen, having a second cup of coffee. Luckily, Maeve and Catherine were upstairs and hadn't heard. Sarah was

47

always afraid Mrs. Ellsworth's superstitions would frighten them, although they hadn't seemed to so far. In fact, they often found them amusing.

Mrs. Ellsworth didn't seem to have paid any attention to Sarah's protest. "Something to change your luck," she mused, rubbing her chin thoughtfully. "That's what we need. Oh, I know! If a bird leaves a dropping on you, that's good luck."

Sarah gaped at her. "Are you suggesting I go outside and try to get a bird to plop on my head?"

"What?" Mrs. Ellsworth asked, distracted. "Oh, dear me, no. That was just a thought. I'm sure there are other ways to do it. Besides, if you *wanted* a bird to do that, it never would."

Sarah continued to gape. She was serious! "Mrs. Ellsworth, I'm not worried about this. These women weren't in love with Tom anyway."

"I thought you said one of them was. What was her name? Edith or Evelyn or—"

"Edna, but she's not even involved in Tom's death. And if she wanted to kill me, she's had ample opportunities over the last four years. Why would she suddenly decide to harm me now?"

"I have no idea," Mrs. Ellsworth said, "but nothing else these women do makes sense either, so I wouldn't count on that."

"Oh, I'll certainly be sensible."

"More sensible than you've been in the past?" Mrs. Ellsworth asked with raised eyebrows.

Sarah winced. She could remember a time or two

when she'd been in physical danger. "Yes, more sensible than I've been in the past," she promised. "I have a family now."

"You most certainly do," Mrs. Ellsworth said. "Did that lawyer ever bring over those papers for you to sign?"

"Oh, yes," Sarah assured her. "I'm Catherine's legal guardian now."

"You're Catherine's *mother*," Mrs. Ellsworth corrected her, "whether the state of New York will recognize that or not. I just can't see why they won't let you adopt the child and be done with it."

"They have their rules," Sarah reminded her. "A child needs a mother *and* a father."

"How many children in this city get by with just one or the other? Or none at all, for that matter? If you and Dr. Brandt had had a child, you'd be raising it on your own now. The state wouldn't come along and take it from you just because your husband died."

Sarah smiled sadly. "You don't have to convince *me*, Mrs. Ellsworth."

"I know I don't. I just get so mad about things sometimes. For instance, what would've happened to that beautiful child upstairs if you hadn't taken her in?"

Sarah didn't like to think about that. "No sense in wondering about it, because I did take her in, and she's my daughter whether the state recognizes it or not."

"Of course she is. Now, I've got to put my mind to thinking about a good luck charm, something to protect you."

Sarah opened her mouth to protest again, but then she remembered that Mrs. Ellsworth had given her a protective charm once before. She wasn't sure it had actually saved her life, but she'd certainly survived an attack. "I still have the handkerchief . . ."

"Oh, no, we need something much stronger," she decided. "Are you sure you don't want to try going for a walk? The birds are coming back for the spring."

Sarah started to tell the older woman exactly what she thought of the idea but then she saw the teasing glint in Mrs. Ellsworth's eye. She grinned back wickedly. "Only if you'll go with me."

THIS TIME FRANK DIDN'T EVEN TRY KNOCKING on the front door of the Werner house. He figured Mrs. Rossmann had told him everything she was going to, at least for the time being. No, he wanted to talk to someone else in the household who knew all the family secrets but who might not be so reluctant to reveal them.

He was lucky. Just as he reached the back gate, it opened and a middle-aged woman stepped out. She wore a plain dress and a shabby coat that marked her as a servant. She'd apparently inherited a hat from the lady of the house, one the mistress no longer considered stylish enough, and had it

50

perched on her head. She'd tied a wool scarf around it, though, to keep her ears warm, even though the weather was fairly mild today, with a hint of spring in the air. She had a market basket on her arm. Frank guessed that she was the cook. She closed the gate behind her carefully.

"Good morning," Frank greeted her.

She looked up, startled, then took him in from head to foot the way the maid had yesterday. "You'll be that policeman what was here yesterday, talking to the missus," she said with disapproval. "Well, you're wasting your time. She ain't home today."

"I didn't come to see her," he told her cheerfully. "I came to see you."

"Me? Whatever for?" she asked, not sure whether to be alarmed or not.

"I need to find out more about Miss Ordella," he said.

"Well, you won't find it out from me," she sniffed. "I ain't one to talk about them that feeds me." She turned away and started down the alley.

"That's too bad. I was hoping I could find out something that would help Miss Ordella."

That stopped her in her tracks. She looked back over her shoulder, and her eyes narrowed suspiciously. "What would you want to help her for?"

"To keep her out of jail. There's some that want to put her away for good, but if I can find out why she did it . . . Maybe she had a good reason. If she did, they wouldn't have to lock her up."

51

"And what if she didn't have no good reason?" she challenged.

Frank shrugged. "You think she should be locked up?"

"Heavens, no. That poor child, after what she's been through, nobody should blame her for anything."

"How about if I walk with you to the market and carry your basket, and you can tell me all about it."

She thought it over. "Suit yourself," she said after a moment, heading down the alley again.

Frank noticed she was limping a bit. "Or maybe I could get us a cab so we can talk in private," he suggested.

From the way her eyes brightened, he knew he'd won her over.

Her name was Mrs. Flynn, and she'd worked for the Werner family since Ordella was a little girl.

"She never was much to look at, even when she was a wee bit of a thing," Mrs. Flynn confided when they were tucked up into the cab and clattering along the cobblestone street. "Most children are appealing when they're little, you understand, but she never was. Looked too much like her da, she did. Still does, come to that. He could never deny her, and that's a fact."

Frank murmured something encouraging.

"Sometimes I wonder if things would've been different if her mother had lived, but she wasn't much different from him. A cold woman, almost as cold as him. I always wondered how they'd managed to get Miss Ordella in the first place, if you know what I mean."

Frank chuckled politely. "She was their only child, then?"

"Oh, yes. She wasn't spoiled, though, not like you'd expect. I never even heard either of them say one kind word to the child. Always 'don't do this' and 'don't do that.' Then she started growing and got so tall and gawky. The other children made fun of her, the way they do when somebody's not pretty, you know?"

Frank allowed that he did know.

"The child hardly ever smiled, now that I think on it. She always was trying to please them, but nothing she did was good enough."

"Did she have friends?"

"None that I ever saw," Mrs. Flynn said, disappointing Frank. He was hoping for another source of information. "They wouldn't have liked her having anybody over anyway. They didn't like a mess."

"No suitors, then?" Frank pressed.

"Oh, heavens, no." She shook her head at the silliness of the question. "I told you, she wasn't much to look at, and she didn't improve with age. She's shy, too, and backward with people."

"Her family has money, though," Frank argued. "Wasn't anybody interested in that, at least?"

"If there was, we never saw him. I don't expect Mr. Werner would take too kindly to somebody sniffing around after his money. Neither would he believe somebody was interested in Miss Ordella for her kind heart," she added sarcastically.

"Was Dr. Brandt interested in her kind heart?" Frank asked mildly.

Mrs. Flynn looked at him in surprise. "Who did you say?"

"Dr. Brandt. You remember him, don't you?"

"I ain't likely to forget. He's the one started all the trouble."

# 3

FRANK MANAGED NOT TO REACT. "I THOUGHT Miss Ordella had started causing trouble long before Dr. Brandt came along."

Mrs. Flynn made a rude noise. "She wasn't much trouble before that, at least once they figured out why she kept wanting them to call Dr. Leiter."

"Why was that?"

She looked at him like he wasn't quite right. "Didn't anybody tell you? She was batty over the poor man. Can't blame her, I guess. He might be the first man who was ever nice to her."

"So she'd pretend she was sick?"

"Oh, yes. She got real good at it, too. You'd of thought she was dying. Then he'd come, and she'd be all meek and happy for a day or two. He finally had to tell her father she wasn't really sick. Mr. Werner was that mad!"

"I guess he was," Frank said. "Didn't like paying for a doctor if she wasn't really sick."

"Heavens, no!" she exclaimed with a chortle. "He's so tight, he squeaks. He told Miss Ordella he wouldn't call the doctor again no matter what was wrong with her."

"So that was the end of it, I guess."

"Not at all," Mrs. Flynn assured him. "If he couldn't come to her, she'd go to him, and so she did."

"She went to his office?"

"Oh, yes. Every time she went out, which was almost every day. Said she was visiting the sick from church. She'd take food with her, little things I'd baked. Then she'd give them to Dr. Leiter."

"And he accepted them?"

"The first few times, I guess. He thought she was just grateful for him taking care of her when she was sick. After a few times, though, his nurse wouldn't let her in to see him, so she'd leave the gifts."

"That doesn't sound so bad," Frank said.

"That's because you don't know about the notes."

"She sent notes?"

"Oh, yes. I never saw one, mind, but the whole staff heard Mr. Werner yelling about them. I guess Dr. Leiter finally had to tell him what she'd been doing. Mr. Werner told Miss Ordella she was a disgrace to all females and called her unnatural and a harlot and I don't know what all. Said she'd never be let out of the house alone again."

"She managed, though, didn't she?"

"Oh, yes. Nobody ever said she wasn't clever. She waited until they thought she'd forgotten all about Dr. Leiter. She didn't even talk about him anymore, although she'd kept writing him letters. They found them in her room. But she never mailed them or anything, so they thought she'd gotten over him. Then, one Sunday when they was walking out of the church, she slipped away. They didn't even notice she was gone until they got outside. By then, she'd disappeared. You know where they found her?"

"At Dr. Leiter's house."

She nodded in approval that he'd guessed correctly. "She'd broke a window to get in. We never did find out if she knew the family had gone away or not, but they wasn't home. They was off visiting his wife's parents, as I remember."

"How long was she there before they found her?"

*"Two days,"* Mrs. Flynn reported with appropriate amazement. "She just acted like she lived there. She even slept in the doctor's bed," she added in a scandalized whisper.

"Her father must have been worried when they couldn't find her for so long," Frank said.

Mrs. Flynn pulled a face. "I wouldn't call it *worried*. At least he wasn't worried about *her*."

"Who was he worried about, then?"

"Himself, of course. Worried that she'd make some kind of scandal, which of course she did. I think he would've been happier if they'd found her floating in the river. He said as much to Mrs. Rossmann when Miss Ordella first went missing."

Frank couldn't wait to meet Mr. Werner. "What happened when they did find her?"

"I didn't hear right away what happened at the doctor's house. All I knew was they brought Miss Ordella home one day and locked her in her room. They didn't act real glad to have her home neither. We had to take her meals up to her, though, and she'd talk to the maids. She told them the most outlandish things, about how she'd been with Dr. Leiter the whole time she was gone, and how he was going to leave his wife and run away with her to Europe, where nobody would know them. The girls didn't know what to think, but pretty soon I got the whole story."

"I suppose the Leiters' servants spread the word."

"Oh, yes. They was with the family when they got home and found her living in the house. Mrs. Leiter, she was wild. The doctor had to give her some laudanum to make her stop screaming. The children was scared out of their wits, too. The police had to come and take Miss Ordella away. The housekeeper, she told me later that Mrs. Leiter made them scrub every inch of the house with lye soap. She didn't want no trace of Miss Ordella left."

She fell silent and gave Frank a sidelong glance full of apprehension.

"What is it?" he asked gently.

"I shouldn't of done it."

"Done what?"

She fiddled with the handle of her basket for a moment. "I shouldn't of told her."

"Told who?"

Mrs. Flynn sighed. "Told Miss Ordella. I told her about the lye soap." She looked up at Frank plaintively. "I thought if she knew, she'd . . . I was just trying to make her understand that Dr. Leiter didn't want nothing to do with her. I know Mrs. Rossmann and Mr. Werner had told her, but she wouldn't believe them. I thought she'd believe me. She's known me almost all her life, and I always treated her kind."

Frank nodded. He remembered his conversation with Edna White and how he'd tried to convince her Tom Brandt was dead. The woman had accused him of being an actor hired by her brother to trick her. If he hadn't had that experience, he never would have understood how frustrating it was to talk to women like that. "She didn't believe you, though, did she?"

"Oh, she believed me about the lye soap and Mrs. Leiter making the servants scrub the house. She hated Mrs. Leiter because she was standing in the way of her being with Dr. Leiter. I tried to tell her Dr. Leiter didn't want her, but she wouldn't listen. She just kept saying how mean Mrs. Leiter was for not divorcing him so he could be with Miss Ordella."

Frank waited, knowing if he did, she would probably reveal more than if he asked a question. The sounds from the street around them filled the silence, the shouts from the drivers of the vehicles around them, the horses whinnying, the clatter of wheels and hooves on the cobbles, the cries of street vendors advertising their wares.

Finally, Mrs. Flynn looked up at him again. "Do you think it was my fault?"

"Do I think what was your fault?"

"Miss Ordella trying to hurt Mrs. Leiter. Maybe if I hadn't told her about the lye soap . . ."

"I thought everybody blamed Dr. Brandt for that," Frank said.

Relief smoothed her face. "Oh, well, he *did* get her all stirred up."

"How did he do that?"

"He tried to talk reason to her is how," she said in disgust. "I could've told him not to bother, but nobody asked me."

"What did he talk to her about?"

"He tried to explain how Dr. Leiter didn't love her and wasn't never going to leave his family for her. The same thing we'd been trying to tell her all along."

"And that upset her?"

"She was beside herself. She tried to scratch his eyes out. Mr. Werner had to pull her off of him."

"Did she always get like that when somebody talked to her about it?"

"She'd get mad sometimes, but mostly she'd just argue with you. She thought we was all lying about Dr. Leiter because he was married and we didn't want her making a scandal. Funny thing, she was right about that, at least. Mr. Werner sure didn't want no scandal."

"Why do you think Dr. Brandt made her so mad?"

Mrs. Flynn sighed as she thought it over. "I wasn't there, of course, but I think maybe he just wouldn't give up. He was that sure he could convince her. Mrs. Rossmann and Mr. Werner, when she'd start arguing with them, they'd just give up and go away, but not Dr. Brandt. He stayed with her for such a long time, but then she started screaming, and that's when Mr. Werner run in and stopped it."

"What happened after that?"

"He left. Dr. Brandt, that is. He apologized to Mr. Werner and Mrs. Rossmann, and he left."

"What happened with Miss Ordella?"

Mrs. Flynn frowned. "It was the oddest thing, but at first she seemed to get better. After she got calmed down again, she was real quiet. She didn't even talk about Dr. Leiter anymore. Everybody thought . . . Well, maybe we just hoped that he'd gotten through to her somehow, but it wasn't that at all. She was just waiting, biding her time. She'd decided to do something, and she needed to make everybody think she wasn't going to be any trouble to anybody anymore. Then one day, she tricks one of the maids into leaving her door unlocked, just for a minute while she runs downstairs to get something, and Miss Ordella is gone, just like that. She'd been planning it all along."

"She went straight for Dr. Leiter's house," Frank guessed.

"Oh, yes. She couldn't have been there long when they found her. She'd broke the same window to get in again. They found her hiding in the cellar. She'd got a knife from the kitchen, and she was waiting for Mrs. Leiter, she said. I heard they had a terrible time getting the knife away from her. She cut a policeman pretty bad."

Frank winced. Nobody had mentioned that. "She admitted she wanted to kill the doctor's wife?"

"She did. Told anybody who'd listen. That's when they sent her away."

"Where did they send her?"

"One of them asylums. She never said what happened to her there, but it must've been awful." Mrs. Flynn shuddered inside her shabby coat.

"Why do you think so?"

"Because she was so changed when she come home. Or at least we thought she was. Meek as a lamb, and never spoke another word about the doctor. Mr. Werner, he didn't trust her at first, but after a while, even he started to believe she was over it, so when Miss Ordella asked could she go to church with them, they said she could."

"Wasn't that how she'd gotten away from them the first time?"

"Oh, they didn't take no chances with her. They watched her real close, and for a long time, she was just fine. They'd got a new minister, and they thought she just liked his sermons. Everybody liked him, come to that. He was real friendly, and handsome, too, I don't mind saying. He come to the house a time or two. Mr. Werner, he's an important man, so of course he'd get notice from his minister."

Frank could easily guess what happened next. "Miss Ordella wasn't just interested in his sermons, though, was she?"

"Oh, no. Remember I said she was clever? Well, she'd learned from before not to tell anybody what she was thinking. She didn't want them to send her back to that place, so she kept it to herself, but later it all came out. She thought he was in love with her because he was nice to her. I doubt he ever said more than a few words to her, but that was enough, I guess." Mrs. Flynn looked up at Frank, wide-eyed. "She thought he was sending her secret messages in his sermons."

Frank managed not to wince this time. "How did she come to stab the minister's wife?"

Mrs. Flynn shook her head. "She found out the woman was going to have a baby. She thought . . . Well, I don't suppose nobody really knows what she thought. She got a knife from the kitchen and somehow sneaked it out of the house. She stabbed the poor woman when she was coming down the aisle after the service. Right in front of everybody."

"How did she expect to get away with it?" Frank asked without thinking.

"I don't have no idea," Mrs. Flynn said sadly.

"Where is she now?"

Mrs. Flynn sighed again. "They took her back to that place. I don't suppose they'll ever let her out now."

Sarah was surprised to find her mother on her doorstep later that morning. Elizabeth Decker might now be a middle-aged matron, but her beauty hadn't faded any more than her spirit had.

"Mother, what a lovely surprise," Sarah said as Mrs. Decker made her entrance. Outside, her carriage clattered away, indicating she planned to stay for a while. Mrs. Decker had chosen a relatively plain gown for her visit, but she was still wildly overdressed for a visit to this part of town.

"I'm so glad I found you home," Mrs. Decker said, although she wasn't looking at Sarah at all. She was looking at the small girl hovering shyly in the shadows of the stairway. "Catherine, is that you, child?" she asked.

Catherine giggled.

"Come out and give Mrs. Decker a proper curtsey," Maeve urged her. "Show her what a big girl you are."

The child stepped cautiously out into the hallway, acutely aware that everyone was staring at her, and loving every moment of it. Obediently, she bobbed the way Mrs. Ellsworth had taught her, then looked up hopefully for Mrs. Decker's approval.

"That was well-done, Miss Catherine," Mrs. Decker decreed, "but I would much prefer a kiss."

Catherine giggled again, this time in delight, and she scampered over, stood on tiptoe, and kissed Mrs. Decker's offered cheek.

Sarah had to blink hard at the sting of tears. If anyone had ever suggested to her that Elizabeth Decker, a member of one of the oldest and wealthiest families in New York City, would consent to being kissed by a child from the streets, she would have called them insane.

"Thank you, my dear," Mrs. Decker was saying. "Now I'm going to need your help with something," she added as she started to remove the velvet cape she was wearing against the early spring chill. That's when they noticed she was carrying a small carpetbag over one arm.

Catherine waited expectantly as Sarah took her mother's cape and hung it up. Then Mrs. Decker opened the bag and looked inside. "I have some doll clothes here, but I'm not sure they will fit your baby. Will you help me try them on her to see?"

Catherine's eyes lit up and she nodded vigorously. In another moment, the two of them were climbing the stairs to the second floor to

Catherine's room. Sarah thought perhaps she should be insulted that her mother had virtually ignored her own child in favor of a little girl who was no relation to her at all. She wasn't, though. She felt only gratitude that her mother had taken Catherine into her heart the same way Sarah had.

Sarah glanced at Maeve, who was grinning hugely. "I think Mrs. Decker likes her," Maeve whispered.

Sarah was sure of it.

Sarah sent Maeve off to spend some time to herself, and gave Catherine and her mother a while alone before going up to see how they were doing. When she got to Catherine's room, the girl looked up and proudly held up her doll, now dressed quite fashionably in a new walking suit every bit as elaborate as the one Mrs. Decker wore. Sarah could only shake her head at her mother's extravagance.

"Your baby looks beautiful, darling," Sarah marveled. "Did you thank Mrs. Decker?"

Catherine nodded vigorously.

"She most certainly did," Mrs. Decker said. She was sitting in the rocking chair that she had insisted every nursery needed, even though Catherine had been far too big to need rocking when she arrived at Sarah's. Mrs. Decker had insisted on most of the rest of the furnishings as well, and they had arrived here one day to Sarah's surprise and Catherine's delight. She had also sent over Sarah's old dollhouse, which had a place of honor in one corner.

The three of them spent the next hour admiring the doll's various outfits as Catherine dressed and undressed her. When Mrs. Decker had first brought Catherine the doll, with its soft fabric body and fine china head, hands, and feet, Sarah had been afraid it would be too fragile, but Catherine handled her with loving care.

Finally, Maeve appeared in the doorway. "Catherine, can you come down and help me fix some luncheon? We can show Mrs. Decker what we've learned since she was here last."

Catherine gave Mrs. Decker a questioning glance. "I'd like to see what you've learned," the older woman said. "Go on now and help Maeve. We can play some more after lunch."

When they were alone, Sarah looked over at her mother, who was smoothing the doll's current outfit. "I don't remember you ever visiting me in the nursery to play dolls," she teased.

Her mother looked up, and Sarah saw a shadow cross her face. "It's never too late to correct past mistakes," she said.

Instantly contrite, Sarah said, "I'm sorry. I didn't mean—"

"No, that's all right. I know you didn't mean anything. I was just thinking how much I missed with you and . . . and Margaret."

Sarah's sister Maggie had chosen a life far different from the one her parents had wanted for her, and she'd died as a result. For many years, Sarah had blamed her parents and had herself rebelled against them. She was glad now that she had become reconciled with them at last. "I never felt that you neglected us," Sarah said.

Her mother finished adjusting the doll's dress and gently laid her aside. "I'm sure I could have done better," she said, then quickly added, "and I intend to do so with Catherine."

"I'm very grateful, Mother. Catherine is genuinely fond of you."

"And I am genuinely fond of her," Mrs. Decker said. Then she took a deep breath and quickly said, "Sarah, you must never allow yourself to be in need. You know I will help you in any way possible."

Sarah blinked in surprise. "You don't need to worry about us, Mother. I'd never allow pride to stand in the way of Catherine's well-being, but I don't expect to ever find myself in need."

Mrs. Decker frowned. "You can't possibly know what will happen in the future. Oh, I know you manage to earn a living," she added when Sarah would have protested. "But your work is so dangerous. Being called out at all hours, going to sections of the city where no decent woman should ever go . . ."

"I'm not going to give up my work," Sarah said, holding on to her temper because she knew her mother was concerned only for her safety.

Mrs. Decker smiled sadly. "I know better than to

ask it of you, but you are always welcome to return home, and to bring Catherine with you, if you should ever change your mind."

Sarah couldn't help smiling in return. "I see it all now. You're just trying to get Catherine all to yourself."

Mrs. Decker feigned shock. "Am I that obvious?"

"Of course you are."

Mrs. Decker shook her head in wonder. "I must admit, it came as a surprise . . . my feelings for Catherine, that is. I never expected . . . But she *is* the closest thing to a grandchild that I have. I suppose that could explain it."

For a long moment, they recalled Maggie and her child, both long dead. "You don't need to explain it," Sarah assured her. "You simply need to enjoy it."

Mrs. Decker managed a smile. "And I suppose I shouldn't give up hope entirely. You're still young. If you were to remarry . . ."

"But I'm not going to remarry," Sarah said, trying not to think about whom she might marry if she did.

Mrs. Decker picked an invisible piece of lint off her skirt. "And how is Mr. Malloy doing these days?" she asked with elaborate casualness.

Sarah hated the heat she felt flooding her face. "He . . . he's fine, I suppose."

Her mother pretended not to notice her dismay. "You suppose? Haven't you seen him lately?" She tried to look innocent, but Sarah wasn't fooled.

"I saw him just last evening, as a matter of fact,"

Sarah admitted grudgingly. "Mr. Malloy was perfectly fine."

"Last evening?" Mrs. Decker's lovely face creased in concern. "Are you . . . ? Has there been another murder?"

If her mother worried about her work as a midwife being dangerous, she must be terrified at the prospect of Sarah's investigating another murder. "Not a new one," Sarah said. "He . . . he's looking into Tom's death."

"Tom?" she echoed in surprise. "You mean your husband, Tom? After all this time?"

"Yes, he . . . he found some new information."

"How could he find new information now when the police couldn't find it back then?"

"The police didn't look back then."

"What do you mean, they didn't look?"

"I mean they didn't investigate Tom's death at all."

Mrs. Decker frowned. "Why on earth not?"

"Because Father didn't pay them to."

"Pay them? What do you mean, *pay them*?"

"I'm sure you would have no reason to know this, Mother, and I certainly didn't at the time, but the police don't investigate a crime unless they are paid to do so. Sometimes this payment is called a reward, but it's actually nothing more than a bribe."

"Well, of course your father didn't pay a bribe," Mrs. Decker said in outrage. "He would never do such a thing! That's scandalous!"

"Yes, it is," Sarah agreed. "But that's how busi-

69

ness is done in this city, and because no one paid a bribe, no one found Tom's killer."

Mrs. Decker considered this information for a moment. "And now Mr. Malloy has decided to investigate."

"Yes."

"I don't suppose I need wonder why," she tried, but Sarah refused to react. After a moment of silence, Mrs. Decker said, "Does he have any idea who might have killed Dr. Brandt?"

"Not yet, but he believes it has something to do with some women who were Tom's patients at the time."

"Does he think a woman killed him?" she asked in surprise.

"No, he's sure it was a man, but he thinks it may have been the father of one of his patients."

"Did the woman die?"

Sarah sighed. She was going to have to tell her mother the whole story. "It all started with this woman named Edna White." As briefly as possible, she told her mother the tale.

"I can't believe this," Mrs. Decker said when Sarah had finished. "Dr. Brandt must have done something to encourage her."

"He was merely kind to her. She was his patient, after all."

"And you say she believes he is still alive and that they are still *lovers*?" she asked with obvious distaste. "I can hardly credit it!"

"Nevertheless, she does."

"And Mr. Malloy thinks this woman's father killed Dr. Brandt?"

"No, Miss White's father was dead long before then. You see, Tom wanted very badly to find out how to cure Miss White of her delusions, so he started asking his colleagues if they'd ever encountered anything like her case. He found at least three other females who had developed similar attachments to their own doctors."

"*Three?* How amazing!"

"Apparently, females often develop affection for their physicians, but these women imagined themselves madly in love and even believed the doctors were in love with them, no matter how much the gentlemen in question denied it."

"But that's just . . ." Mrs. Decker searched for a word.

"Insane," Sarah supplied. "Yes, it is."

"Not to mention unladylike," Mrs. Decker added ironically. "How could a female be so . . . so undignified?"

"I can't understand either," Sarah admitted, "but it's true."

"So Mr. Malloy believes the father of one of these women killed Dr. Brandt?"

"Yes, he does."

"And how does he hope to find out which one did and then prove it and bring the man to justice?"

"I'm not sure. In fact, I'm not sure he could

bring the man to justice even if he can prove who did it."

"Why ever not?"

"Because the killer is probably a well-respected man of means. Men like that seldom are charged with crimes, no matter how guilty they may be."

Mrs. Decker considered this for a long moment. "Probably because no one would take a charge from an Irish Catholic police detective against a man like that seriously, I suppose."

"Probably not," Sarah admitted.

"Unless . . ."

"Unless what?" Sarah prodded when her mother hesitated.

"Unless someone like Felix Decker stood behind him."

Sarah shook her head. "Father would never want to be involved in something so sordid. Besides, if he wanted Tom's murder solved, he would have paid the bribe in the first place."

"What do you mean?" her mother asked in surprise.

"I mean, he must have known how justice is dispensed in New York City, even if we didn't. Mother, he didn't want Tom's death solved then, so he probably isn't interested in solving it now."

FELIX DECKER LOOKED UP FROM THE PAPERS spread on his desk as Frank entered his office. Decker's secretary closed the door behind him with a nearly silent click.

72

"Sit down, Mr. Malloy," Decker offered.

Frank took one of the well-worn leather chairs that faced Decker's desk. The office bore little indication that Decker was one of the wealthiest men in the city. Frank supposed he didn't need to impress anyone. The mere fact that Deckers had lived in New York City for a century before anyone had even thought of rebelling against the English crown was probably impressive enough.

"What have you learned?" Decker asked when Frank was seated.

"I've learned your Pinkertons didn't do a very good job."

"Allan Pinkerton's agents are supposed to be excellent," Decker protested, referring to the detective who had made his reputation as a Union spy during the war and gone on to found a professional detective agency. Decker had hired the agency to find out everything they could about Tom Brandt's besotted female patients.

"They missed a few important details about Miss Ordella Werner," Frank said. "For instance, how she tried to murder her doctor's wife."

"Murder?" Decker echoed in surprise. "Are you serious?"

"Yes, I'm serious. She also tried to kill her minister's wife, but that only happened a few weeks ago, so they wouldn't have known about it."

Decker was genuinely shocked. "Why did she try to kill her minister's wife?"

"When things didn't work out for her and the doctor, she decided she loved the minister. It doesn't matter. The point is, your Pinkertons didn't do their job, so now I've got to worry about what else I don't know."

Decker drummed his manicured fingers on the desk. "What do you want me to do?"

Frank had to admire the way Decker always got right to the point. "First of all, how much time do I have before Roosevelt leaves office?" Police Commissioner Roosevelt had campaigned vigorously for newly inaugurated President McKinley, and everyone expected he would soon be given a presidential appointment in Washington, D.C. Roosevelt had given Frank his personal permission to work full-time on solving Tom Brandt's murder, but Decker had warned Frank that Roosevelt wouldn't be around much longer as police commissioner. Once Roosevelt was gone, chances were slim Frank would be able to continue the investigation.

"I haven't heard anything definite yet," Decker said. "You'll probably hear the same time I do, though, when the newspapers report it. I don't expect it will be more than a few more weeks."

"I guess he'll leave immediately then."

"Most likely. That doesn't give you much time."

Although it galled him to admit it, Frank said, "I may need some help."

"What kind of help?"

"The kind of help another cop would give me, if I had a partner on this case. Somebody to find witnesses and track down people I need to see. Somebody to go outside the city, if I need that."

"Can you get someone in the department to help?"

"Not likely. Roosevelt won't want to annoy the chief of detectives by taking another of his men for a four-year-old case."

Decker leaned back in his chair and considered. "Would you consent to working with a Pinkerton?"

Even though that's what Frank had come to suggest, the very idea still stuck in his craw. "He's got to know I'm in charge. He takes his orders from me and doesn't do anything unless I tell him to."

Decker allowed himself a small smile. "I see you've already given the matter some thought."

Frank didn't bother to reply. He just waited for Decker's decision.

"This Miss Werner, what's become of her since she tried to kill two defenseless females?" Decker asked instead.

"She's been sent to an asylum upstate somewhere."

"You'd like to question her, I assume."

"Not particularly. Dr. Brandt's killer was alone with him in that alley, and I doubt he confessed to his crazy daughter after he did it. She wouldn't know anything, even if she was in her right mind, which she isn't. But one of the other families has moved out of the city, and I might find out the other women have been locked up someplace. I can cover more ground if I have a partner."

"Very well. I'll contact the Pinkerton office. I will ask them to send their best man, and you can have him as long as you need him."

Frank should have felt relief, but Decker's agreement only made him angry. "I want him to give his reports directly to me," he added.

Decker raised his eyebrows. A man like him didn't need to huff and puff to demonstrate his displeasure. Frank felt it like a hot wind blowing across the desk. "So *you* can decide what information I receive and therefore what information my daughter receives?"

Frank didn't like having things so clearly stated, but he said, "Yes."

"Mr. Malloy, I believe we have both been guilty of trying to protect my daughter in the past. You should know as well as I that it is a thankless—and often fruitless—task."

Frank did know it. "People have made some pretty ugly accusations against Dr. Brandt. There's no sense in her hearing any more of them if they aren't true."

"And if they are?"

Frank wanted to punch Decker, but he held on to his temper tightly and only said, "They aren't."

Decker just stared at him for a long moment, giving no indication of a reaction. Then he said, "I'll call the Pinkertons. Where shall I have his man meet you?"

# 4

FRANK SCANNED THE BUSY COFFEE SHOP three times before he saw the man he was looking for. The fellow was so ordinary looking, he could have blended into the background in any situation. No one would ever remember exactly what he looked like or even if they'd seen him at all. And no one would *ever* mistake the man for a cop, Frank thought with annoyance. People *always* knew he was a cop, no matter how ordinary he thought he looked.

The fellow looked up as Frank approached his table, and Frank realized to his chagrin that he'd been watching him since the moment he'd entered the shop but without giving any indication of his interest.

"You must be the Pink," Frank said, his annoyance giving his voice an edge.

A smile flickered in the man's average brown eyes but never touched his expression. "And you must be Detective Sergeant Malloy." His voice held no edge, but his tone held a notable absence of respect, which could have been mistaken for contempt if the man had betrayed the slightest hint of emotion. He did not.

Frank took a chair opposite him at the table and signaled to the waitress to bring him some coffee. He waited until she had brought him a cup before speaking. He used the time to study the man sitting across from him and try to decide what made him so nondescript.

The clothes were part of it. His cheap brown suit hung loosely on the man's thin frame, as if he'd inherited it from a well-padded cousin. His thinning brown hair was pomaded to his head, and a brown derby hat that had seen a lot of wear rested on the table. He sat with his shoulders hunched apologetically, as if he were afraid of taking up too much space in the world. Only his eyes betrayed any hint of whatever intelligence might lie beneath his bland exterior, and that hint was very small.

When the waitress had gone on to serve other customers, Frank said, "They were supposed to send over their best man."

"They did," he replied mildly.

That was when Frank made up his mind about him. "You got a name?"

"You can call me Douglas Victor."

"Or Victor Douglas?" The name was another ploy to render him unmemorable. No one would recall it exactly, or he could change it at will to confuse.

"Whatever is easier to remember," he agreed amiably. He hadn't made up his mind about Frank yet. No reason he should expect Frank to be more than a dumb and drunken Irish cop who'd made his way to detective by paying the appropriate bribe to the appropriate captain.

78

"Are they paying you extra to take orders from a Mick?" Frank asked.

"Should they?" Victor countered.

"I'll let you decide that. Have you read the reports your fellows gave Mr. Decker?"

"Of course."

"Did they tell you about Ordella Werner?"

"She stabbed some woman. That wasn't in the report."

"She stabbed her minister's wife a few weeks ago, but they wouldn't have known about that. She tried to kill her doctor's wife a few years back. That's the part they missed."

Victor was looking interested now. "What else did they miss?"

"I don't know. I haven't questioned anybody about the other two women yet, and there may be some more about the Werner woman I haven't found out."

"And this Dr. Brandt, he's supposed to have seduced all these women?"

Frank felt the frustration welling up in his chest, but he swallowed it down. "No, he didn't seduce any of them."

Victor's eyebrows rose. "Then why did somebody kill him?"

Frank ran a hand over his face. "He had this patient, Edna White. You read about her."

Victor nodded.

Frank explained his meeting with Miss White and her strange obsession with Tom Brandt.

"Are you saying she imagined the whole thing?" Victor asked skeptically.

"She *did* imagine the whole thing. Dr. Brandt was a married man and—"

"Married men enjoy a little piece on the side just like anybody else."

"You never met Edna White. She's not a little piece. She's a homely old maid, and no man ever looked twice at her in her entire life. She imagined the whole thing."

Victor looked unconvinced. "Then why did Brandt go out and find more females to seduce?"

That was, of course, what the original reports had said. "Like I said, your men got a lot of things wrong. These other women, they weren't in love with Brandt at all. They were in love with their own doctors."

"All of them?"

"Yes, and with different doctors."

"So their doctors seduced them," he guessed.

"No. They're just like Edna White. Their doctors didn't have anything to do with them. They imagined all of it."

Victor frowned and leaned back in his chair. "This doesn't make any sense at all. And what does any of it have to do with Brandt getting killed?"

"I told you. Brandt was trying to figure out how to cure this Edna White. He went to see these other women to see if he could talk them out of their crazy notions or at least figure out a way to help cure them. Near as I can find out, he caused more harm than good, at least with Ordella Werner, and probably with the others, too. The father of one of these women got so mad at him, he murdered him."

"You know that for a fact?"

"Yes, I do. I have a witness." Frank didn't explain that his witness was a street Arab whose testimony would be worthless in a court of law, even if he could locate him again.

"Then why don't you ask this witness who the killer is?"

"He never knew the man's name, and I can't exactly ask these respectable gentlemen to come down to Police Headquarters so he can take a look at them, even if he remembers what the fellow looks like after four years."

Victor scratched his chin. "Then how do you plan to figure out which one of them it is?"

"That's my lookout."

Victor didn't like that answer. "Then what's mine?" he challenged.

"To do what I tell you."

Douglas Victor, or whatever his real name was, looked far more interested than he had a few minutes ago. "And what are you going to tell me to do?"

"First, I want you to find out everything you can about Oscar Werner, Ordella's father."

Victor reached into his coat and pulled out a small notebook and the stub of a pencil. He made a note of the man's address and the facts Frank knew about him.

"You can't talk to him directly or let him know you're asking questions about him," Frank added when he'd finished giving all the information.

For the first time, Victor displayed emotion. He glared at Frank. "I'm a professional."

"So were the Pinks who did those other reports," Frank reminded him.

Victor ignored the provocation. "What else?"

"That's all for now. I'll meet you here day after tomorrow, same time, to see what you've found out."

Victor tucked his notebook and pencil away and looked back at Frank. This time his expression was shrewd. "Decker must be paying you a lot of money, but what I can't figure is why he'd bother. Why pay us both, when he could just hire me to do it?"

Frank felt the heat crawling up his neck as he fought down his anger. "Decker isn't paying me anything, and if he thought the Pinks could do the job right, he would've asked you."

This time Victor let his own anger show. "If mistakes were made before, they weren't mine."

"I'm glad to hear it. Now you've got a chance to show what you can do."

SARAH HAD BEEN OUT VISITING SOME NEW mothers that morning, checking on their progress.

As she turned down Bank Street on her way home, she was surprised to see her neighbor Mrs. Ellsworth outside sweeping her front porch. For most of the years Sarah had lived on Bank Street, Mrs. Ellsworth had busied herself with this chore for far too many hours while in reality keeping track of the comings and goings of the residents who shared the street. With only a grown son to care for, Mrs. Ellsworth had not been able to find enough to keep her truly busy, until Catherine and Maeve had come live with Sarah.

Usually, at this time of day, Mrs. Ellsworth would be with the girls, teaching them one of the mysteries of successful homemaking. Instead, she seemed to be keeping an eye out for Sarah's return.

"Good morning, Mrs. Ellsworth," she called when she was close enough.

The older woman pretended to be surprised, although Sarah knew she'd probably been aware of her presence since she'd turned in at the corner. "Good morning, Mrs. Brandt! I hope you haven't been out all night."

"Oh, no. I was just doing some follow-up visits."

"I'm so glad," she said, although Sarah had the oddest feeling she wasn't paying much attention to the conversation at all.

"Oh, my, I think if you look around your bottom step there, you'll see something of interest," Mrs. Ellsworth said in a poor attempt to appear casual.

Intrigued, Sarah walked over to her own porch

and dutifully looked around. Her porch wasn't as clean as Mrs. Ellsworth's, so she saw lots of things lying about but nothing of particular interest. She leaned over to get a closer look.

"Down this way a bit," Mrs. Ellsworth suggested anxiously.

Sarah bit back a smile and turned her gaze in the appropriate direction. That's when she saw it. At first she thought it was a pebble, but closer inspection revealed it to be . . .

"A tooth?" she asked, straightening in amazement and looking up to where Mrs. Ellsworth still stood on her own porch, now casually pretending to sweep again.

"Oh, my, did you find a tooth?" she exclaimed in feigned surprise. "What good luck!" She hurried down her steps and over to where Sarah stood, frowning. "Teeth aren't good fortune by themselves, you know, but if you just happen to find one, they're very good luck indeed." She looked down at the object in question, as if to confirm its existence.

"How would a tooth happen to be lying in front of my house?" Sarah asked skeptically. "Could it have just fallen out of someone's mouth as they walked by?"

"Who knows?" Mrs. Ellsworth asked, plainly not willing to explain. "The important thing is for you to pick it up and carry it with you."

Sarah sighed. No matter how hard she tried, she

couldn't seem to escape Mrs. Ellsworth's superstitions. "I wouldn't want the girls to know about this," she said with just a hint of warning in her voice.

"There's no reason why they should," Mrs. Ellsworth readily agreed.

At least they wouldn't be led to think Sarah believed any of this nonsense. She reached down and picked up the tooth with her gloved fingers and held it up for closer examination. It was a molar, but quite small.

"It looks like someone's baby tooth," Mrs. Ellsworth observed. "I saved all of Nelson's baby teeth. He was so embarrassed by that." She chuckled at the memory.

Sarah felt a small sense of relief. At least Mrs. Ellsworth hadn't stolen a tooth from some innocent person's mouth! "I suppose I need to carry it in my pocket?" she asked in defeat.

"If you tie it in the corner of your handkerchief, you'll combine two charms and double the effect," she suggested happily.

When she had accomplished this, Sarah tucked the handkerchief away. "Won't you come inside for a while?"

"Oh, my, no, not now," she protested. "Your mother is visiting the girls. I wouldn't dream of disturbing you."

Her mother? Back again so soon? Sarah felt a small frisson of alarm. "You wouldn't be disturbing us. You know you're always welcome," Sarah said politely.

"I'll come by later," the older woman said. "You'd better hurry. I'm sure your mother is anxious to see you. She rarely comes two days in a row, so it must be important."

Sarah didn't remind her that she would have been inside long since if not for the fiction of finding the tooth on her doorstep. Biting back a smile, she climbed the steps to her front stoop and unlocked the front door.

As usual, Catherine ran to greet her, and Maeve followed closely behind. By the time she'd hugged Catherine and removed her hat and gloves, her mother had reached the bottom of the stairs as well. As Maeve helpfully explained, the three of them had already spent several happy hours rearranging the furniture in Catherine's dollhouse. When Sarah had admired the results and given the appropriate amount of praise, her mother asked Maeve and Catherine to fix them all some lunch.

Once again, Sarah and her mother were alone in Catherine's room.

"I spoke to your father last night," Mrs. Decker said when the sound of the girls' footsteps had died away.

"You usually do, don't you?" Sarah said, trying to lighten the mood. She wasn't sure she wanted to know what her mother and father had discussed.

Her mother did not smile. "I told him Mr.

Malloy is investigating Dr. Brandt's death."

Sarah didn't know if she approved or not. "What did he say?"

"He told me I shouldn't involve myself in such unpleasant matters, or some such drivel, just as he always does when I want to discuss something serious with him," she said, waving away her husband's concerns with one slender hand. "That's not the important part. The important part is that he wasn't surprised by this information."

"So you think he already knew about it?"

"Oh, yes. Would Mr. Malloy have told him?"

Sarah hesitated, trying to remember if Malloy had said anything about her father being involved. "Mr. Malloy told me that the boy who witnessed Tom's murder thought he had heard one of them say the name *Decker*," she recalled, then remembered something else. "Malloy also said Father had received a letter shortly before Tom died, accusing Tom of seducing young women."

"Good heavens! How horrible!" her mother exclaimed.

"Isn't it?" Sarah agreed, still outraged. "But I just realized that Malloy couldn't have known about the letter unless Father told him."

"You're right, of course. Although I suppose the policemen who originally investigated Dr. Brandt's death could have known about it and put it in the reports or something," Mrs. Decker suggested.

"I don't think so. According to Malloy, Father

decided not to mention the letter at all. He . . . Mr. Malloy said Father didn't want me to be hurt by it."

Her mother's beautiful blue eyes narrowed. "How very kind of him," she said doubtfully.

"I didn't believe it either," Sarah admitted. "But now that I think about it again, perhaps it's true."

"What makes you think so?"

"Because after Tom died, Father and I quarreled," Sarah reminded her. Her mother winced slightly at the memory of that awful time. "Father wanted me to forget all about Tom's work and my own and come home. He wanted me to return to the life I'd had before I married, and so did you."

"We only wanted you to be happy, Sarah," her mother said defensively. "We couldn't imagine you living all alone and . . . and earning your own living." Her tone suggested she still wasn't completely convinced Sarah had made the right choice.

"Did you think I'd starve?" Sarah asked, still stung by their failure to believe in her.

"We were afraid you'd be too proud to come to us for help if you weren't successful," she corrected her.

"The way Maggie was," Sarah said and instantly regretted her words when she saw the blood drain from her mother's face. Maggie's pride had cost her her life. "I'm so sorry! I didn't mean—"

"No, you're right," Mrs. Decker admitted, holding up her hand to stop Sarah from apologizing. "That's exactly what we feared when you married Dr. Brandt. Of course, he was much different from . . . from . . ." She couldn't bring herself to name Maggie's husband, who had been unable to support her at all, through no fault of his own. Mrs. Decker swallowed. "Dr. Brandt had a profession. He would have taken care of you. But when he died . . . Sarah, we only wanted you to be safe."

Sarah's heart ached to see her mother's anguish. "I know that now," Sarah admitted. "Now that I have Catherine, I can understand how terrified you can be for your child."

"You're so much like your father, too," Mrs. Decker said.

Sarah stiffened in automatic resistance to such an idea. "In what way?" she challenged.

Mrs. Decker smiled. "In many ways, but the *faults* you share are pride and stubbornness."

Sarah opened her mouth to protest and then caught herself. Her mother was only too right. "I wouldn't necessarily call stubbornness a *fault*," she demurred. "That's why I've been successful helping Malloy on his cases."

"I'm not sure Mr. Malloy would agree with you about stubbornness not being a fault," her mother said wryly, "but you are, no doubt, correct. In that light, perhaps we should call it something else."

"Persistence," Sarah offered.

"Persistence it shall be," Mrs. Decker confirmed. "Oh, my, how on earth did we get on this subject?"

"You were telling me that Father knew about Mr. Malloy investigating Tom's death," Sarah recalled.

"Oh, yes. And you told me about that awful letter he received. We still don't know the real reason he didn't tell anyone about it, though."

Sarah considered. "I may have to change my mind about Father," she said after a moment.

"About what?"

"I said I didn't believe he kept the letter a secret to protect me, but looking back . . . After we quarreled, he could have shown me the letter to make me think ill of Tom and make me doubt my decision to carry on his work. He could have used it to destroy my memories of Tom and persuade me to return home, but he didn't."

Her mother's face brightened. "You're right! Oh, Sarah, you're absolutely right. We've both misjudged him. He was protecting you all along. In fact . . ." She frowned thoughtfully.

"In fact what?" Sarah prodded when she hesitated.

"Remember when you told me that the police never solved Dr. Brandt's murder because your father didn't pay a . . . a *reward*. You couldn't believe he didn't know that was necessary."

"That's right," Sarah said, feeling the bitterness welling up again.

"You thought he did it out of spite, but remember, he'd just received that letter telling him awful things about Dr. Brandt. Perhaps the reason he didn't pay the reward was because he was afraid of what an investigation would uncover about Dr. Brandt. Perhaps he was still only trying to protect you."

Sarah had to admit that argument made a lot of sense. She just wasn't sure if it was enough to change her whole opinion of her father.

FRANK WAITED UNTIL THE LAST PATIENT HAD left, and Dr. Unger's office had closed for the day. The middle-aged woman in the waiting room wore a stiffly starched apron over her striped dress and a pince-nez hanging from a string pinned to her bodice. Her hair had been scraped back into a severe bun. She glared at Frank down her long nose.

"The office is closed. We open again at nine tomorrow."

"I'm not a patient. I'm Detective Sergeant Frank Malloy with the New York City Police. I need to ask the doctor a few questions."

"Concerning what matter?" she demanded. Plainly, she was used to controlling who got in to see the doctor.

Frank gave her a look that had caused hardened criminals to falter. "If the doctor wants you to know, he'll tell you."

She caught her breath, but whether from shock or fury, Frank couldn't tell. She got up from her desk and quickly disappeared through a nearby door, closing it tightly behind her. In a matter of moments, the door opened again, and this time a man appeared, with the woman in his wake. He was tall and too thin, his face drawn and tired, but his eyes were alive with concern.

"Is one of my patients in trouble?" he asked. His voice was deep and kind, the type of voice that would reassure a sick person, even if the doctor had no idea how to cure him. In Frank's experience, they usually didn't.

"I'd like to talk to you in private, Doctor." Frank glanced meaningfully at the woman, who lifted her chin in silent outrage.

"Oh, of course, of course," the doctor said, oblivious to the woman's reaction. "Come in, please."

The woman moved out of the way with obvious reluctance, allowing Frank to follow the doctor through the door and down a short hallway. Dr. Unger led Frank into a small, cluttered room furnished as an office. A glass-doored bookcase held many thick volumes. The desktop was covered with stacks of folders similar to the ones Tom Brandt had kept for his patients.

"Sit down," Dr. Unger said as he closed the office door behind them. "I'm sorry, I didn't get your name."

Frank gave it again as he sat down in one of the straight-backed chairs opposite the doctor's desk. Dr. Unger took his place behind it.

"What's this all about, Mr. Malloy?"

"I need to ask you some questions about Amelia Goodwin."

For a moment, Dr. Unger just stared back at him blankly as he tried to place the name. Then he remembered. "Oh, yes, Miss Goodwin." He shook his head. "Sad case, and rather embarrassing for me, I'm afraid."

Not the response Frank had been expecting. "How was it embarrassing?"

"The poor girl fancied herself in love with me, if you can imagine," he admitted with some chagrin. "She was only eighteen, if I remember correctly. I'm older than her father, and as you can see, not the kind of man to inspire a young girl's affections."

He was right. Dr. Unger had never been handsome, and the years had not been kind to him. His suit, while originally of good quality, had not been cleaned or pressed in some time. Frank could almost believe he slept in it. Except for the kind manner Frank had originally noted, he could see nothing that would fulfill a young girl's fantasies of true love. "What can you tell me about her?"

"Is she in trouble? Has she done something?" the doctor asked with a frown.

"No, not that I know of. It's in connection with another case I'm investigating."

"I'm not sure I can help you very much. I only saw her once, and that was years ago."

"You only saw her *once*?" Frank echoed in surprise.

"Yes, that was what made it so strange. Her family summoned me for some complaint or other. She was crippled, you see."

"Crippled?"

"Yes. She was born with a deformed leg or foot, I can't recall exactly. Wait, let me see if I can find her chart." He got up and disappeared for several minutes. When he returned, he was flipping through the pages in a folder like the ones on his desk. "That's right," he mused, scanning one of the few sheets of paper in the folder. "She had a clubfoot."

Frank couldn't help his flinch. His son Brian had been born with a clubfoot. "Didn't they try to operate on it?" Surgery had recently corrected Brian's deformity.

Dr. Unger looked up in surprise that Frank would know the treatment for clubfoot. "No, they didn't. Truth to tell, we really have only developed operations that work for clubfoot in recent years. Back when she was born, they would occasionally try to operate on them but were seldom able to help much. Sometimes the surgery would even make it worse. Miss Goodwin's parents had never tried any treatment at all, and by the time I saw her, it was far too late to do any good in any case."

"Why did she need to see you?"

He sat back down at his desk and studied the paper again. "She was subject to moods, according to her grandmother, but lately she had fallen into a decline. She wouldn't eat and never wanted to get out of bed, even though she didn't appear to have any illness. She claimed sunlight hurt her eyes, and she cried over everything anyone said to her."

"What did you do for her?"

He was still looking at his notes. "I couldn't find anything wrong with her. Except for her foot, she was perfectly healthy, although she was thin and pale from not eating and refusing to get out of bed. According to this, I prescribed a tonic."

"That's all?"

Dr. Unger frowned with remembered frustration. "After what happened later, I tried to recall what I could have done to mislead the poor girl, but I was never able to determine what it might have been. As I said, I only saw her the one time. I did talk to her for a few minutes. In cases like that, it's all you *can* do. I probably told her she needed to get up and eat. I may have said something about a pretty girl like her not wasting her life lying in the dark."

"Was she pretty?" Frank asked.

He made an apologetic gesture. "Not really, but she was young. I was being kind, you see. One tries to be kind when a young person is ill, especially one whose life was so sad already."

"What do you mean?"

"Oh, her family . . ." He shuffled through the papers in the folder, looking for more information. "Her mother had died, and her grandmother had charge of her. The old woman didn't think much of her, because of her foot, you see. Her father didn't either, from what I could tell. They were ashamed, I think. Thought she reflected poorly on them or something. They kept her at home. Not much of a life for a young girl. No wonder she took to her bed."

"If you only saw her once, how did you know she'd developed an affection for you?" Frank asked.

Dr. Unger shifted uncomfortably in his chair. "Her father came to see me one day a few weeks later. He was enraged. Nearly attacked me. Fortunately, some of the patients in the waiting room were able to subdue him. When he calmed down, he accused me of seducing his daughter," he admitted with a chagrined wince.

"What made him think that?"

"She'd told him I did! It was the most fantastic thing I'd ever heard. She'd told her father and grandmother and anyone else who would listen that I came to her room at night and . . . and made love to her!" Plainly, the admission mortified him.

"And they believed her?" Frank asked in amazement.

"Why would she invent a story like that? How would a girl like that even know of such things?"

"Did you ever find out?"

"Oh, yes. She'd overheard the maids talking, apparently, and picked up enough that she was able to imagine what a lover might do, and she could talk about it quite convincingly."

"How did you convince her father you hadn't violated her?"

"It wasn't easy!" Dr. Unger remembered. "I called in my wife . . . you met her outside. She vouched for my faithfulness. I slept beside her all night, every night. I think her fury at the thought that she would tolerate an unfaithful husband who went out at night carousing was what convinced him."

"Did the girl have a lover at all?"

"As difficult as it is to believe, considering how much she seemed to know about the act of lovemaking, no, she didn't. I suggested her father have the house watched to see if anyone was able to sneak in or out during the night. No one did, but still she persisted in her tales of midnight assignations. She even insisted that I had spirited her away one night for a clandestine marriage ceremony."

"She claimed you were *married* to her?"

"Oh, yes! According to her, we were going to run away together to France, I think it was. Or perhaps California. I'm afraid I've forgotten all the details. I'd hoped never to think of it again, as a matter of fact."

"I'm sorry to *make* you think about it again," Frank said quite honestly. The doctor's distress was obvious.

"Why have you, then?" he asked curiously. "You said she hasn't done anything untoward."

"No, she hasn't, or at least not that I know about. I'm here because of Dr. Tom Brandt."

Once again Dr. Unger returned a blank stare.

"He was the one who was investigating cases like Miss Goodwin's," Frank offered helpfully. "He had a patient like this Amelia Goodwin who'd fallen in love with him. I think he came to consult with you."

"Oh, my God, yes," Dr. Unger finally remembered. "I'd forgotten his name. Poor devil. He was murdered, wasn't he, not long afterwards?"

"That's right."

Now Dr. Unger was really confused. "And you're still investigating Dr. Brandt's murder, after all these years?"

"Yes, I've found some new information."

"Information that brought you to me?"

"Yes, because Dr. Brandt was trying to find other women who suffered from the same malady as Amelia Goodwin. How did he find out about Miss Goodwin?"

"If I recall correctly, he'd been asking other physicians if they'd ever heard of a situation like his, and one of my friends sent him to me." He thought for a moment. "I seem to remember he told me he'd found *several* similar cases. I could hardly believe there were others, although it was somewhat of a comfort to know I wasn't alone."

"He did find other cases like hers. In fact, it's common enough to have a name. It's called Old Maid's Disease."

"Old Maid's Disease," Unger echoed thoughtfully. "Probably because the sufferers are unmarried. Was he able to find a cure?"

"I don't think so, but even if he did, he died before he could tell anyone."

"What a pity. He was a young man, too, if I recall."

Frank felt a pang of sympathy for Sarah's loss. "Like I told you, I found some new information about his death. I have reason to believe that Dr. Brandt's killer was the father of one of these women."

"The women with this Old Maid's Disease?" Dr. Unger asked in surprise.

"Yes. A witness heard Dr. Brandt's killer accuse him of ruining his daughter."

"Oh, my, that's exactly what Amelia Goodwin's father accused me of doing." Unger shuddered slightly at the thought that he might have escaped being murdered as Dr. Brandt had been.

Frank felt the hairs on the back of his neck rise. "What kind of a man is this Mr. Goodwin?"

Unger stiffened defensively. "What do you mean?"

"You said he attacked you when he thought you'd seduced his daughter. Were you afraid of him?"

"Of course I was, at least then. But he was very upset. He thought I'd violated his daughter. Any man would be furious."

"Do you know how he reacted when Dr. Brandt tried to treat Amelia?"

Unger shook his head. "No, I never spoke with

Dr. Brandt again after his first visit to me. I told him all I knew about Amelia Goodwin, and he promised he'd report back to me if he was able to help her at all. Of course, I never heard from him again."

"What do you know about Goodwin?"

The doctor frowned. Plainly, he didn't like the idea of implicating a man in murder, even one who had been so unpleasant to him. "He's a successful businessman, I believe. They lived in a good neighborhood, at least. Nice house with a few servants. The girl didn't want for anything, even if they kept her hidden away. I only met him the one time he came to my office to thrash me, so I'm afraid I didn't form a very thorough opinion of him."

Opinions weren't worth much, in any case, Frank thought. A man who believed he was protecting his child would do things he would never do otherwise.

"If you asked me about the grandmother, though," Unger remarked into the silence, "I'd have to say I could believe her capable of anything."

"Amelia's grandmother?" Frank had met her briefly and shared that opinion. "Why do you think so?"

"She's a very angry woman. Thought her son married beneath him, or so I gathered. The girl being crippled was his punishment."

Frank felt an unreasonable anger at such a thought. His son, Brian, wasn't a punishment for anything. "You said the girl's mother had died. Do you know how long ago?"

100

"I'm going to say I don't think she'd been dead long before I saw Amelia, but I don't know why I thought that. Something the grandmother said, perhaps." He flipped through the papers in her folder again, then shook his head. "Nothing in here about it, but if that was so, it would explain the girl taking to her bed like that in the first place."

"Yes, it would," Frank said. He wondered if he'd gotten everything from the doctor that he could, but since he couldn't think of anything else to ask, he rose to his feet. "Thanks for your help, Dr. Unger."

"I don't think I was very helpful, but I wish you success in finding Dr. Brandt's killer. No one has a right to take another's life, no matter what the provocation."

"In Dr. Brandt's case, I don't think there really was any provocation either," Frank said.

"All the more reason to find his killer, then."

# 5

FINDING ORDELLA WERNER'S DOCTOR WAS A bit more difficult than Frank had anticipated. He wasn't listed in the city directory as a practicing physician, and Frank had to go to three hospitals before he found someone who had heard of Dr. Leiter. A small bribe bought him an address, but when he went to the house, the Leiters didn't live there anymore.

The maid who answered the door wasn't sure

anyone would want to speak with him, so she left him standing on the front stoop for ten minutes. He was just considering going around to the back to try his luck with the servants' entrance when she opened the front door again.

"The two Mrs. Paisleys will see you," she reported and let him in. When she'd taken his hat and coat, she led him into a small front parlor where everything looked a bit too tidy. Frank was sure no one ever relaxed in this room. Two women sat side by side on the horsehair sofa. The younger Mrs. Paisley was plump and comely with hair the color of straw done up in fancy curls. The older Mrs. Paisley bore no trace of any past comeliness, and Frank could see that she had never tolerated foolishness from anyone in her entire life. She held an intricately carved cane that did *not* have a silver handle. The younger one was frightened, and the older one, angry.

"Mr. Malloy from the police," the maid said a bit uncertainly. Obviously, she rarely introduced anyone from the police.

"Detective Sergeant Frank Malloy," he clarified as the maid slipped away hurriedly. "I was looking for Dr. Leiter."

The younger Mrs. Paisley turned to the older one. "I knew there'd be trouble."

"Nonsense, Doris!" the older woman snapped. She glowered up at Frank. "What do you want with him?"

"I'm investigating a murder."

The younger Mrs. Paisley let out an undignified squeak, earning her a black look from her mother-in-law.

"Has Dr. Leiter murdered someone?" the older woman asked.

"No."

This time she glared at Frank and banged her cane on the floor, causing her daughter-in-law to jump. "Come, come, young man. If you want cooperation from us, you must cooperate in return."

Frank bit back a smile. "May I sit down?"

"Oh, yes, of course," she said impatiently, indicating a chair opposite them with a wave of her hand. "I'm not going to offer you refreshment, though. That would encourage you to stay, and we can't have the police lingering around the place, now can we?" She didn't wait for an answer. Why on earth are you looking for poor Dr. Leiter?"

"I told you," Frank said when he was seated. "I'm investigating a murder . . . the murder of another doctor," he added before she could chide him again.

"Did that madwoman kill him?" she asked, startling another squeak from Doris.

"What madwoman is that?" Frank asked with credible innocence.

She was having none of it. "The madwoman who broke into this house twice when Dr. Leiter lived here, of course. What was her name again, Doris?"

"Miss Werner," Doris reported faintly.

"Did you know Miss Werner?" Frank asked.

Doris looked so horrified, Frank was afraid she might faint, but Mrs. Paisley said, "Of course we don't know her. One does not *know* madwomen, no matter who their families might be."

"We certainly didn't know about her when we bought the house," Doris offered, her voice quivering.

"Because if we had, we wouldn't have bought it," Mrs. Paisley added. "Doris is much too imaginative. She thinks every sound she hears is this mad Miss Werner returning to murder us all."

"I don't think you need to worry about her anymore," Frank said.

"Whyever not?" Mrs. Paisley asked. "Is she dead?"

"No, but she recently tried to stab her minister's wife, and she has been locked securely away."

Frank wasn't positive how securely she was locked away, but he wanted to give poor Doris some peace.

"Her *minister's* wife?" Doris echoed, horrified.

"Why would she do such a thing?" Mrs. Paisley demanded.

"She had transferred her affections from Dr. Leiter to her minister. She apparently thought if she killed his wife, he would marry her."

As he had expected, Doris took this news badly. "Why on earth would she think such a thing?" she demanded almost desperately. "It doesn't even make sense!"

"She's a *madwoman*," Mrs. Paisley reminded her impatiently. "It is the nature of madness *not* to make sense. Now, Mr. Malloy, why have you come here today and upset Doris and annoyed me?"

"As I said, I need to speak to Dr. Leiter. I believe he may have some information about another doctor's murder."

"And is Miss Werner involved in this matter in some way?"

"Only because she was a patient of both doctors," Frank said, stretching the truth a bit. "Do you know where I could find Dr. Leiter?"

"Suppose I do," Mrs. Paisley said. "Why should I tell you?"

Frank had to think about that for a moment. "A killer is loose in the city, Mrs. Paisley. You would be helping me put him in prison."

Mrs. Paisley sniffed derisively. "I doubt that very much."

"Oh, just tell him, Mother Paisley," Doris begged, "so he'll leave us alone!"

Mrs. Paisley glared at Doris again, but she turned back to Frank in resignation. "You must promise me that Miss Werner will never find out where he is," she said sternly.

"I wouldn't dream of telling her," Frank assured her. "I know what she did to them."

"Mrs. Leiter has never been the same since they found Miss Werner hiding here," Mrs. Paisley told him. "I've never met the woman, you understand, but the neighbors have been most informative."

"But only *after* we moved in," Doris added bitterly. "You would think someone would have warned us."

"If it's any comfort to you, Miss Werner has lost interest in Dr. Leiter," Frank said. "Like I said, she's in love with her minister now."

"And trying to kill *his* wife," Mrs. Paisley recalled.

"She's probably forgotten all about Dr. Leiter," Frank said. "You really have nothing to worry about."

Doris did not look convinced.

"You said you have Dr. Leiter's address," he reminded them.

Mrs. Paisley gave Doris one of her glares. "Go get it for the man."

Doris hopped up and scurried away, leaving the parlor door standing open.

"She has the constitution of a rabbit, I'm afraid," Mrs. Paisley said sadly.

"Miss Werner is a terrifying creature," Frank allowed. "I'm not sure I'd want to live in this house myself."

Mrs. Paisley frowned thoughtfully. "I told you the neighbors were very informative. I haven't told Doris, but they said Mrs. Leiter had a complete breakdown after they found that woman here the second time. Dr. Leiter had to make sure Miss Werner never found them again, so they moved

106

away and told no one where they were going. Can I trust you to keep their secret?"

Frank didn't hesitate. "You most certainly can. If I had my way, Miss Werner would be in prison for what she's done."

She seemed satisfied with that. They sat in silence for a few more minutes until Doris returned with a sheet of writing paper. She handed it to Frank, and he saw that her hand was trembling. He felt a pang of guilt for upsetting her, but it couldn't be helped. He glanced at the address. The Leiters had gone a long way to escape Ordella Werner.

"Thank you, ladies, for your help. I'm sorry to have bothered you." Frank rose to take his leave, but when he reached the door, he stopped and turned back for one more question. "By the way, you said your neighbors had been helpful. Could you tell me which ones were the *most* helpful?"

THE NEXT MORNING, AS PLANNED, FRANK returned to the coffee shop. This time he saw the Pinkerton agent right away, even though he was hiding behind a newspaper. Victor looked at him with little warmth as Frank sat down opposite him at the small table. The waitress hurried over with coffee, took Frank's order for some donuts, and left.

"What did you find out?" Frank asked.

"Good morning to you, too," Victor said. He reached into his coat and pulled out a packet of papers. He handed them to Frank.

They were neatly typewritten, Frank saw as he unfolded them, just like all the Pinkerton reports. The Pinks must employ a small army of secretaries. He quickly skimmed the words.

"If I had a few more days, I could find out more," Victor said when Frank looked up again.

"I doubt it," Frank said. Victor stiffened with anger, but before he could protest, Frank added, "I don't think there's anything left to find out about him." Indeed, it was the most thorough report Frank could have wished for.

Mollified, Victor sat back again and waited.

"I don't suppose you found out if he's got a silver-headed cane," Frank sighed.

"Why a cane? Does it have something to do with the murder?"

"The killer used one to kill Brandt."

"You said not to go near him," Victor reminded him. "I did follow him for a few hours yesterday, but he wasn't carrying a cane when I saw him. If he has one in his house—"

"If it comes to that, we'll find out. You didn't come across anything that indicated he's violent, did you?"

"No, he only cheats and steals, same as every other businessman in the city. If he ever hit anybody, they didn't complain about it."

Frank sipped his coffee. The waitress delivered his donuts, and he took a bite of one, savoring the burst of sweetness in his mouth.

When he'd waited as long as he could, Victor asked, "What's next?"

"This was a test," Frank said, tapping the report lying on the table. "I had to make sure you were good, before I gave you something important to do."

"You think I don't know that?" Victor snapped.

Frank made him wait a few more moments. "One of the families moved out to Yonkers."

"The Albertons," Victor said, one step ahead of him already. He pulled out his notebook and pencil and began to write.

"I need to find out as much about them as possible before I approach them. The daughter is in an asylum, according to a former neighbor. She had a breakdown when her twin brother died in a bicycle accident."

"Damn things should be outlawed," Victor muttered. "One of 'em near ran me over a few weeks ago."

"According to the old woman I talked to, Christina Alberton was perfectly normal before her brother died. Then she started hearing voices and going outside in her nightclothes and doing other crazy things."

"She try to stab anybody?"

"Not that I know of," Frank reported grimly. "I'm not real sure who she was attached to, either. Dr. Brandt's file on her didn't say."

"Must have been her doctor, don't you think? All the others were."

"I don't want to guess. I want to *know*."

Victor raised his eyebrows. "Yes, sir," he mocked. "His file did say she had dementia praecox."

"Is that like the clap?" Victor asked in disgust, surprising a laugh from Frank.

"Not even close," Frank assured him. "Just means she's extra crazy. Hears voices, like I said. Imagines things that aren't there."

"But she doesn't stab wives?"

"She may have since she moved to Yonkers. It's not likely we'd have heard about it down here if she did."

"If she did, I'll find out. When do you want a report?"

"Yesterday, but I'll settle for day after tomorrow. I know you can't find out much in that time," Frank added quickly when Victor started to protest. "Just find out everything you can and report back."

"What'll you be doing in the meantime?"

"I'm going to talk to Dr. Leiter, Ordella Werner's first love." Briefly, he told Victor of his encounter with the two Mrs. Paisleys.

"When are you going to question Werner himself? I'd like to see that."

"Not until I've found out everything I can," Frank said. "I'll only get one chance with him. If I can't get him to confess then, I never will, because he'll bring down the wrath of God on me after that."

"You think he's the one?" Victor asked in surprise.

"I haven't decided yet, but I'm not going to talk

110

to *any* of the suspects directly until I know everything about them. I'm hoping I'll find out which one did it, or at least have a pretty good idea, before I have to confront any of them, but that might not be possible. So I'll go to each one and accuse him with all the facts and see if the guilty one will break."

Victor frowned. "You really think that'll work?"

"It's worked before," Frank said. "Remember, these are men who never broke the law before or since. Well, never killed anybody at least," Frank corrected himself at Victor's grimace. "That's a hard thing to carry around with you for four years."

"Lots of men do it," Victor reminded him.

"Those men don't go to church every Sunday and sit across the table from their families every night."

"But these men sit across the table from daughters who are insane," Victor said. "That's got to change you."

Frank shrugged. "You got a better idea?"

"Not yet, but if I get one, you'll be the first to know." He rose from his chair. "Day after tomorrow right here?"

Frank nodded. Victor sauntered out of the coffee shop and disappeared into the crowd, a man no one would notice or remember. Frank sighed, wishing he could figure out an excuse to go see Sarah.

# • • •

"**I** WISH THERE WAS SOMETHING I COULD DO TO help," Maeve said as she finished clearing the breakfast table.

"You're a tremendous help," Sarah assured her in surprise. She thought surely Maeve knew Sarah couldn't get along without her.

"Oh, I don't mean help *you*," the girl clarified. "I mean help Mr. Malloy. Help him find out who killed Dr. Brandt."

Catherine had gone upstairs to play while Sarah and Maeve washed the dishes and put the kitchen to rights, but Sarah automatically glanced out into the hallway to be sure the child wasn't lurking within earshot. The less Catherine heard about death and murder, the better. "Don't tell anyone, but so do I," Sarah confessed. "It's driving me crazy, not knowing what he's doing."

"I wonder if they'll ever let women be policemen," Maeve wondered aloud as she started washing the dishes.

"They do have matrons who work at the precinct houses," Sarah said. "And Commissioner Roosevelt has a female secretary."

Maeve shook her head. "They don't do what Mr. Malloy does, though. They don't investigate and figure things out."

Sarah couldn't help smiling. "Does that appeal to you?"

"Oh, yes, ma'am! I think it's so interesting when

Mr. Malloy comes to tell you what he's found out and the two of you talk it over."

"It can be dangerous, too. Don't you remember what happened the last time I helped Mr. Malloy solve a murder?"

Maeve looked up, and Sarah saw that the girl remembered only too well the peril that had invaded this very kitchen. "Yes, but bad things can happen to you anywhere you go, even if you haven't done anything to deserve it."

"Are you thinking about your own life, Maeve?" Sarah asked gently.

Maeve looked away and started concentrating on the dish she was scrubbing. "That's over now," she said after a moment. "I don't think about it anymore. What I'm talking about is how trouble can find anybody, so there's no such thing as being safe. And if there's no such thing as being safe, why not take a chance now and then and do some good?"

"You make a good argument," Sarah admitted as she dried the plates Maeve had washed. "Somehow I don't think Mr. Malloy would think a female should take any chances at all, though."

"What do men know about anything?" the girl scoffed. "If most of 'em had their way, females would be locked up in a tower someplace like that princess with the funny name in Catherine's book."

"Rapunzel?" Sarah asked in surprise.

"That's the one. Don't you think Mr. Malloy

113

would be happier if you was in a tower someplace where no killer could ever find you?"

Sarah didn't bother to correct Maeve's grammar. She was too busy picturing what she had described. "Actually, I don't think Mr. Malloy would like it all," Sarah said with a grin, "because if I was locked in a tower, I'd be in an extremely foul temper all the time, and I'd make his life as miserable as I possibly could."

Maeve yelped in surprised laughter. "Then you know I'm right! Why should men get to do all the interesting things, and women just get to take care of children and wash dishes?"

"I get to do interesting things *and* take care of children and wash dishes," Sarah reminded her, holding up a dish to prove her point.

Maeve smiled triumphantly. "That's why I want to be just like you."

FRANK HAD TO ADMIT THAT DR. LEITER HAD chosen well when he escaped the city to get away from Ordella Werner. The long train ride out to Long Island had carried him to a peaceful little town where the air was clean and sweet and the only sounds were gulls calling and the crash of waves on the nearby shore. The porter at the station had pointed him in the right direction and assured him Dr. Leiter's house was just a short walk. This proved to be correct.

The sea breeze was brisk but not cold as Frank

walked down the sandy stretch of road and found the house he was looking for. A weathered shingle hung out front, proclaiming this to be the home and office of Dr. Howard Leiter, M.D. Frank stepped up onto the wraparound porch, chose the door designated as the office, and found it unlocked. Opening the door caused a bell overhead to jangle, and Frank stepped into a small anteroom furnished with several mismatched wooden chairs. In a few moments, a middle-aged man entered the room through another door that apparently led to the main part of the house. He was shrugging into his suit jacket, but he stopped dead in his tracks when he saw Frank.

"May I help you?" he asked uncertainly, straightening his coat and smoothing the lapels nervously. What had alarmed him? The sight of a stranger or had Frank's demeanor betrayed him?

"I'm looking for Dr. Leiter," Frank said.

"I am he." He glanced over his shoulder, as if making sure the door behind him was securely closed.

"I'm Detective Sergeant Frank Malloy from the New York City Police."

Dr. Leiter closed his eyes, drew a deep breath, and let it out in a gusty sigh. Then he opened his eyes again. "What has she done now?"

"What has who done?"

"You know who," he said wearily. "Ordella Werner." Then his expression changed to alarm.

"Or has she escaped?" He looked around anxiously. "Has she found us?"

"No, no," Frank assured him hastily. "She's locked up in an asylum, and as far as I know, she doesn't even know where you are."

He sighed again, this time with profound relief. He glanced uneasily over his shoulder at the door. "Let's go into my office, where we can speak privately."

He ushered Frank through a third door that led to a room furnished as a combination office and examining room. He closed this door, too, after assuring himself that no one had followed them. "Sit down, Mr. . . . I'm sorry, what was your name again?"

"Malloy." Frank took the offered seat opposite Leiter's desk while Leiter took his seat behind it. Frank realized he seemed to be spending a lot of time lately in this very situation.

"I'm right that you've come about Miss Werner, then," Leiter said. Frank marveled at the fear he saw reflected in Leiter's eyes.

"Yes, but not really because of her. I'm investigating Dr. Tom Brandt's murder."

"Brandt?" Leiter's forehead wrinkled as he tried to recall the name.

"He's the doctor who had a patient who fell in love with him like Miss Werner did with you," Frank reminded him.

"Oh, my God, yes. I remember now—he was

murdered shortly afterwards. But I thought that was solved. Wasn't it a robbery or something?"

"No one ever investigated. They just assumed it was a robbery, but we have some new information."

"Do you think the Werner woman had something to do with it?" Leiter asked. Frank noticed his hands were trembling, and he was making no effort to hide it.

"Not her personally, no. I have a witness who said the killer was a man."

"Thank God for that, at least," Leiter said, rubbing at his forehead. He reached down to open a desk drawer, and he brought out a bottle and a glass. "Can I offer you a drink, Mr. Malloy?" he asked, not even looking up as he poured several fingers of whiskey into the glass.

"No, thanks," Frank said and watched as Leiter emptied the glass in one long gulp.

He set the glass back on the desk with a thunk, then looked up at Frank as if expecting to see disapproval. "You don't know what that woman has put us through."

"I heard the story from Ordella's aunt and one of the servants," Frank said. "How she got into your house and lived there while you were out of town."

He shuddered at the memory. "They thought I must have done something to encourage her," Leiter said somewhat desperately.

"Who did?"

"Everyone! The police, my neighbors, her family, even my wife at first. No one could believe she'd do such a thing unless we really were having some sort of affair."

"But you weren't."

"Heavens, no! I'd never even been alone with the woman. Her aunt always stayed in the room when I visited the house, and I never saw her as a patient at my office. By the time she started coming around, we knew that she fancied herself in love with me, so my nurse would send her away without letting her see me. I'd still find notes from her slipped under my office door, though. She'd come by when no one was around and leave them. Sometimes she'd leave little cakes or cookies or loaves of bread, too. I kept thinking if I continued to ignore her, she'd get discouraged and stop."

"But she never did."

"No, she didn't." The whiskey seemed to have helped. He was a little calmer now. "In fact, the more I refused to see her, the more convinced she became that I wanted to leave my wife and run off with her."

"How did her father act during all this?"

The question surprised Leiter, and he had to think for a moment. "He was embarrassed at first. When her aunt told him that Miss Werner was only pretending to be ill so I would come to see her, he actually apologized to me. He asked if I would try to keep it quiet, so it wouldn't reflect badly on the family. Of course I agreed. I didn't want anyone to know either. We thought that was the end of it. When she started coming to the office, I just ignored her at first, but after a while, I had to notify him of what she was doing. He was mortified."

"Not angry?"

"Not with me, at least not that he ever showed until she came to our home the first time."

"You said her family thought you must have led her on."

"Yes, as I said, no one believed she would do that otherwise, and of course she told them we were lovers. That was the worst part." He rubbed his head again.

"How did you convince them you weren't?"

"I had to convince my wife first. She knew I came home and spent every evening with her and the children, so Miss Werner's claims that I met her someplace were obviously false. Her family quickly realized that she could not have been meeting me either, once my nurse informed them that she was never allowed to see me at the office. I'm not sure the police believed it even then. It was humiliating to be accused of something so vile when I was completely innocent."

"I'm sure it was," Frank sympathized. "How did Dr. Brandt get involved in all this?"

He needed a moment to remember. "He called on me one day and told me he was having the same sort of problems with one of his patients. I had confided in one of my friends, and he had told Dr. Brandt. Brandt told me others were having the same issues. I could hardly believe it at first . . . that others had experienced the same thing. I suppose I could hardly believe there were other women like Miss Werner."

"What did he want from you?"

"He wanted to interview Miss Werner. He thought he could help her."

"Did you think he could?"

"I had no idea, but I was certainly willing to let him try. I didn't think it could do any harm," he added bitterly.

"The Werners' cook told me he got her pretty upset."

"I never heard anything about that. I didn't know anything at all until the police came to my office and told me she'd broken into our house again." His voice broke, and he reached for the bottle again. This time he didn't bother with the glass. He took a long swallow and set the bottle down, wiping his mouth with the back of his hand. "It took three policemen to subdue her."

"I heard she cut one of them."

"She had a butcher knife. She was . . ." Leiter had to swallow loudly before he could continue. "She was going to kill my wife with it so she and I could be together." He looked up at Frank with horror-filled eyes. "How could she imagine I would run off with the woman who had murdered my wife?"

"She's a madwoman." Frank heard himself quoting Mrs. Paisley. "It's the nature of madness not to make any sense."

"My wife was . . . *shattered*," he said brokenly. "Her nerves are destroyed, and my children still have nightmares. This house . . . this house has no cellar. She won't live in a house with a cellar any longer. Luckily, my wife inherited some money when her parents died, so I was able to bring my family out here, where I thought Miss Werner couldn't find me, where I thought we'd be safe. But you found me," he added sadly.

"I know how to find people," Frank said. "And even then, it took a long time, and I had to bribe a few people at the hospital where you worked." He wouldn't mention how Mrs. Paisley had assisted. "Miss Werner would never be able to do it. Besides, she's found a new victim."

"What?" he asked incredulously.

"They sent her away to an asylum, and after a while she convinced them she was cured, so they brought her home again. About the only place they let her go was church, so she fell in love with the minister."

"Poor bastard," Leiter said with feeling.

"His wife was the one who suffered," Frank said.

"Oh, no! Don't say she killed the poor woman!" Leiter cried, his face ashen.

"No, no," Frank assured him. "Ordella did try to stab her in church one Sunday, though."

Dr. Leiter swore a colorful oath. "Was she badly hurt?"

"No, her corset protected her, but now they've locked Miss Werner away again, and this time she probably won't get out."

Dr. Leiter used the glass this time, but he gulped the liquor just as quickly. Then he set the glass down very carefully. "Why have you come all the way out here, Mr. Malloy? Surely, you didn't go to all this trouble just to make me relive the most horrible chapter of my life or to tell me some other woman's life was endangered by this . . . What did you call her? This *madwoman*?"

"I told you, I'm investigating Dr. Brandt's death."

"And you think I can help you?" he asked doubtfully.

"Dr. Brandt had found three women like Miss Werner. He had visited all of them, and he was trying to figure out how to cure them. I believe Dr. Brandt was killed by the father of one of these women."

Leiter stared at him for a long moment. "Do you think Mr. Werner might have killed him?"

"He's one of my three main suspects. What kind of man is he?"

Leiter leaned forward, folding his hands on his desk. He wasn't showing any sign that the whiskey had affected him except that he had grown calm again. "I'm not sure what you mean."

"He blamed Dr. Brandt for upsetting his daughter.

He believed that Brandt was responsible for her escaping and trying to kill your wife. How do you think he would react to that?"

Leiter considered the question carefully. "He seemed to be a reasonable man, at least at first. He didn't want anyone to find out what his daughter had been doing, sneaking over to my office and leaving the notes. The notes were rather . . . Well, I have to confess they shocked me. For a maiden lady, she seemed quite knowledgeable about matters of the flesh."

"But when he thought that you really were having an affair with his daughter, how did he behave?"

The color rose in Dr. Leiter's face. "He was furious, of course. He . . . Well, he had to be restrained at one point, or he would have attacked me."

This was interesting. "Do you think he would have killed you?"

Dr. Leiter rubbed his hand over his jaw. "I don't know if he would have gone that far, but he was certainly very emotional."

Frank worded his next remark carefully. "Any man would be if he thought someone had ruined his daughter."

"Oh, I don't think he cared about that so much," Leiter said, surprising Frank.

"What do you mean?"

"I mean he didn't seem to care about the girl at all. She was simply an annoyance to him. He was furious that I'd embarrassed *him* in front of other people. Or rather that my affair with her had driven her to embarrass him. He was worried it would be in the newspapers and his business associates would find out."

Frank sighed. That didn't sound like an outraged father at all.

# 6

SARAH AWOKE TO THE SOUNDS OF GIRLISH giggles. She'd been out until dawn the night before on a delivery and had slept most of the day. She smiled, thinking of all the times she'd awakened to silence in an empty house. This was so much better! She washed her face in the cold water left in the pitcher from her hasty wash hours earlier, brushed out her hair, and threw on a robe. Then she followed the sound of giggling.

She found Catherine and Maeve in the kitchen with Mrs. Ellsworth. They had their backs to her, and the three of them had just put a baking sheet into the oven. "Something smells good," she said by way of greeting.

"Mama!" Catherine cried and ran to greet her, wrapping her small arms tightly around Sarah's legs.

"What are you making for supper?" she asked Catherine after the girl had released her from her hug of greeting.

Catherine glanced over her shoulder at Mrs. Ellsworth and Maeve, but they remained silent, giving her the opportunity to reply. "Stew," Catherine said when she turned back to Sarah.

"I hope you're making a lot, because I'm starving," Sarah said. "I think I could eat the table."

This sent Catherine into a fit of giggles again.

"Sit down, Mrs. Brandt," Mrs. Ellsworth said cheerfully. "I'll make you a pot of tea while we're waiting for the biscuits."

"Who made the biscuits?" Sarah asked, taking the offered seat.

"Miss Catherine did," Mrs. Ellsworth reported.

Catherine smiled shyly but proudly.

"You're becoming quite a cook," Sarah observed. Catherine climbed up in her lap and snuggled in until she was comfortable. Sarah sighed with contentment.

"The girls said Mr. Malloy hasn't been around," Mrs. Ellsworth observed as she put some water on the stove to boil.

"I really haven't expected him," Sarah said, trying not to sound disappointed.

"I wish he'd come," Maeve admitted. "I keep wondering if he's found out anything."

"If he had, I'm sure he would have told us," Sarah said. "Tell me what you've been doing all day," she added to change the subject.

Maeve described their activities with a little help from Catherine whenever Maeve prodded her. By then the water had boiled and the tea had brewed. Mrs. Ellsworth poured three cups and set them on the table. As she set down the last one, the spoon lying on the saucer slipped off and clattered to the table.

"Oh, my, we're going to have a visitor," Mrs. Ellsworth said.

"I thought a spoon falling meant disappointment," Maeve said, making Sarah wince. She'd have to remind the girl again about not believing superstitions.

"Only if it lands on the floor with the bowl facing down," Mrs. Ellsworth explained, oblivious to Sarah's disapproval. "If it lands on the table, it means a visitor."

Catherine sat up straight in Sarah's lap and whispered hopefully, "Mr. Malloy," making everyone laugh.

"I hope not," Sarah said. "I'm not even dressed."

Just then, they heard the chime of her front doorbell.

Catherine scrambled down from Sarah's lap. "Mr. Malloy," she repeated with much more confidence.

"Don't open the door!" Sarah called after her as she raced out of the room. "Wait for Maeve!"

"You'd better get dressed," Mrs. Ellsworth advised Sarah knowingly.

Biting back a groan, Sarah hurried out and into the safety of her bedroom. She was already stripping out of her nightdress when she heard the

126

familiar rumble of Malloy's voice. She couldn't seem to stop smiling as she dressed.

By the time she got back to the kitchen, decently clothed and moderately well groomed, Malloy was sitting at the table with Catherine in his lap.

"Good evening, Mr. Malloy," she said, managing to sound only mildly glad to see him.

He returned her greeting with an equally moderate enthusiasm, although she thought she saw a slight sparkle in his dark eyes.

"I'm afraid we burned the biscuits a bit in all the excitement," Mrs. Ellsworth said. "But we won't let that stop us from enjoying them, will we?"

Catherine shook her head. The table had been set in Sarah's absence, and they all crowded around while Mrs. Ellsworth served them. Although Sarah and Mrs. Ellsworth wanted to question Malloy, they were too well mannered to grill him while he was eating. Maeve had no such reservations.

"What have you found out, Mr. Malloy?" she asked when everyone was settled and served.

"Let the poor man eat his supper," Mrs. Ellsworth scolded. She also nodded toward Catherine, a reminder not to talk about death and murder in front of the child.

"I'm sorry," Maeve said meekly. Then, "What did you do today?"

The two women gasped in exasperation, but Malloy chuckled. "I was out on Long Island."

"Where's that?" Maeve asked.

"It's out past Brooklyn," Malloy told her.

*"Past Brooklyn?"* Maeve marveled. Clearly, she'd never thought about anything being farther away from the city than that. "How far past?"

"You get on the train and just keep going," Malloy said with a straight face.

"How long were you there?"

"I left this morning and just got back. I had to see a doctor out there."

Catherine's head popped up from where she'd been concentrating on the stew. "Are you sick?" she whispered with a worried frown.

"No, darlin'," he assured her. "I needed to ask him some questions, that's all."

Catherine nodded, satisfied, and went back to eating her supper.

"Why was he way out there?" Maeve asked.

"Maeve . . ." Mrs. Ellsworth started, but Malloy stopped her.

"It's all right. He moved out there after . . . Well, he wanted to get away from the city."

"Whose doctor was he?" Sarah asked casually, but not casually enough. Everyone looked at her in surprise.

Maeve bit back a giggle. "I thought we were going to let him eat his supper."

Malloy took a bite of his stew and chewed it slowly and deliberately, making Sarah wait, which she did patiently. Finally, he said, "He was Ordella Werner's doctor."

"No wonder he left town," Maeve said solemnly.

Catherine looked up again, interested now, but Mrs. Ellsworth said, "That's enough. Let's talk about something more pleasant."

Later, after the table was cleared, Maeve took Catherine to get her ready for bed, but she cast a wistful look back as she left the kitchen, silently reminding them she wanted to hear all about Malloy's investigation, too.

When they were gone, Mrs. Ellsworth sat back down at the table. "The dishes can wait," she decreed. "Tell us what you've found out."

"Not much, except that Ordella Werner is insane and her father doesn't care about much except for his reputation in the city."

"This is the doctor whose wife Ordella tried to kill, isn't it?" Sarah asked.

"That's right. His wife never really got over the shock, so he moved her out to the country. They live in a house without a cellar, because she's afraid Ordella will come back and hide down there again."

Mrs. Ellsworth made a sympathetic noise, and Sarah shivered at the thought. "I can't blame her. I wonder she can feel safe at all after what happened. Did he tell you anything new?"

"Not really, but I did learn one important thing. Dr. Leiter and his family are scared to death of Ordella Werner, even after all these years. Leiter was actually shaking when he was telling me the story."

"Imagine how frightened that poor minister's wife must be," Mrs. Ellsworth said. "She was actually stabbed. Her baby will be marked for sure, or she could even lose it."

"Miss Werner has done a lot of damage," Sarah agreed. "Thank heaven she's safely locked away."

"What have you found out about the other women?" Mrs. Ellsworth asked.

"I talked to Amelia Goodwin's doctor. You won't believe this, but he only saw the girl *one time*."

"One time?" Sarah echoed. "Are you saying she fell in love with him after only seeing him once?"

"That's right. He's a middle-aged man and not the least bit handsome, but she told her father and grandmother that he came to her every night, and that they'd even run away and gotten married."

"What!" Mrs. Ellsworth exclaimed in amazement.

"She sounds very much like Edna White," Sarah said, naming the woman who had fallen in love with Tom.

"Yes. She imagined all of it. Of course, her father believed her and was ready to do the poor doctor bodily harm."

Sarah felt the hairs on the back of her neck stand up. "He's a violent man, then?"

Malloy's gaze was steady. "When he thinks his daughter has been harmed. Of course, Mr. Werner was violent, too, when he thought his daughter's doctor had taken advantage of her."

"What about the other girl?" Mrs. Ellsworth

asked. "What have you found out about her?"

Malloy looked uncomfortable for a moment. "Nothing yet. I . . . I've got another detective working on that."

"*Another* detective?" Sarah asked in surprise.

"Did Commissioner Roosevelt give you some help?" Mrs. Ellsworth asked, delighted.

"Not exactly. But I've got some just the same."

"What will you do now?" Mrs. Ellsworth asked.

Malloy hesitated when they heard footsteps. Maeve and Catherine had returned. Catherine was all ready for bed with her hair braided and her face scrubbed. She held her nightdress up with one fist so she wouldn't trip on it.

"Catherine wants you to read her a story and tuck her in," Maeve announced to Sarah. Sarah couldn't help wondering whose idea that had been, since she was sure Maeve wanted to hear what Malloy had to say, but she was always happy to spend time with Catherine.

As Sarah rose from her chair, Maeve quickly slipped into one of the other chairs, already leaning forward to silently invite Malloy to bring her up-to-date on his investigation. By the time Sarah returned from putting Catherine to bed, the dishes were washed and dried, and Malloy was on his second cup of coffee, looking very much at home in her kitchen. Maeve was no longer asking questions, so Sarah thought her curiosity about the case must now be satisfied.

"You were just about to tell us what you're going to do next," Sarah reminded him as she took her own seat at the table.

"I'm still investigating," he hedged. "I've got to find out as much as I can about each of the suspects before I confront them."

"I think you should just search their houses to see if they have a silver-headed cane," Maeve said.

"That wouldn't prove anything," Malloy explained patiently. "Anybody can have a cane like that. And not having one wouldn't make you innocent, either. If you'd killed somebody with your cane, would you keep it? So an innocent man might have a similar cane, and the guilty man might not have one at all."

Maeve frowned. "I didn't think of that. The killer probably threw it in the river or something."

"If he was smart, he did," Mrs. Ellsworth offered. "But maybe he's not that smart."

Sarah didn't want to talk anymore about the weapon that had taken her husband's life. "How will you decide which one you think is the killer?" she asked to change the subject.

He fiddled with his cup, not meeting her eye. "I may not be able to. If I can't, I'm just going to confront each one and see if I can get the guilty one to confess."

"That's risky, isn't it?" Sarah asked with a worried frown. "What if he lies? Without any evidence—"

"I thought you had a witness," Maeve recalled. "Wasn't there a boy who saw him?"

"A street Arab," Malloy said, his discouragement obvious. "Nobody would take his word over a respectable citizen's."

Sarah hadn't really considered how very difficult this would be. "Then how will you frighten him into confessing?"

To show his disapproval of her lack of confidence in his abilities, Malloy gave her one of his looks.

Sarah barely blinked, but Maeve and Mrs. Ellsworth gasped aloud. She looked over at them in surprise and saw genuine shock on their faces. "Oh, my," Sarah mused to Malloy. "I'd forgotten how terrifying you can be."

"You're the only one who does," he informed her with disapproval.

Maeve recovered quickly. "I still think you need to find the cane . . . if you can," she added quickly at Malloy's frown. "Or something."

To his credit, he remained patient. "I can't just go barging into somebody's house looking for it. They'd have my job or worse."

"What would be worse?" Maeve wanted to know.

Malloy gave her a sly grin. "They might arrest me."

That amused her. "How funny to be arrested for trying to prove somebody was a murderer!"

"It wouldn't be funny at all, child," Mrs. Ellsworth assured her solemnly. "Mr. Malloy, I'm afraid I don't see how you're going to succeed in this. So much time has passed . . . How will anyone even remember if these men were out that night or home with their families or attending a play or something?"

"They won't, which is why I've got to be careful. I'll only have one chance with each of them. And even if the killer lies," he said, looking straight at Sarah this time, "I think I'll be able to tell. These men aren't criminals who've been lying all their lives. They'll be surprised to be confronted after all this time. The killer will have been carrying his secret guilt around for four years. Sometimes a man is actually grateful for the chance to confess."

The three women considered his statement for a long moment. Finally, Maeve broke the silence.

"I think you should let us help."

He raised his eyebrows in surprise. *"Us?"* he echoed skeptically. "Is Mrs. Ellsworth anxious to get involved in the investigation? Or maybe you meant you and Catherine," he teased.

Maeve just glared at him in a fair imitation of the look he'd given Sarah a few moments ago.

"Maeve thinks they should have female detectives," Sarah informed him quite seriously. "She thinks I've done a good job helping you solve some of your cases."

This time the look he gave her was more disgruntled than terrifying.

"She has, too," Maeve argued.

Mrs. Ellsworth coughed suspiciously behind her hand.

Malloy drew a fortifying breath. "Even if she has, that doesn't mean females should get involved in murders. It's dangerous. Remember what happened the last time?"

"He's right, you know," Mrs. Ellsworth said, but Maeve ignored her.

"Just living in this city is dangerous," Maeve said. "I could get run over by a wagon tomorrow."

"Not if you watch where you're going," Malloy argued back. "And that would be an accident. Having somebody come after you with a knife because you're trying to prove he's a killer is a very different thing."

"I'm not afraid," Maeve insisted.

"Well, *I am*," Malloy countered.

"Mr. Malloy is right, child," Mrs. Ellsworth said, patting Maeve's arm where it lay on the table. "I know all this sounds like fun when you're sitting here in Mrs. Brandt's kitchen, but—"

"Killers have been in Mrs. Brandt's kitchen," Maeve reminded her.

"Which is a good reason for you not to give any *more* of them a reason to come here," Malloy said in disgust.

"I'm sure Mr. Malloy would let you help if he had something safe that you could do," Sarah said with a conciliatory smile. "Wouldn't you?"

Malloy glared at her. "What would you suggest?"

"I could search their houses," Maeve offered before Sarah could reply.

Everyone looked at her in surprise.

"Mr. Malloy couldn't, but I could. I wouldn't get arrested either, not if I worked there."

They just continued to stare.

Maeve sighed in frustration at their lack of perception. "If I was a servant in their houses, I could look around anyplace I pleased. They'd never suspect a thing!"

Mrs. Ellsworth was the first to recover. "How would you become a servant in their houses?"

Maeve shrugged. "I don't know. Knock on their doors and ask for work. I know how to cook and clean house now. You taught me yourself," she reminded the old woman. "Mrs. Brandt could write me a reference—"

"No, she couldn't," Malloy said firmly.

"Why not?" Sarah challenged, getting into the spirit.

"Because they know the name *Brandt*, that's why. One of them killed your husband," he reminded her brutally, making her wince.

"Then Mrs. Ellsworth could write me one," Maeve argued. "I'd only have to be there a few days, just long enough to search the house."

*"No,"* Malloy said, slapping his hand on the table and making them all jump. "You are *not* going to put yourself in danger, and that's the end of it."

He was right, of course. Sarah looked at Maeve,

ready to offer sympathy to the girl whose enthusiasm had been dashed. Mrs. Ellsworth was already murmuring consolation and patting her hand again.

But Maeve didn't look the least bit upset. She just stared back at Malloy with a fiercely determined scowl, reminding Sarah that Maeve wasn't some innocent child to be terrorized by a relatively mild rebuke. When she said she wasn't afraid, she wasn't being foolishly brave; she was telling the truth. She'd seen more of life than Sarah probably ever would, and she'd survived.

"I'm afraid Mr. Malloy is right," Sarah said. "I know I'm a fine one to say it, but investigating a murder is too dangerous. I wouldn't want anything to happen to you, Maeve. Catherine loves you too much to lose you, and so do I."

Maeve's eyes widened in surprise. "You do?"

Sarah smiled at the girl's amazement. "Of course I do. Mrs. Ellsworth does, too."

Maeve looked at Mrs. Ellsworth as if expecting her to deny it, but the old woman nodded.

Tears flooded the girl's eyes, and she uttered a strangled cry before bolting from her chair and running from the room.

Sarah was half out of her own chair when Mrs. Ellsworth caught her arm. "She probably needs to be alone," the older woman said. "She most likely never had anyone say they loved her before."

Sarah sank back into her chair, blinking at her own tears.

Malloy sighed. "I just hope it's enough to keep her from doing something stupid."

FRANK KNOCKED ON A LOT OF DOORS THE next morning before he found the person he'd been looking for. He hadn't known her name until she revealed it to him, but he'd already known a lot about her. Most neighborhoods had someone like her, and she always proved an invaluable source of information. In Sarah's neighborhood, she was Mrs. Ellsworth, who made it her life's work to know everything that happened to everyone who lived on Bank Street. Or at least that had been true until Sarah brought Catherine home. Since then, Mrs. Ellsworth had been far too busy with Maeve and Catherine to pay nearly enough attention to the rest of her neighbors. Frank wondered idly if anyone had taken up her duties as resident busybody.

The resident busybody on the street where Ordella Werner's family lived didn't sweep her own porch, as Mrs. Ellsworth did. In this part of the city, servants performed that task. But she did sit by the front window, where she had an excellent view of the comings and goings. He had already knocked on several doors before he'd spotted the curtain moving in her front window.

Frank had concocted a fairly believable story for why a police detective would be calling on respectable people. Few respectable people would admit a policeman into their homes unless compelled to do so, even with his fairly believable story, and none of the people on this street had admitted him so far. But he knew that the woman he was looking for would happily invite him in and even serve him refreshments. When he saw the curtain flutter the first time, he knew he'd found her. Still, he kept knocking on each door in turn, knowing that her curiosity would be at a fever pitch by the time he reached hers.

A maid answered his knock, but Frank knew immediately that she was expecting him. All the other maids had expressed surprise or suspicion or both while they listened to his explanation. This one listened carefully, as she had been instructed to do.

"I'll ask Mrs. Taylor if she'll see you," she said when he had finished, and then let him inside to wait. It was the first doorstep he had actually crossed this morning.

The girl slipped through one of the doors that opened onto the entrance hall, and reappeared almost at once. "Mrs. Taylor will see you," she said. She held the door open for him and accepted his hat as he passed.

"Good morning, Mrs. Taylor," he said, making a slight bow at the tiny, wizened woman sitting in the overstuffed chair by the fireplace. It was too far from the window to be her regular seat, so he knew she'd moved in order to make a better impression.

From the corner of his eye, he could see the chair from which she had been watching him. It had a comfortable, well-worn appearance. "I'm Detective Sergeant Frank Malloy from the New York City Police."

She lifted her chin to look up at him, reminding him of a bird with her sharp chin and tiny eyes. "My girl said you're investigating a burglary in the neighborhood." Her voice was as sharp as her chin. The girl hadn't had time to tell her all this. She must have been listening at the door when he'd been talking to the maid.

"Yes, ma'am, that's right. It was two streets over, but we're asking everyone around if they remember seeing anything unusual."

"Well, now, I don't know what you'd call unusual, but I suppose I should help if I can. Please sit down, Mr. Malloy. Liza, bring us some tea. Would you like some tea, Mr. Malloy, or would you prefer coffee?"

"Coffee, please," Frank said, taking a seat on the horsehair sofa.

"Coffee instead, Liza. And some of those scones from breakfast."

Liza disappeared, closing the door behind her.

"Now tell me who was robbed, Mr. Malloy." Mrs. Taylor was wearing a simple gray housedress adorned with a rather large cameo pin fastened at her throat. Her clawlike hands lay folded in her lap, and she wore several elaborate rings.

140

Her small eyes sparkled with excitement as Frank related the details of a robbery that had happened six months ago and had turned out to be the work of a disgruntled groom. He didn't mention the age of the crime or that it had already been solved, however.

"Good heavens!" Mrs. Taylor exclaimed. "What is the world coming to? The next thing you know, we'll all be murdered in our beds!"

"I wouldn't worry too much," Frank assured her. "The thief didn't hurt anyone. But we don't want anybody else to get robbed, so we're trying to get information to help us find the thief. Maybe you or someone in your family saw somebody sneaking around. Or maybe you noticed something missing around the house but didn't report it to the police."

Now he had her complete attention. "Missing? You mean you think the thief might have robbed other people without their even knowing it?"

"Sometimes, if the thief is young or inexperienced, he might start out by just trying back doors at night to see if one was left open by accident."

"Oh, I'm always reminding the girls to make sure the doors are locked," Mrs. Taylor assured him.

"When he finds an unlocked door, he'll sneak in and just take what he can carry in his pockets. After he's been successful at that, he'll get bolder, and next time he'll bring a sack to carry away more valuables. Finally, he'll start breaking locks or windows and get a partner, so they can carry twice as much."

Mrs. Taylor shuddered dramatically. "I know I won't sleep a wink tonight, worrying about sneak thieves. I keep telling my son we should move out of the city, but of course, his work is here."

"So," Frank prodded, "have you noticed anything missing?"

"Oh, no," she said quite confidently. "I'm very careful about counting the silver and checking the cupboards. Servants, you know. They'll steal you blind, if you let them."

Frank didn't know, of course, but he nodded agreeably. "Have you heard any of your neighbors mention anything out of the ordinary?"

She tipped her head to the side, reinforcing Frank's impression of a bird. "What do you mean?"

Frank pretended to consider the question. "Well, like I said, have you seen anyone sneaking around where they shouldn't be or behaving suspiciously? Or maybe one of your neighbors mentioned something?"

The parlor door opened, and Liza was back with the tray. Mrs. Taylor served him his coffee and took some for herself. She also insisted he try a scone, so he did. When the girl had gone and Frank had expressed his satisfaction with the scone, he said, "Now, where were we?"

"I'm sure I don't remember," Mrs. Taylor lied. Frank was pretty sure she remembered perfectly well.

"Oh, yes," Frank said. "I was asking if you'd

noticed anything out of the ordinary in the neighborhood."

Then he waited, knowing that the longer he remained quiet, the more likely she was to fill the silence. He didn't have to wait long.

"There was something," she admitted with apparent reluctance. "It probably has nothing to do with the robbery, though."

Frank leaned forward slightly, silently expressing his interest. "You never know," he said. "The smallest thing can help us solve a case like this."

"Well, as I said, it probably has nothing at all to do with the robbery, but one of our neighbors . . ."

"Yes?" Frank prodded with just the proper amount of eagerness.

Mrs. Taylor's birdlike gaze darted around the room, as if searching for eavesdroppers. Then she leaned in a bit, too, as if confiding a secret. "The Werner family," she said softly.

Frank managed not to react. "What about them?"

She hesitated, as if loath to speak of it, but the sparkle in her eyes betrayed her. "The daughter, Ordella. She tried to murder two women!"

Frank drew back, appropriately shocked. "*Murder?* Are you sure?"

"Oh, I'm very sure," she said. "I'm surprised you haven't heard about it, you being with the police and all."

"I hadn't heard a thing," Frank lied. "When did this happen?"

"Oh, the first one was years ago, but the second one happened just recently." She proceeded to tell him a fairly accurate version of the stories he'd heard from his other sources. She didn't have the details exactly right, but close enough. To her credit, she appeared appalled by the events, although she couldn't quite conceal her delight in repeating them.

"Did they arrest this Miss Werner?" Frank asked when she had finished.

"I have no idea," she said with a sniff. "She just disappeared, as she did the first time. I heard they'd sent her to some asylum after that business with the doctor, but no one seems to know where she is now. I'm just relieved she's no longer living here. If she'd do that in a church, heaven knows whom she might attack next!"

Frank shook his head in dismay. "When something like this happens, you have to wonder how her parents could have been so careless."

"Oh, well," Mrs. Taylor said, her disapproval evident. "Her mother died a long time ago. She never would have allowed this to happen, I'm sure, and Mr. Werner was busy with his business. He couldn't be expected to know what the girl was up to. His sister lives with them, though. Rossmann is her name, I think. She seems like a respectable sort of person, but one never knows."

"Her father should have taken a firmer hand," Frank said. "He probably spoiled the girl after her mother died."

144

"Oh, no, you can't blame him," Mrs. Taylor assured him. "He never tolerated any nonsense from her at all. 'Spare the rod and spoil the child,'" she quoted piously. "And he never spared it. He actually accused me of being too lenient with my own children, although I'm sure my children never attacked anyone with a knife."

"He was a violent man, then?"

"Violent?" she echoed in surprise. "I wouldn't say he was violent just because he whipped his daughter."

"Did you ever know him to be violent against other people?"

"Other people?" she mused. "No, not other people. Just that one time . . . ."

Frank clenched his teeth to keep from jumping up out of his chair and shaking the story from her bony frame. "What time was that?" he asked with just the slightest trace of interest.

"Oh, he beat a groom. The boy hadn't done something to his satisfaction, so he . . . Well, some people thought he was too harsh, but if you can't keep your servants in line, your life will be unbearable."

"So he beat the groom?" Frank prodded her.

"Oh, yes. Everyone was talking about it. Broke the boy's arm, I think it was."

"Does the boy still work for him?"

"No, no," she said, dashing his hopes. "He disappeared after that. Mr. Werner probably dismissed him. Can't have incompetent help, can you?"

"You wouldn't know the boy's name, would you?"

She looked at him as if he were insane. "Certainly not. I can hardly keep track of my own servants without learning the names of everyone else's." Suddenly she stopped and looked at Frank again, as if seeing him for the first time. Or as if realizing his inquiries had nothing to do with the reason he had supposedly called on her. "We've certainly gone a long way from the subject of a burglary in the neighborhood."

Frank knew he'd asked too many questions and made her suspicious. He wasn't worried about that, though. He feigned surprise. "Yes, we have." He set his cup back on the tray. "I'm afraid I've taken up too much of your time, Mrs. Taylor." He rose from his chair. "I'll leave my card. If you see or hear anything that would be helpful in solving the robbery, please let me know."

"I certainly will," she said, but she was still peering up at him curiously, as if she was taking his measure all over again and not liking what she saw.

Frank departed and conveniently forgot to leave his card.

# 7

THIS MORNING FRANK WAS THE FIRST TO arrive at the coffee shop. The girl had automatically brought him coffee and a plate of donuts. He'd finished the first one when the Pinkerton agent came in. He spotted Frank immediately and strolled over to the table.

"Good morning," Frank said, surprising him. Victor returned the greeting. The girl brought him his own cup of coffee and retreated.

Victor claimed a donut without asking. "How's your end of things going?" he inquired with mild interest.

"Let's just say I hope you've had better luck," Frank said, unwilling to give anything away.

Victor reached into his coat and brought out another neatly typed report. "The Albertons are a very interesting family," he remarked as he laid the sheets of paper on the table.

He was going to make Frank ask. "What did you find out?"

Victor pretended to scan the papers in front of him, although Frank was sure he knew every detail by heart. "You know the girl had a twin brother, name of Sam."

"And he was killed in a bicycle accident. I think I told you that part myself," Frank said impatiently.

"Oh, yes," he said, unruffled. "The girl Christina had some sort of nervous collapse after the brother died. The family moved out to the country a few years ago. Thought the quiet would be good for her."

"Yes, Yonkers, wasn't it?" Frank managed not to sound as frustrated as he felt.

"That's right. Nice and quiet out there. They've

got a big house and a few servants who don't go out much."

"Which means you didn't talk to them."

If Victor felt criticized, he gave no sign of it. "The family keep to themselves, too, so the neighbors don't know much, what neighbors they have. What I do know is that the girl is living with them."

This was news. "She's not in an asylum?"

"Not now. I can't say what happened before, but she's home now."

"What else do you know?"

"Her father's got some kind of importing business. He goes into the city during the week and stays at the house on the weekends. He's rich."

Rich was a relative thing, as Frank knew. He earned enough from his salary and the "rewards" he received to support his mother and son comfortably. They never went hungry and had a decent place to live and clothes on their backs. Many in the city who slept in flophouses only when they were lucky enough to have the nickel to spare and on the street the rest of the time, and who were nearly always hungry, would consider Frank rich. He wasn't rich compared to men like Felix Decker, however. "How rich is he?"

"He don't go to Mrs. Astor's parties, if that's what you mean," Victor said, naming the leading society hostess in the city. "But he's doing all right."

"What kind of man is he?"

"I didn't get a handle on him yet. Not enough time, and like I said, they keep to themselves socially. I couldn't go around asking the people who work for his business either. You said not to let him know we're investigating. If I ask one fellow, next thing you know, everybody in his company hears about it."

"What else?" Frank's foot was tapping impatiently.

"What do you want to know?" Victor snapped, equally annoyed.

"Who lives in the house? How many in the family? How many servants?"

"Not many servants. A couple maids, a cook, a fellow, and some boys who work in the stable, and they got a girl who looks after the crazy one exclusively. Doesn't do anything else. I don't know who takes care of the kid. Maybe they got a nursemaid, but—"

"What kid?" Frank asked with a frown.

"The kid. A little girl, about so high." Victor held out his hand about a yard from the floor. "Saw her out in the yard running around."

"They just had the two children, the boy who died and the crazy girl," Frank reminded him.

"Maybe they only had those two when they lived in the city, but now they've got another one. She looks young enough, maybe she wasn't born until they moved out to the country. You know what they say about the country air."

"And she's a sister to the crazy girl?" Frank asked, ignoring Victor's sly grin.

"I guess so."

"You don't get paid to *guess*," Frank snapped, furious now.

Victor bristled again. "And I told you, I didn't have time to find out all the details. They keep to themselves and don't let anybody mind their business for them."

"So the mother and father, the crazy girl, and this little girl are the only family in the house. No grandparents or maiden aunts?"

"Not that I could find out about, but they might keep one locked up in the attic for all I know. I told you—"

"I know, they keep to themselves," Frank said in disgust.

"We've got some female agents," Victor offered. "Maybe one of them could . . ."

"Could what?" Frank demanded when he hesitated.

"I don't know. I'm just thinking. Maybe one of them could get inside the house somehow."

"You mean get a job as a maid or something," Frank said, aware of the irony of his suggesting the very thing he had refused to let Maeve do.

Victor seemed to like the suggestion. "Yeah, that might work. Even if they don't hire her, she could chat with the other maids, maybe find out something."

"Maybe she could even search the house, see if she could find the silver-headed cane that killed Brandt."

Victor didn't seem to notice the sarcasm in his voice. "You really think he'll still have it after all this time?"

"No, I don't," Frank said. "I would've thrown it in the river a long time ago, but maybe he's not that smart."

"All these fellows are rich," Victor reminded him. "And probably educated, too."

"Which only means they're smart about books and making money. They might not be smart about other things. I'm guessing this is the only murder this man has committed."

"I thought we didn't get paid to guess," Victor reminded him sourly.

"I said *you* didn't get paid to guess," Frank reminded him just as sourly.

Victor glared, but he didn't lose his temper. "So, do you want me to find a female agent to help or not?"

Frank hoped Maeve never found out about this. She'd probably cut out his liver for stealing her idea and not letting her do it. "All right, but bring her to meet me first. I want to talk to her before she goes out there."

"I'll send you word when she's ready."

"Don't let anybody at Headquarters know you're a Pink," Frank reminded him.

"Afraid of ruining your reputation, Malloy?" Victor taunted.

Frank would be tormented forever if anyone found out he was working with the Pinkertons. "No," he countered. "I'm afraid of ruining yours."

WHEN FRANK STOPPED BY POLICE HEAD-quarters later to check in, he found a message waiting for him. He knew from the smirk on the desk sergeant's face that it was probably from Sarah. The envelope the sergeant handed him was plain, with just his name written on it, but the hand-writing was feminine and the high quality of the paper betrayed her. He tore it open quickly, knowing she wouldn't have contacted him here unless it was important.

He was right. Maeve had disappeared.

WHEN SARAH OPENED HER DOOR TO ADMIT Malloy, Catherine ran straight for him, wrapped her arms around his leg, and burst into tears. He looked up at Sarah in surprise.

"I'm sorry I had to send the note to the station," Sarah said, fighting tears of her own. "But Catherine begged me to send for you. I was afraid if I sent it to your home, you wouldn't be able to come until tomorrow."

Malloy nodded his understanding. "Don't worry," he said, gently stroking Catherine's small head. "We'll find her."

152

"Let Mr. Malloy take his coat off, sweetheart," Sarah urged the child.

Reluctantly, Catherine released him and let Sarah comfort her. The girl's expression when she looked up tore at Sarah's heart.

"What's going on?" Frank asked as he shrugged out of his coat. "Your note just said she disappeared."

"She wasn't in her bed this morning. We found this note on her pillow."

Malloy took the paper from her and read it carefully. It was a sheet of paper from Sarah's desk, the same kind she'd used to send for Malloy. The girlish scrawl apologized for leaving and said she'd be back in a few days and ended with, "I just had to help."

"Do you think she went to try to get a job at one of the houses?" Sarah asked, voicing her worst fear.

"That would be my guess."

"Do you have any idea which one?"

"She did ask me where the women lived," Malloy recalled with a frown. "Last night when you were putting Catherine to bed."

"Did you give her addresses?"

"No, only street names. I thought she just wanted to know the neighborhoods, to know what kind of people they were or something."

"I doubt she'd be familiar with those neighborhoods. And even if she was, how would she find the right house?" Sarah asked, wringing her hands anxiously. Catherine, who was clinging to her skirts, made a small whimper.

"Let's go sit down," Malloy suggested.

"Oh, I'm sorry. Of course," Sarah stammered and led the way to the kitchen.

Catherine slipped her small hand into Malloy's larger one as they made their way through the house.

"Where's Mrs. Ellsworth?" Malloy asked when they were seated at the kitchen table. Catherine had crawled up into his lap and snuggled in close against his shoulder. Sarah wondered if he knew how natural he looked, holding the child. He was even rubbing her small back in silent comfort.

"I went over to get her as soon as I found the note," Sarah said, "but she wasn't home. I suspect she went to the market. She'll probably be over as soon as she gets back, though. She usually brings something for the girls."

Malloy reread the note. "She says she'll be home in a few days," he reminded Sarah.

"Yes, she does," she replied, unable to keep the worry from her voice. Maeve probably intended to return as soon as she'd had an opportunity to search the house or houses, but what if someone caught her snooping? What if she got caught in the killer's house, and he decided to make sure she never told anyone what she'd found? Sarah knew Malloy was thinking the same things, but neither of them wanted to talk about it in front of the child.

"One of the families lives out in Yonkers," Malloy remembered. "I doubt she'd go all that way."

"You're right. She probably doesn't even know where it is," Sarah said. "She didn't know where Long Island was."

"That just leaves the two families in the city." Malloy was staring at the note as if he expected to find an answer hidden there.

"Could we just go and ask for her?" Sarah asked.

"And say what? That you're looking for a run-away maid? She also might be using a phony name. Besides, it might be dangerous to call attention to her."

"It also might warn the . . . the man we're looking for, too," Sarah said, glancing at Catherine, trying to judge how much of this she understood. The poor child looked terrified.

"Is Maeve lost?" she asked in her whispery voice.

"No!" both Sarah and Malloy said at once, frightening her even more.

"Maeve isn't lost at all," Sarah explained quickly, reaching across the table to catch her hand and hold it. "She knows exactly where she is, and she'll be coming home as soon as she . . . as soon as she finishes what she's trying to do."

Catherine nodded solemnly. "Find Dr. Brandt's killer."

Sarah winced and so did Malloy. So much for shielding her. They stared at each other helplessly across the table for a long moment, and then someone knocked on the back door.

Sarah jumped up, absurdly grateful to see Mrs. Ellsworth standing on her back porch. She was carrying a market basket on her arm and smiling expectantly.

"I found the most wonderful . . ." she began, but stopped when she saw Sarah's expression and noticed Malloy sitting at the table. She looked back at Sarah and frowned. "What's wrong?"

"Maeve has run off to play detective," Malloy informed her before Sarah could. He held up the note.

Mrs. Ellsworth hurried past Sarah and snatched the note from his hand. She scanned it quickly, then looked down at Catherine, still sitting in Malloy's lap. "Did she say anything to you about going away?" she asked gently.

Catherine shook her head. Tears flooded her eyes again.

"Oh, now, now, don't cry," Mrs. Ellsworth pleaded, setting her basket on the table and reaching for the child. Malloy eagerly relinquished her to Mrs. Ellsworth, a horrified expression on his face. Sarah quickly pulled out a chair so Mrs. Ellsworth could sit down and take Catherine into her own lap. The child buried her face on the old woman's shoulder and sobbed.

Sarah felt tears running down her own face, and she quickly scrubbed them away. She was furious, although she could not say why or at whom.

"Do we know where she went?" Mrs. Ellsworth asked when she'd calmed Catherine down.

"We think she must have gone to the home of one of the girls," Sarah said.

"To get a job there," Mrs. Ellsworth remembered. "I didn't realize she was so headstrong."

"None of us did," Sarah admitted.

"What can we do?" Mrs. Ellsworth looked at Malloy.

"Not much without putting her in danger," he said. "Or tipping off the killer that we're investigating him."

Mrs. Ellsworth frowned. "So we just wait for her to come home?"

"We'll wait a few days," Malloy said. "After that, we'll go looking for her. At least we have an idea of where to find her."

"You told her where they live," Mrs. Ellsworth recalled. "Do you think she'll even be able to find the right houses?"

"She survived on the streets alone," Malloy reminded her. "She can surely find a house if she knows the street and the name of the people who live there. All she has to do is ask somebody in the neighborhood."

"And if she can't find them, I'm sure she'll have the sense to come home," Sarah said, although it was as much a wish as a statement of belief.

"And until she does, I'll be happy to look after

Miss Catherine here, whenever you need me," Mrs. Ellsworth said.

"That's so kind of you," Sarah said, feeling the sting of threatening tears again.

"No, it isn't kind at all," Mrs. Ellsworth informed her. "I'm being completely selfish. There's nothing I'd rather do than spend time with Miss Catherine." Catherine looked up at her with shining eyes. "Oh, my, I almost forgot! I brought you some sweets from the market. Look here." She reached across to where the basket sat on the table and pulled out a paper-wrapped packet. For a moment, at least, Catherine forgot her missing friend.

MAEVE FELT A FLUTTER OF APPREHENSION IN her stomach as she looked up at the big house. She'd never been in this part of the city before, even though she'd lived here all of her life. Girls like her had no business on a street like this unless they were employed in one of these big houses. The man delivering the mail had been happy to point out where the Werners lived when she'd told him she was visiting her sister who worked for them. She should have been ashamed of lying like that. The nice ladies at the Prodigal Son Mission would have scolded her for it. In fact, she'd been a bit surprised at how easily the lie had come. Time was, her very survival had depended on her ability to make other people believe her untruths, but she hadn't practiced in a long time. Good thing she hadn't lost her touch. She'd be lying a lot in the next few days.

The alley behind the row of houses was nicer and cleaner than the streets where she'd spent her childhood. She had no trouble at all finding the rear entrance to the house she wanted. Her knock brought a stocky middle-aged woman to the door. She wore a stained apron and looked Maeve up and down critically. "And what would you be wanting, then?" she asked without the slightest hint of welcome.

"I'm looking for a job, and I was wondering if you might have something for me." Good, she thought. She sounded just slightly desperate but not too much. She'd also dressed the part, choosing the skirt and shirtwaist that she wore when taking care of Catherine and borrowing an old jacket from Mrs. Brandt that had seen much better days. She'd brought a change of clothes tied in a bundle.

"We don't need any help right now," the woman said and started to close the door.

"I'll work for my keep," Maeve cried. "You don't have to pay me wages, at least not until I prove myself."

The woman looked her over again. "Oh, hungry, are you?" she said with a trace of compassion. "Well, I suppose I could spare you something to eat at least. Can't have you fainting on the doorstep, now can I?"

Maeve didn't have to fake her sigh of relief when

the woman admitted her into the warmth of her kitchen. The smell of baking bread made her mouth water. She really was hungry. She'd left in the middle of the night, with no thought of breakfast, and she'd forgotten to take any food with her.

"What's your name, girl?" the woman asked.

"Maeve Smith," she said, half-truthfully.

"I'm Mrs. Flynn," the woman said.

"Pleased to meet you, I'm sure," Maeve said with a small curtsey.

Mrs. Flynn pulled a face. "Pretty manners," she said. "Where'd you learn that?"

"From my last mistress. I know how to clean house and cook, too."

"We've got a cook here already," Mrs. Flynn reminded her. "Take off your coat and sit down."

Maeve did as she was told while Mrs. Flynn gathered up a makeshift meal and set it before her. Day-old bread but real butter and jam to spread on it.

"Do you have a big family living here?" Maeve asked, sounding hopeful. A large family would require more servants.

"No, just the master and his sister."

Maeve tried to look surprised. "It's a big house for just two people."

"Oh, the master's family used to live here, too, but they're all gone now."

"Dead, are they?" Maeve asked between bites.

Mrs. Flynn gave her a disapproving look. "You ask a lot of questions, girl."

"I'm just making conversation," Maeve lied genially. "If you like me, maybe you'll find a place for me," she added with a winsome grin.

The older woman chuckled at that, and Maeve knew she was making headway.

"How do you come to be looking for work?" Mrs. Flynn asked.

"My mistress died, sudden like," Maeve said sadly. She'd given some thought to this story since she'd known she'd be asked. "She didn't have no family, so the law came and just put us out, me and Mary. She was the housekeeper. Didn't have a chance to get a reference letter from her or anything." Maeve paused, letting her eyes fill with tears.

"So that's why you're going door to door," Mrs. Flynn surmised. "There now, don't cry."

"I'm sorry," Maeve said, scrubbing at her eyes with her sleeve. "I try not to feel too bad. I'm still young. Poor Mary, she's getting along in years, and she's got the rheumatism, too. Went to stay with her sister, but they can't keep her for long. Don't know what'll become of her."

"Don't you be borrowing her trouble. You got enough of your own, girl."

"I'm a hard worker," Maeve offered again. "I could show you, if you give me a chance. You don't have to pay me anything except maybe . . ."

"Maybe what?" Mrs. Flynn asked suspiciously.

"Maybe I could work here a week or so, and you

161

could write me a reference." Maeve had once practiced her facial expressions to learn just the right one to use in specific instances. This time she chose the desperately hopeful one that had often swayed a mark.

"I can't write you nothing," Mrs. Flynn said, dashing her hopes. "Only Mrs. Rossmann can do that."

"Do you think she would?" Maeve asked, pleading silently with her entire body. "Do you think she'd let me work for a few days and then write me a reference?"

"I'll have to ask her."

Maeve sat back in her chair as a second wave of relief flooded through her. She was halfway to her goal.

Frank DECIDED HE WOULD NEXT VISIT THE neighborhood where Amelia Goodwin lived. He tried not to think that he could run into Maeve there. She might just as easily have gone to the Werner house first, or even tried to find Yonkers to go to the Alberton house. Even if she were here, she'd be too careful to let him see her. Still, he caught himself looking around as he worked his way down the street, looking for the gossipy neighbor who would tell him things he didn't know about the Goodwin family.

Twice he caught a glimpse of a young woman, but neither of them was Maeve.

When he found the gossipy neighbor, it turned out to be two sisters this time. One was a widow and the other a spinster who had lived with her for many years, he discovered once he was settled in their stuffy and overstuffed parlor. They knew everyone and everything that happened, although they were quite surprised to learn about the robbery that had taken place on the next street.

"I don't know what the world is coming to," Mrs. Stewart remarked to no one in particular when Frank had finished his story.

"I know that I'm afraid to leave the house anymore," her sister added. Miss Plimpton was a round, pink lady whose snow white hair lent her the air of an aging cherub. "I told you to remarry after William died, Sister, but now we're here all alone."

"Me?" Mrs. Stewart said in surprise. "If you'd married yourself, you wouldn't have to be worried about relying on *my* husband to protect you."

"I could have married any number of gentlemen, as you well know," Miss Plimpton reminded her primly, "but none of them suited Father."

"William didn't suit Father either," Mrs. Stewart replied tartly. "But I had no intention of ending up an old maid."

Frank could see they were entering very dangerous territory, so he stepped in to distract them from what was apparently an old argument. "Neither of you will have to be concerned, if we can find the thief," he reminded them. "Now, can you tell me if you've noticed anything out of the ordinary?"

"When did you say the robbery occurred?" Mrs. Stewart asked. Unlike her sister, she had no softness about her. She was all angles and elbows with a gaze that could cut glass.

"A week ago last Wednesday," Frank lied.

"I don't know how we can be expected to remember that far back," Miss Plimpton protested. "I can hardly remember what happened yesterday."

"If you kept a diary as Mama taught us, you'd know exactly what you were doing on that day," Mrs. Stewart said. "Fortunately, I do keep a diary, Mr. Malloy." She rang a small bell that had been sitting on the table beside her, then instructed the maid who appeared to fetch her diary from her bedchamber.

While they waited, Frank took the opportunity to make some small talk. "Have any of your neighbors mentioned having something go missing?"

"I'm sure I haven't heard a thing. Has anyone said anything to you, Sister?" Miss Plimpton asked.

"Certainly not."

"Maybe you haven't spoken to them recently," Frank suggested.

"Oh, my, we see our neighbors quite regularly, do we not, Sister?" Miss Plimpton said. "Everyone is most friendly."

"Indeed they are. Why, just last week Mrs. Gates hosted a tea. Almost everyone on the street attended."

"And no one mentioned—?"

"Anything missing?" Mrs. Stewart supplied. "Most certainly not. I'm sure we would have remembered something so shocking."

"You said *almost* everybody attended. Who wasn't there?" Frank asked.

The sisters had to think a moment.

"Was Mrs. Noble there?" Miss Plimpton asked.

"Oh, yes. She was wearing that horrible green gown that makes her look bilious."

"That's right. I'd forgotten. What about Mrs. Anderson?"

"The rust-colored batiste with all the ruffles," Mrs. Stewart recalled with distaste.

Miss Plimpton nodded knowingly. "I'm afraid I can't recall anyone else . . ."

"Mrs. Goodwin!" Mrs. Stewart announced triumphantly.

"Are you sure?" Miss Plimpton asked with a tiny frown.

"Absolutely."

"When was the last time you saw this Mrs. Goodwin?" Frank asked with just the proper amount of concern.

"Not recently," Mrs. Stewart reported confidently. "The family keeps to themselves. Not sociable at all."

Frank reached into his coat and took out a small notebook and the stub of a pencil and proceeded to take notes. This process usually caused his audience either to clam up completely for fear of saying something that would harm someone else or to begin blurting out as much information as they could think of in an attempt to demonstrate their helpfulness and knowledge. Frank had judged the sisters to be the kind who would blurt, and he was right.

"Mrs. Goodwin is a widow," Mrs. Stewart informed him, waiting while he wrote down this information.

"Does she live alone?" Frank asked.

"Oh, no," Mrs. Stewart said. "She lives with her son and her granddaughter."

"Poor little thing," Miss Plimpton murmured.

"Why is Mrs. Goodwin a poor little thing?" Frank asked with apparent concern.

"Oh, not her," Miss Plimpton clarified. "The granddaughter."

"Is something wrong with the girl?" Frank asked.

"She's a cripple," Mrs. Stewart said with disapproval, as if reporting the girl had violated some rule of proper conduct.

"It's her foot," Miss Plimpton added quickly. "She was born that way, poor thing. Couldn't help it, I imagine."

"No, I'm sure she couldn't," Frank agreed without showing his disdain.

"She never goes out," Mrs. Stewart said. "The girl, I mean. They keep her at home, which is only proper. Wouldn't want her to be an object of ridicule, now would they?"

"No," Frank agreed. "But if she's at home all the time, maybe she noticed something on the day of the robbery. Do you think the family would let me speak to her?"

"I doubt it," Mrs. Stewart said. "As I said, they're not sociable."

"Ellie was," Miss Plimpton said.

"Who is Ellie?" Frank asked, still writing in his book.

"The girl's mother," Mrs. Stewart said with a frown of disapproval at her sister.

"Well, she was," Miss Plimpton said defensively. "She always seemed like such a nice person. I never believed what they said about her."

"What did they say about her?" Frank asked, not having to feign his interest.

The two sisters exchanged a glance, silently debating the wisdom of telling him.

"I'll never reveal who gave me the information," Frank assured them, "but it's always helpful to understand the situation before I question someone."

Mrs. Stewart made a small show of reluctance, his gaze avoiding and fiddling with the trim on her skirt for a moment while Frank waited patiently to hear what she was dying to tell him. But before she could, Miss Plimpton could stand the suspense no longer.

"They say she committed suicide!" she said in a horrified whisper.

167

Just then someone knocked on the parlor door, and after giving her sister a murderous glare, Mrs. Stewart bade the person enter. The maid had brought her diary. When Mrs. Stewart had thanked her, and the girl was gone, she turned on her sister again. "No one ever said so officially," she said sharply.

"Everyone knows it, though," Miss Plimpton defended herself. "She drank arsenic," she confided to Frank in her whisper.

"That's what her servants told our servants, at least," Mrs. Stewart clarified. "We never heard anything from the family."

"Of course they wouldn't speak of it, would they?" Miss Plimpton pointed out. "No one wants a scandal like that."

"When was this?" Frank asked, as if seeking only to complete his information gathering.

"At least three years ago," Miss Plimpton said.

"Oh, no," Mrs. Stewart corrected her. "Closer to five years. William had only been dead a few months. We still had the crepe hanging on the door."

"That's right," Miss Plimpton agreed. "We went to offer our condolences to Mr. Goodwin. Who better to comfort him than one who only recently lost her own spouse?" she explained to Frank. "But he was horrid to us."

"Oh, yes," Mrs. Stewart agreed. "Barely civil. We left after only a few minutes."

"They did let the girl come to the funeral, at least," Miss Plimpton recalled. "They had it at home, of course, and she was there. She was sitting in her chair when everyone arrived, and she never moved from it. I'm sure I wondered how she was able to walk with her foot and all, but she never rose from her chair."

"Didn't go to the cemetery either," Mrs. Stewart said. "I suppose if she can't walk, they couldn't take her."

"Did she seem upset over her mother's death?" Frank asked. He had done the math and realized that the mother's suicide had probably caused Amelia Goodwin's decline, the one for which Dr. Unger had treated her.

"She was devastated, poor thing," Miss Plimpton confirmed. "Cried inconsolably, even when her grandmother told her to stop."

"Mrs. Goodwin isn't a kind person," Mrs. Stewart reported with disapproval. "She didn't even try to comfort the girl. Just snapped at her to be quiet so everyone could hear the minister."

"Didn't her father try to comfort her?" Frank asked.

"Heavens, no," Miss Plimpton said, dismissing such a preposterous idea with a wave of her hand.

"He's as bad as his mother," Mrs. Stewart said. "If his wife really did kill herself, he was the one who drove her to it, I'm sure."

"What makes you say that?" Frank asked, still managing to sound only mildly interested.

"He's a hard man," Miss Plimpton said with a puckered frown.

"He always blamed her for the girl, too," Mrs. Stewart added. "For her being crippled. As if it was somehow her fault."

"Would you say he was a violent man?" Frank asked, and the instant he asked, he knew he'd gone too far.

Both women looked at him in surprise, as if suddenly remembering why he was there.

"I'm sure we'd have no way of knowing that," Mrs. Stewart informed him stiffly.

"Certainly not," Miss Plimpton said.

Frank closed his notebook and returned it to his pocket to reassure them he was finished with the topic of the Goodwin family. "Does your diary note anything that might be helpful about the day of the robbery?" he asked, turning their attention to something else.

"Oh, my, I'd almost forgotten," Mrs. Stewart said, looking down at the book in her lap as if she had no idea how it had come to be there.

It was a small book bound in brown leather with her initials embossed discreetly in gold leaf in the lower right corner of the cover. She opened it to a page marked with a yellow ribbon, presumably her last entry, and flipped back several pages to the correct day.

She read it over carefully before reporting. "That was the day we called on Cousin Priscilla. She lives

170

in Harlem," she added, naming a northern area of the city that was still somewhat rural. "We returned home rather late, had a light supper, and retired. I'm sure we didn't notice anything of significance, since we were away from home the entire day."

She closed the book with a snap, signaling to Frank that his visit was over.

"Thank you for your help, ladies. If you notice anything at all or hear of anything out of the ordinary, I'll leave my card so you can contact me."

The maid came to show him out, and this time he did leave his card. If the ladies got bored enough, perhaps they would remember something interesting, even if it had nothing at all to do with the mythical robbery.

Only when he was on the street did he realize he should have asked if they'd noticed any new servants in the area. But it was too early for that. If Maeve had managed to get herself hired, no one would have had time to see her around.

# 8

MAEVE WAS BONE TIRED, BUT SHE KEPT scrubbing. Mrs. Flynn had set her to the task of cleaning the floor of the pantry. Plainly, it was a job Mrs. Flynn neglected, probably because the cramped quarters and the clutter of bags and boxes and shelves made maneuvering difficult, and Mrs. Flynn was not a small woman. Determined to banish every speck of dirt and every stray crumb, Maeve had swept and now was applying lye soap suds with more than a little elbow grease to stains both old and new.

"There she is, ma'am," Mrs. Flynn said, making Maeve jump.

She looked over her shoulder to find a well-dressed middle-aged woman observing her solemnly. Mrs. Flynn stood at the woman's elbow.

Maeve scrambled to her feet, self-consciously smoothing her skirt.

"What's your name, girl?" the woman asked. Maeve knew she must be Mrs. Rossmann, Ordella Werner's aunt.

"Maeve Smith," Maeve said, trying out her curtsey again.

"Mrs. Flynn says you've fallen on hard times." Her voice was nice and sweet, like Mrs. Brandt's, like she never yelled at anybody, ever.

"Yes, ma'am." Maeve glanced at Mrs. Flynn, trying to judge whether the woman had put in a good word for her or not.

"She's done a good job on the floor there," the cook observed.

"Yes, she has," Mrs. Rossmann confirmed.

Maeve's instinct was to repeat her request for a few days' work to earn a reference, but she knew enough to keep her mouth shut. Mrs. Flynn had no doubt already conveyed her request. If she asked for something specific, she'd get that or less.

If she waited, she might get more. She waited.

"We don't have a place for you," Mrs. Rossmann said.

"No, ma'am," Maeve agreed.

"But I'm sure Mrs. Flynn can find some work for you for a few days," she added.

"Oh, thank you, ma'am," Maeve said, not having to feign her gratitude. "You won't be sorry. I'm a hard worker."

"I can see that." She smiled slightly, then turned and was gone.

"Oh, thank you, Mrs. Flynn," Maeve said.

"Don't thank me," the old woman sniffed. "You worked hard, so I thought you should have a chance. Finish the floor. I'll call you when supper's ready."

Maeve drew a deep breath and let it out in a sigh. Then she got back down on her knees and started scrubbing again.

Sometime later, when she'd finished the floor and cleaned out the bucket, Mrs. Flynn called her to eat. Supper was a hearty beef stew, probably left over from what Mrs. Rossmann and her brother had eaten the day before.

Two girls in maid's uniforms were already seated at the kitchen table, helping themselves. They looked Maeve over suspiciously.

Just like at the Prodigal Son Mission, Maeve thought with an inward smile. The girls were always suspicious of newcomers. You never knew what to expect from them, so nobody got too friendly at first. Here it would be even worse. If Maeve turned out to be a better worker than one of them, that girl might lose her place. Of course, Maeve wasn't interested in taking their jobs, but she didn't dare reassure them of that.

She took the empty chair where Mrs. Flynn had set a place for her, and waited for her turn with the stew bowl. There wasn't much left when it passed to her, but she didn't complain. She didn't say a word, just took what remained.

"This is Maeve," Mrs. Flynn told them. "She'll be here a few days. She's gonna do some of the jobs you don't like."

This pleased them, although they were still suspicious.

"Say hello, then," the old woman snapped when neither spoke.

"I'm Becky," the younger one said. She was a thin, pockmarked girl with watery blue eyes and bad teeth.

"I'm Gert." She was older, a solid stump of a woman who didn't look like she smiled much.

"Pleased to meet you," Maeve said, earning frowns from both of them. She made a mental note to steer clear of them as much as possible.

The four females tucked into their food, and for a few minutes, no one spoke.

"Mrs. Rossmann wants to start spring cleaning, doesn't she?" Becky asked after a while.

"It's early for that," Mrs. Flynn said.

"She could start on some of the heavy work, though," Becky argued.

"We'll see," Mrs. Flynn said, silencing the speculation, but Maeve could see the girls were already plotting. Maeve would probably be cleaning the privy tomorrow.

THE MESSAGE FROM DOUGLAS VICTOR WAS waiting for Frank when he got back to Police Headquarters. The plain sheet of paper had been folded over once with his name scrawled on the outside, and for a moment Frank felt his hackles rising in fury over Victor's carelessness. But when he opened the note, he found only an address written inside, and nothing else to indicate who had written it.

"Who delivered this?" he asked the desk sergeant.

"Some bum."

Frank wondered idly if the bum was a Pinkerton agent, too.

The address was a respectable-looking boardinghouse near Washington Square. The door opened before Frank could even knock. The Irish-looking woman who stood in the doorway was as nondescript as Douglas Victor, with a plain face and plain clothes. He guessed her age to be somewhere between thirty and fifty. She could probably become whatever age she needed to be. Her light brown hair had been carelessly pinned up, and her clothes had a slightly disheveled look, as if she took no care at all for her appearance, but she looked him up and down with a thoroughness that raised his hackles again.

"You'll be Malloy," she said. "Come on inside."

The front parlor had the shabby, lived-in look of a place where many people made themselves at home without giving it the care they'd give their home.

"I'm Allie," she said.

"Allie what?" he asked.

"Allie Shea," she replied with a sly look that told him this wasn't really her name. "Sit yourself down and tell me what the job is."

"Didn't Victor tell you?" Frank was getting annoyed.

"Of course he did. Now *you* tell me." She sat down in one of the wing-backed chairs by the fireplace. The coals had burned down to ash, but Frank welcomed even the feeble warmth. He took the chair opposite her, only to discover the seat was sprung. "This one's not much better," she said when he made a face.

Frank drew a breath and told her, "You know I'm investigating a murder?"

"A doctor, yes. Got killed about four years ago, over some woman."

"*Not* over some woman," Frank snapped. He would have cheerfully strangled Victor. "He was

176

trying to figure out how to cure something called Old Maid's Disease."

"Have they made it a disease now?" she scoffed with obvious amusement.

"Are you afraid you'll catch it?" he threw back at her.

Her eyes widened with a moment of appreciation. "All right, then, what's this Old Maid's Disease?"

Frank explained as briefly as he could.

"That don't make no sense at all," she insisted when he was finished. "Why would a woman carry on like that over a man she hardly knows or one who's married and don't want any part of her?"

"A normal woman wouldn't," Frank agreed, "but these women are insane. The one who tried to kill her rivals is locked up in an asylum now. The other two are locked away in their homes."

"And you want me to go inside one of the homes," she said.

"That's right. I need to find out as much about the family as I can before I confront the man I think is the killer, but Victor couldn't get much information on them."

"He said they keep to themselves, and they live out in the country, so they don't have a lot of neighbors."

"Yeah, that's what he told me," Frank agreed.

"They say that's good for crazy people."

"What's good for crazy people?" Frank asked, confused.

"Living in the country, where it's quiet. That's probably why they moved out there."

Frank looked at her sharply. "You know a lot about crazy people?"

"I know some. I know the quieter you can keep them, the better. They won't want some stranger coming into the house either."

"Victor said you could get in."

"Victor says a lot of things. He told me you want somebody inside the house, working as a servant. I can do that, if I can get them to let me in. Trouble is, they might not. People like that don't tend to be too trusting."

Frank sighed in exasperation. "Then why did you send for me?"

"To find out for sure. I didn't say I wouldn't try. If they've got a crazy girl in the house, it can't be easy to keep servants. Maybe they need help. So I'll try. What will I be looking for if I do get in?"

"A silver-headed cane," Frank said, unable to keep the sarcasm from his voice.

"That what the doc was killed with?"

"Yes."

"You think he'll still have it?" she asked doubtfully.

"No, but look for it anyway."

"Lots of silver-headed canes around," she observed. "Any idea what it looks like?"

"None at all."

She rolled her eyes. "What else?"

178

"Find out what kind of man the father is. How does he feel about his daughter? Is he the kind who would plot to murder somebody he thought had hurt her?"

"That could take some time," she warned.

Time was what Frank didn't have. He kept expecting any day to hear the newsboys calling out that Theodore Roosevelt had resigned from the Police Commission and was taking a job in Washington, D.C. When that happened, Frank would have only as much time as it took somebody to figure out he was working on a four-year-old case when new crimes were happening every day. "Do what you can," was all he could say.

"To WHAT DO I OWE THIS HONOR?" SARAH'S mother asked in amazement when Sarah and Catherine entered her sitting room. "Come and give me a kiss, Catherine," she added, not waiting for an answer.

Catherine ran to where Mrs. Decker sat, and obediently kissed the offered cheek. In another instant, Catherine was comfortably ensconced in Mrs. Decker's lap and getting kisses of her own.

Sarah was surprised by the twinge of jealousy she felt. She was long past needing her mother's adoration, so why should the fact that she was giving it so generously to another cause her discomfort? Would she have felt the same if Catherine had been born to her? Or was she just reacting to her own

179

regret that she couldn't recall her mother ever welcoming her with so much enthusiasm? Whatever the cause of her momentary distress, she squelched it and smiled a greeting.

Her smile must have looked strained, however, because her mother didn't return it.

"What brings you here at the crack of dawn, my darlings?" Mrs. Decker asked.

"So you would be home," Catherine replied solemnly before Sarah could think of a diplomatic reply.

Sarah ignored her mother's raised eyebrows. "We had to come before you left for your visits." Sarah knew this wasn't one of her mother's usual mornings to be "at home" to visitors, so she would probably have left at some point to pay calls of her own. "And it's far from the crack of dawn," she added. Only a lady of leisure like her mother would find nine o'clock early.

"I'm not complaining, mind you," Mrs. Decker assured them both. "I'm always happy to see you. I'm just surprised. What have you been up to?" she asked Catherine.

"Maeve left," the child reported.

"Maeve *left*?" Mrs. Decker echoed in surprise. "Where did she go?" She looked up to where Sarah still stood, a worried frown marring her lovely face.

"She had some personal business to take care of," Sarah tried. "We expect her back in a day or two."

Her lie hadn't fooled her mother, but Mrs. Decker

180

wanted to protect Catherine, too, so she accepted it for the moment. "So you've come to visit me," Mrs. Decker concluded. "How lovely. Catherine, my dear, would you like to go upstairs and play in the nursery for a while? We'll come up soon and join you."

Catherine looked to Sarah, silently asking permission. Sarah gave it with a smile and a nod.

"Sarah, dear, will you ring for the maid?" her mother asked, then chatted with Catherine about inconsequential things until the girl came to fetch her.

When they were gone, Mrs. Decker frowned. "What on earth happened with Maeve? Did she run away?"

"I almost wish she had," Sarah said, taking a seat next to her mother on the sofa. "She's gone off to help Mr. Malloy solve Tom's murder."

"How on earth can she do that?"

"She decided she could help Malloy by getting a job as a maid in the house of one of the suspects."

Her mother stared back at her, incredulous. She needed a few moments just to be able to frame a question. "Mr. Malloy permitted this?"

"Of course not," Sarah assured her. "He absolutely refused to even consider such a plan, but she decided to do it anyway. When we woke up yesterday, she was gone."

"How do you know that's where she went?"

"She left a note. She did promise to return soon."

"But what does she hope to accomplish? Surely, she doesn't think she can get some man to admit to murder."

"She thinks she can search the house for a silver-headed cane, which is what . . ." Sarah's voice broke, and she had to clap her hand over her mouth to keep from weeping.

"Oh, my dear, how heartless of me." Mrs. Decker reached out and took Sarah in her arms. "This must be so awful for you, reliving Dr. Brandt's death all over again."

Sarah hadn't allowed herself to admit just how very difficult it had been, but when she tried to reply, her words came out in an incoherent sob. The next thing she knew, she was weeping out all the pain and anguish on her mother's shoulder. For several long minutes, Sarah allowed the grief she'd thought she'd conquered to overwhelm her while her mother murmured the appropriate words of comfort and gave the appropriately soothing pats.

When she could weep no more, she sat up and accepted the delicate handkerchief her mother offered. While Sarah composed herself, her mother rang for a maid again and ordered tea for them both.

"I'm so sorry," Sarah said when she could speak.

"There's no reason to be," her mother said. "It's perfectly understandable, and I'm actually surprised you haven't broken down before now. I'm sure Mr. Malloy thinks he's doing you a great favor

182

by trying to solve Dr. Brandt's murder, but sometimes finding out the truth is more painful than not knowing."

"I hadn't realized that until now," Sarah said. "I think Maeve's leaving was the last straw."

"Of course it was. You must be terrified for her. Do you know where she went? Which house, I mean?"

"No. If we did, we'd make some effort to contact her and bring her home. We're fairly certain she's still in the city. The third family lives in Yonkers, and I doubt she would have ventured that far from home."

"So you know it's one of two places, then."

"Yes, but not which one. Malloy doesn't want to draw attention to her by looking for her either. One of these men has killed once and presumably wouldn't hesitate to kill again to protect himself."

"I'm sure Mr. Malloy is right to be concerned, but every instinct demands that we find her, doesn't it?"

"Yes, it does," Sarah admitted. "I don't think I realized how much I'd come to care for her until she was gone."

"You say she left yesterday morning?"

"That's right, before we were even awake."

"Then she must have succeeded in getting into one of the houses, or she'd have come back by now. What did you say she was planning to do?"

"She wants to search the house to see if she can

183

find the cane that killed Tom." Sarah was pleased that she could say the words without breaking down again.

"How do you know it was a cane?" Mrs. Decker asked with a frown.

"Mr. Malloy found a witness. He said the killer was carrying a silver-headed cane, and Maeve thinks if she can find it, she will solve the case."

"Good heavens, that won't prove a thing. Your father owns at least one cane with a silver head, perhaps more. Probably half the men in the city do."

Sarah thought this unlikely, but probably half of the *wealthy* men in the city did. "Malloy seems to think the real killer would have gotten rid of it in any case."

"Oh, of course he would," her mother realized. "Any sensible person would. Didn't you point this out to Maeve?"

"Yes, we did, but she was determined to help. I think . . ."

"What do you think?"

Sarah sighed in frustration. "I think I may have given Maeve a bad example with my own involvement in solving murders."

Her mother raised her eyebrows again. "I never thought I'd hear you admit that. Of course, I can certainly understand the appeal. Ordinary life seldom provides any excitement at all . . . nothing that would compare to investigating a murder, at least." Her mother's expression was slightly wistful. She was probably remembering the time she'd assisted in one of Malloy's cases.

"Oh, Mother, surely trying to decide what to wear to Mrs. Astor's latest ball is terribly exciting," Sarah teased.

"No, it's terrifying," her mother corrected her. "One must look one's best without outshining the hostess, a process fraught with peril . . . but not as much peril as searching for a killer."

"No," Sarah agreed with another sigh. "But Maeve doesn't worry about danger. She's a brave girl. She'd have to be to have survived on the streets."

"And the young always think they're invincible."

For a moment, they both remembered Sarah's sister, Maggie, and how her courage had cost her life.

"But Maeve knows how to take care of herself," Mrs. Decker reminded them both. "She's a clever girl, and as you said, she knows how to survive on the streets."

"I just hope she knows how to survive in a killer's house."

MAEVE WASN'T SURE WHAT SHE'D EXPECTED a killer to look like. Mr. Werner just looked like an ordinary swell. She'd happened to see him when she was outside in the yard, beating carpets. The other maids had been only too happy to delegate the dirty and exhausting job to "the new girl," and she'd been glad for a chance to get away from their scrutiny for a while. They watched her every move, like they expected her to run off with the silver or something. If she didn't win their confidence soon, she'd never have a chance to sneak away and search Mr. Werner's rooms.

He must have just gotten home from a trip, because she was fairly certain he hadn't been in the house last night. She hadn't wanted to ask too many questions after being taken to task by Mrs. Flynn for her curiosity. Now he was back, and she might have missed her best chance to search his rooms with no danger of him catching her. Silently cursing her luck, she kept hitting the carpet that had been slung over the clothesline with the sturdy wire beater while stealing glances over to where Mr. Werner stood talking with the groom.

Mr. Malloy had said Mr. Werner had once beaten a groom. She tried to see any evidence that this young man was afraid of Werner, but she saw nothing aside from the usual deference a servant gave his master. If Werner really did beat a groom, it wasn't this one. The groom was nodding and then disappeared back into the stable. Mr. Werner started down the flagstone path that ran between the stable and the house.

Maeve positioned herself to be behind the carpet so he wouldn't notice her and therefore wouldn't notice her watching him.

He was a hard man. She could see that in his face as he went by. He'd have no patience with mistakes and no mercy for failure. A man like that would never tolerate weakness in any form. She didn't ask herself how she knew all this. She'd been taught from birth to judge people at a glance. Her grandfather had warned her as soon as she was old enough to understand that her very survival might depend on this ability. Of course, he'd also told her that nobody was truly honest or truly good. He'd been wrong about that, as she now knew from living with Mrs. Brandt, but he'd been right about almost everything else. So she knew that when she did have an opportunity to search Mr. Werner's rooms, she'd better not get caught.

She hid behind the carpet, waiting while he passed, his well-made shoes tapping forcefully on the stones as he walked purposefully to the house. He never so much as glanced in her direction. When he disappeared into the house, Maeve looked over at the barn and wondered how she might strike up a conversation with the groom. He'd know Mr. Werner as well as his valet, but his valet would think himself too good to talk to the likes of her. Maybe she'd offer to carry out the slops after supper. No one would fight her for that task, and she'd have a few moments alone in the yard.

Then she saw the groom come out of the stable carrying a suitcase. Mr. Werner really had been on a trip. Maeve let him go by, then smiled to herself.

He'd be back in a few minutes, and he wouldn't be in any hurry.

She didn't have to wait long. Probably, the house servants wouldn't allow him to carry the bag upstairs himself. His assigned territory was the stable, after all, so he'd left the bag in the kitchen for someone worthy to take it up to Mr. Werner's room.

Maeve judged the boy to be about her own age, sixteen. He was spotty and his front teeth stuck out a bit, but he kept his uniform neat and clean, no small achievement when you worked with animals. He didn't seem aware of her presence until she called out, "Hello!"

He looked around in surprise and frowned when he saw her. "Who're you?"

"I'm new," Maeve said. "Just started yesterday. What's your name?" She took a step closer, but only one.

He looked around, probably checking to see if they were being observed. Then he took two steps closer to her, just as she'd known he would. "Jamie," he said, his plain face lighting with interest. "How come you ain't wearing a uniform?"

"They didn't give me one yet."

"Then how do I know you really work here?" he asked suspiciously.

"You don't," she said coyly. "Maybe I was just wandering by and thought I'd get some exercise by sneaking into the yard and beating some stranger's rugs."

He grinned at her logic. "I guess nobody'd do that," he allowed.

"No, they wouldn't." She tilted her head toward the house. "Was that the master who went by?"

"Yeah, he just got back from Albany," he informed her.

"Where's Albany?"

"A long ways from here. It's the state capital. The master had business there. Important business," he added, in case she was in doubt.

"What's he like?" she asked. "He looked mean to me."

He shrugged one bony shoulder. "He's all right, I guess, if you do your work. Better than some I've known."

Maeve glanced at the house as if making sure they were still alone. "One of the other girls told me he beat a stable boy to death," she said in a shocked whisper.

"He never!" Jamie protested in outrage. "Who was it said so? I'll set her straight."

"I can't tell them apart," Maeve lied. "But she was sure. Said the boy let a horse break his leg or something."

"Oh, that." Jamie waved it away with his hand. "The horse pulled a tendon. Almost ruined him, but he got all right in the end."

"What happened to the boy?"

"I think Mr. Werner let him have a few licks with a riding crop, but he didn't kill him, not by a long shot. Sent him packing is all."

"They said he beat him with a walking stick," Maeve said.

"A walking stick? I never heard that."

"They said it was," Maeve insisted. "Had a silver handle on it. Near broke the boy's skull."

"That's not how it happened at all."

"You saw it, did you?" she challenged.

Jamie frowned uncertainly. "Well, no, I never seen it. Happened before I come. But I heard tell."

"Then you don't know for sure, do you?"

Jamie didn't want to admit that. "I know he never raised his hand to *me*."

"But he could've hit the boy with a stick, couldn't he? I've seen sticks like that, with a big round knob on the end. You could kill somebody with one of those."

"He don't even use a walking stick, and he'd never hit anybody with one if he did. He don't even like me to whip the horses when they need it."

Maeve couldn't have been that far wrong in her assessment of Werner's character. "He didn't look exactly kind to me," she said.

"I didn't say he was *kind*," Jamie clarified. "I said he didn't beat me or the animals."

"I heard he sent his own daughter away. Had her locked up someplace."

Jamie's eyes widened with shock, and this time when he looked toward the house, he seemed frightened. "We don't talk about her."

190

"Why not?"

He took another step closer and whispered, "Because she's crazy."

Maeve feigned surprise. "Is she? How do you know?"

"She tried to kill some lady. Stabbed her with a kitchen knife."

"Stabbed her?" Maeve shivered deliciously. "Did she die?"

"No, just cut her pretty bad. The police came to the house," he told her.

"Police?" she echoed in disbelief. No one like the Werners should ever have a visit from the police. "What did they want?"

"I guess they wanted to arrest Miss Ordella. That's Mr. Werner's daughter."

"You mean put her in jail?" Maeve pretended to think of something. "Is that what they meant when they said she was sent away? Did she go to Blackwell's Island?" she asked, naming the notorious small island off New York City that housed several hospitals, insane asylums, and institutes of correction.

"Naw, they'd never send her to a place like that," Jamie scoffed.

Maeve knew that, of course. "But if she tried to kill somebody—"

"People like the Werners don't go to places like Blackwell's."

"Where'd they put her, then?" Maeve challenged.

"The police didn't put her nowhere," Jamie informed her. "They just went away and never came back. It was Mr. Werner what done it. He made arrangements. That's what he calls it. He says he's making *arrangements*. Then this big carriage comes to the house one day and takes Miss Ordella away. Don't expect she'll ever be back neither."

Maeve shivered again. "I hope he never makes arrangements for me."

"Not likely, unless you're crazy. You think you're crazy?" he teased, coming even closer.

He'd taken a shine to her. He'd tell her anything he knew. Trouble was, he'd also make up what he didn't know just to impress her. She'd have to be careful with him.

"I'm not crazy yet," she allowed, giving him a flirtatious look. "I just wanted to know if I should stay on here. Mrs. Rossmann seems nice enough, but if the master's too mean or if he's got an eye for the girls . . ."

"He don't even look at the girls," Jamie assured her. "He's real religious. Don't hold with drinking or swearing neither. Makes us all go to church of a Sunday, too."

Maeve feigned uncertainty. "Still, I saw his face. I didn't like him."

"You don't have to like him. Just stay out of his way, and you'll be fine."

She pretended to consider. "I guess I'll give it a try. Like I said, Mrs. Rossmann is nice."

"Yes, she is," he agreed.

They both jumped at the sound of the back door opening. Jamie didn't even glance back to see who was there. He just took off for the stable and in a moment was out of sight. Maeve turned and started beating her rug again, raising a cloud of dust that sent her scurrying backward to wait for it to settle again.

While she waited, Gert came up beside her and dropped a rolled-up rug at her feet. "Here's another one when you're through with that one."

She sounded belligerent. Maeve looked at her curiously.

"Don't you be getting any thoughts in your head about Jamie," Gert warned after a moment.

"I didn't have any thoughts about him at all," Maeve said quite honestly.

"I saw you talking to him," Gert snapped. "Mrs. Rossmann, she don't allow nothing funny to go on."

"I know," Maeve said. "We have to go to church and behave ourselves."

"Don't you make fun of Mrs. Rossmann," Gert warned, her face taking on an unbecoming flush.

"I'm not making fun," Maeve protested. "Jamie told me we have to go to church, only he said it was Mr. Werner who made that rule."

"I don't know who made it, but we do it."

"Seems kind of funny to me, a man who makes his servants go to church but sends his daughter away."

Gert's flush grew crimson. "Who told you that? Was it Jamie?"

"No, one of the neighbors," Maeve lied.

Gert didn't believe her. "When was you talking to the neighbors?"

"I've been looking for a job for a couple of days. I asked at some of the other houses on the street, and they warned me away from here. Said a crazy woman used to live here."

"Well, she don't live here now, so what do you care?"

"That's what I thought," Maeve agreed reasonably. "I was just asking Jamie if she might come back, though. I'd be scared to work where there was a crazy woman."

"She never did any harm," Gert said.

Maeve stared at her in amazement. "Jamie said she stabbed a lady nearly to death!"

"Not nearly to death!" Gert protested. "She was hardly scratched."

"With a kitchen knife?" Maeve asked skeptically. "I bet you wouldn't want to be scratched with a kitchen knife."

"What I meant was, she never did any harm as long as she was at home. She tricked the girls that had charge of her before I came. They left her door unlocked one time and she ran away. But once they got her back again, she was gentle as a lamb."

"Until she got loose again and stabbed some lady," Maeve reminded her.

"She didn't get loose that time, not while we was watching her," Gert insisted. "She just wanted to go to church. That's all she talked about. They kept her locked up in her room most of the time, but she was so calm, so they decided to let her go to church with them. Mr. Werner, he's real religious."

"I know, he don't drink or swear," Maeve said. Gert wasn't sure if Maeve was making fun of Mr. Werner or not. Maeve wasn't sure herself, so she said, "Don't tell me she stabbed that lady in church."

Gert didn't want to admit it. "She didn't act like she was crazy," she said instead. "Not ever. She'd talk to you just like anybody else. She even fooled Mr. Werner and Mrs. Rossmann. They thought she was better. That's the only reason they let her go."

Maeve wasn't interested in Ordella Werner. She was only interested in Ordella's father. "Did you ever see Mr. Werner act crazy?"

"Mr. Werner?" Gert echoed, horrified. "No! Not ever."

"Not even when he beat that stable boy to death with his cane?"

"Did Jamie tell you that?" Gert asked in amazement.

"Yes," Maeve lied.

"He was lying, then. Nothing like that ever happened. In fact," Gert informed her with a great deal of satisfaction, "Mr. Werner don't even have a cane."

195

# 9

FRANK WASN'T SURE WHY HE'D GONE TO Police Headquarters that morning. He didn't want to get involved in investigating any new crimes, and he was unlikely to find any information there that would help him find Tom Brandt's killer. Maybe it was just habit to report there. Whatever had drawn him, he found another note waiting for him. This one had a cryptic message that only he would understand: "I have new information. Meet me at the same place." It was signed "Allie."

"Got a new woman, Malloy?" the desk sergeant asked with a sly grin. "Does Mrs. Brandt know about her?"

Frank gave him one of his murderous glares, but the grizzled police veteran didn't even blink. "I'll be back later," Frank said and left the building, nodding to Tom the doorman on his way out.

He wasn't very encouraged. If Allie had gotten a job in the Alberton household, she wouldn't be back so soon, and if she *had* gotten a job, she wouldn't have had time to learn much. He doubted she'd wrung a confession out of Mr. Alberton that quickly, so any other news would hardly count.

This morning he had to knock on the door of the boardinghouse and wait until a harried young maid pulled open the door and glared at him rudely. "What do you want?" she demanded.

"I came to see Allie Shea," he said.

"Oh," she said in surprise. "Excuse me, then. Come on inside. I'll fetch her."

She didn't offer to take his hat and left him standing in the entryway while she hurried up the stairs. In another minute the woman he knew as Allie came down the stairs. She didn't look as self-assured as she had on his first visit. In fact, she looked a little sheepish. Frank tried not to sigh out loud.

"Good morning, Mr. Malloy," she said. "Let's go in the parlor, where we can talk."

She led the way and closed the door behind them. This time, she sat on the horsehair sofa and patted the seat beside her. Frank didn't think she wanted to cozy up to him, so he had to conclude she just didn't want to have to speak very loudly when she told him her "new information." The sofa was old and worn, and the horsehair had worked its way through the upholstery so that sitting on it was like sitting on a hairbrush.

"You didn't get hired on, did you?" he asked before she could offer any excuses.

"No," she admitted. "I went in with a letter of reference to be a maid. I talked to the housekeeper, and she was real polite, but she said they didn't need any maids. Too bad, she said, that I didn't have experience with children. She said they needed someone to look after a little girl."

Frank remembered that Victor had told them the

Albertons had a young child who had probably been born after they left the city. "Why didn't you tell them you could take care of her?" he asked, trying not to sound as annoyed as he felt.

"I did, but the woman thought I was lying because I needed a job. She said she'd have to see real references before Mrs. Alberton would trust anyone with the girl. I got the impression the family dotes on the child."

Frank rubbed his eyes, feeling the frustration building behind them. Two days wasted. "Do you have somebody in the Pinkertons who can be a nursemaid?"

"I already told Victor to find someone, but that could take a while. Anybody can clean house or pretend to for a few days, but looking after a child is different. Most people are careful who takes charge of their children, and if it's a case like this . . ."

"What do you mean?"

"Well, think about what happened to the two older children. The boy died in an accident and the girl lost her mind. Then this one comes along, sort of like a second chance God gave them. They'll be real particular about who takes care of her."

"I should've gone myself," he muttered.

"They'd never hire the likes of you for anything, Malloy," Allie said with a smirk.

Frank was in no mood for teasing. "I meant I should've gone up there to investigate in the first place, instead of trusting Victor."

"He's a good man," Allie said, offended.

"He was supposed to be the best you've got," Frank said. "That's what we're paying for."

"He *is* the best," Allie insisted. "If there was anything to be found, he found it."

"There's only one way to be sure," Frank said, rising from the sofa.

"You're going out there yourself?" Her disapproval was obvious.

"I don't have any choice," Malloy said.

"Do you still want us to find a nursemaid?" she asked as he strode to the door.

He stopped and looked back. He shouldn't be annoyed with her. She'd done what he'd asked her. The trouble was, he'd asked her to do the wrong thing. "Yeah, go ahead. Let me know when you've found somebody."

The walk back to Headquarters gave him a chance to think. He couldn't see any way around it. He'd have to go to Yonkers himself. He'd have to question people. He'd have to talk to the neighbors and their servants, the way Victor was supposed to, and if Victor had, then they'd be suspicious of somebody asking the same questions again. To make matters worse, they didn't live on a city street where everybody saw everybody else coming and going and where servants gossiped over the back fence. He wasn't the sort of man who could blend in like Douglas Victor either. Everyone knew he was Irish and most took him for a cop at first sight.

He'd also be a stranger, and no one liked strangers nosing around.

And finally, what if Victor was right, and the neighbors really didn't know anything about the Albertons? What if they kept to themselves so well that *nobody* could find out about them without moving into their house?

Well, it wasn't like he knew for a fact that Mr. Alberton had killed Tom Brandt. He was only one of three suspects. The other two were just as likely to be the killer. Frank was getting close to being ready to confront them, too. If one of them turned out to be guilty, he could forget all about the Albertons. The only thing keeping him from confronting the other two now was figuring out where Maeve was so he could get her out safely. He found himself wondering if he couldn't use Allie for that somehow, at least to find out where Maeve was. A woman could go knocking on doors, looking for her runaway daughter or something. Allie could pull that off. She might as well earn some of the money Felix Decker had paid her.

He was still mulling over this possibility when Tom opened the door for him and he walked back into Police Headquarters. He looked up to find the desk sergeant grinning at him. He'd seen that grin before and it never meant anything good. If somebody had locked Sarah Brandt into an interrogation room again . . .

"You've got a visitor, Malloy," the desk sergeant

said and nodded toward one of the benches where newly arrested felons sat, waiting to be processed.

Frank turned, expecting to see someone he didn't want to see, but this time he was wrong.

She lifted her head with obvious reluctance and gave him a sheepish grin. Relief flooded over him.

"Maeve," he said, not knowing whether to hug her or shake her.

"YOU'RE LUCKY YOU MENTIONED MY NAME," Malloy told her as he ushered her unceremoniously out the door that Tom held open for them. "You wouldn't like being locked up downstairs."

"Those Muldoons who arrested me almost locked me up anyway," she informed him, outraged. She tried to wrench her arm from his grasp, but he wouldn't let her go. "At first they wouldn't believe I know you."

"What changed their minds? And who are you calling *Muldoons*?" he demanded, equally out-raged.

"Dumb Irishmen, then," she said, showing him the kind of sass a street girl would use. He'd forgotten how recently she'd been one of them. "I didn't mean *you*," she added with an apologetic smile.

He ignored her apology. "How did you convince them you know me?" They'd reached the bottom of the front steps and turned uptown. He took a firmer grip on her arm.

201

"I had to threaten them. I told them you'd get them fired if they didn't take me to you. They were gonna take me to the precinct house and then send me to the Tombs."

"Just what you deserve for pulling a stunt like this. They caught you *stealing*."

"I didn't steal anything!" she protested. "You know I didn't!"

"They didn't know it, though. And why else would a girl like you be sneaking around where she didn't belong and looking in closets?"

"You know why I was!"

Frank gave her one of his glares, which momentarily silenced her. "Do you know how scared Mrs. Brandt is? And Catherine? And Mrs. Ellsworth?"

"I told them I'd be back in a few days," she protested weakly.

"You wouldn't have been back at all if they'd sent you to the Tombs."

She had no answer for that. Instead she said, "You're hurting my arm."

He loosed his grip but didn't release her.

"Where are we going?"

"I'm taking you home."

They'd reached the street corner, and he'd stopped to wait for the traffic and to look for a cab. He glanced down at Maeve and was surprised to see tears standing in her eyes.

He released her arm instantly. "Did I hurt you?" he asked in dismay.

202

She shook her head, not trusting her voice.

"What's the matter, then?"

She looked up at him and said, "Home," and burst into tears.

"DON'T OPEN THE DOOR UNTIL I GET THERE," Sarah called as Catherine raced from the kitchen at the sound of the bell. She hurried after the child, who had stopped obediently at the door and stood bouncing from one foot to the other in an agony of impatience. They could see two silhouettes through the frosted glass, and both of them looked blessedly familiar. Sarah pulled open the door to find an angry Malloy and a repentant Maeve on her doorstep.

"Maeve!" Catherine cried and threw herself at the girl. Maeve picked her up and carried her inside. Malloy followed closely behind, carrying a small bundle.

"Oh, Maeve, I'm so glad to see you," Sarah exclaimed, wrapping her arms around both girls and holding them tightly for a long, sweet moment. When she released them, she noticed Maeve's eyes were teary and bloodshot.

"Don't cry," Catherine begged, her small face screwed into a concerned frown, which only made it harder for Maeve *not* to cry.

"Are you hungry?" Sarah asked briskly, giving everyone something else to focus on. "Come on into the kitchen, and we'll all get something to eat."

The front door still stood open, and Mrs. Ellsworth came bustling in, squeezing around Malloy to see what was happening. "I saw you coming down the street," she said, breathless. "Oh, Maeve, thank heaven you're all right!"

More hugs and exclamations of surprise and gratitude ensued, but finally, they all made their way into the kitchen. Mrs. Ellsworth took charge of making sandwiches. Catherine wanted to sit in Maeve's lap, and everyone wanted to ask her questions.

"Where did you go?" Sarah asked.

"I tried the Werner house first," Maeve said.

"And they hired you on, just like that?" Mrs. Ellsworth said, looking up from slicing bread.

"Oh, no," Maeve said. "I was afraid if I asked for a job and they didn't have any, they'd just turn me away. So I told the cook I was looking for work, but that if they didn't have anything, I'd work for my keep. I told her my mistress died sudden, so I didn't have a reference, and I offered to work for free for a few days, so maybe her mistress would at least give me a reference."

"That was very clever," Sarah said without thinking.

Malloy cleared his throat, and when Sarah looked over, he was glaring at her.

"Well, it *was* clever," she excused herself. "But also very dangerous, Maeve. Didn't Mr. Malloy tell you not to get involved?" she added sternly.

"Yes, ma'am, he did," Maeve said with appropriate meekness. "But I wanted to help. After all you've done for me, I couldn't just sit by and do nothing, could I?"

"You most certainly could," Malloy informed her.

She refused to look at him and concentrated on the sandwich Mrs. Ellsworth set down in front of her.

"Go ahead and eat," Mrs. Ellsworth said. "You must be starving."

Maeve tucked into the makeshift meal.

"So they let you into the house," Sarah surmised. "And put you to work."

Maeve nodded. "I even saw Mr. Werner," she said when she'd swallowed her first mouthful. "He doesn't look like a very nice person."

"And he's probably not," Malloy said. "You should be glad he wasn't the one who caught you searching his room."

"I'm not that stupid," Maeve replied, offended. "I waited until he went to work this morning."

"You searched his room?" Sarah asked, horrified.

"I had to see if he had a cane, didn't I?"

"No, you didn't," Malloy said.

Maeve ignored him again. "I know it was dangerous, but I waited until everybody else was busy. I didn't think anybody would miss me."

"Who caught you?" Mrs. Ellsworth asked, setting a sandwich in front of Malloy.

"Gert, one of the maids. She didn't like me. Neither of the girls did, come to that. I think she was just looking for a way to get me in trouble."

"And you gave her one," Malloy said, earning him an exasperated look from Maeve.

"You're right!" she admitted. "But you have to agree that I got into the house with no trouble. I just got too impatient is all. Another day or two and they would've started to trust me. Then I could've done it without getting caught. Next time that's what I'll do."

*"Next time?"* Sarah and Mrs. Ellsworth echoed together.

Maeve looked at them in surprise. "Well, you still need somebody to get into the other two houses, don't you?"

"No, we don't," Sarah said. "You've done what you wanted to do and now you know how dangerous it can be. You're lucky Mr. Malloy was able to . . ." Suddenly Sarah realized she had no idea how Maeve had come to be in Malloy's custody. "How did you find her?"

"Mrs. Rossmann, that's Werner's sister, she called in the police and had her arrested for trying to steal something," Malloy reported grimly. "She could've ended up in prison."

"But I didn't," Maeve pointed out reasonably. "I told them I was working for Mr. Malloy, so they took me down to Police Headquarters."

"It wasn't that easy, though, was it, Maeve?" Malloy reminded her between bites of his own sandwich.

"Well, I did have to argue with them some," she admitted reluctantly, "but even if they'd arrested me, sooner or later you would've found me."

"I might not have been able to get you off, though," Malloy said. Sarah could see how worried he'd been. "And if you're arrested and charged, you'll have a record. You'd never get a position with a decent family after that."

Plainly, Maeve hadn't considered this, and for the first time since she'd returned, she looked uncertain. "I . . . Well, maybe I don't want to get a position like that. Maybe I could find some other kind of work." Maeve looked around the table, silently daring anyone to challenge her. When no one did, she asked, "Doesn't anyone want to know what I found out, at least?"

"You never said you'd found out *anything*," Malloy said, somewhat irritated.

"You never gave me a chance," she replied, returning his irritated glare with one of her own.

"All right, dear," Sarah said in an attempt to placate them both. "What did you find out?"

"I found out that Mr. Werner doesn't use a walking stick and never has. They said he don't even own any."

They all recognized this as important information, even Catherine.

"Then why did you search his rooms?" Malloy asked intently, no longer irritated at all.

Maeve blinked at his challenge but quickly

regained her confidence. "I had to make sure, didn't I? I didn't have time to make up to his valet, who's the only one who would really know. The rest of them, they're just servants, and they might not know everything about him, so I had to check."

Malloy sat back in his chair and studied her through narrowed eyes.

Sarah was concerned he was going to chasten her again so she quickly jumped in. "Maeve, dear, that was very resourceful of you, and I know how much you want to help," Sarah said, "but you won't be any help at all if you're in jail."

"And I don't think I can survive another scare like that," Mrs. Ellsworth said. "We were beside ourselves when we found out you'd run off."

"I didn't run off," Maeve protested. "I told you I'd be back."

"But you almost weren't," Sarah reminded her. "Suppose you hadn't been able to convince those policemen to take you to Headquarters?"

Maeve didn't want to think about that. "Next time I won't get caught."

"No sense talking about a next time," Mrs. Ellsworth said, setting sandwiches down for Sarah and Catherine. "There won't be any next time, will there, Mr. Malloy?"

Sarah looked up, hoping to catch Malloy's eye before he replied so he wouldn't be too hard on the girl. She had obviously learned her lesson. But

Malloy didn't even seem to be paying much attention to the conversation. He was staring at Maeve as if he'd never seen her before. Maeve had noticed, too, and she lifted her chin defiantly, probably expecting to be taken to task again.

But instead of responding to Mrs. Ellsworth's question, he suddenly rose from his seat. "I've got some business to attend to," he said. He looked straight at Maeve. "Don't go anywhere or do anything until I get back. Understand?"

Startled by the harsh command, she nodded. Then Malloy was gone, without so much as a by-your-leave. Sarah recovered quickly enough to catch him at the front door, putting on his hat. "What is it, Malloy?" she asked.

"I just thought of something I need to check on," was all he would say. He left her standing in her doorway with a puzzled frown, watching him hurrying down Bank Street.

THAT EVENING, CATHERINE WANTED MAEVE and only Maeve to put her to bed, and she demanded that Maeve hold her hand until she fell asleep. When she had finally extricated herself, Maeve found Sarah sitting in the kitchen. Mrs. Ellsworth had gone home, and it was the first time they'd been alone since Maeve's return.

"I'm real sorry, Mrs. Brandt," Maeve said as she sat down opposite Sarah at the kitchen table. "I didn't mean to scare everybody."

"I know you didn't mean to," Sarah said, "but you did. I hope you'll talk to me before you do anything like that again."

Maeve smiled wanly. "If I'd talked to you about it, you would've told me not to do it."

"Yes, I would have," Sarah admitted with a smile of her own. "Investigating a murder is dangerous. I know I've set a bad example," she added when the girl would have protested. "You've seen me get involved with Mr. Malloy's cases, but that's different."

"How is it different?"

Sarah should have anticipated this question and been ready with an answer, but she hadn't. She had to settle for, "Because I'm an adult."

"Do you think I'm a child?" Maeve countered. "Because if you do, why do you trust me to look after Catherine?"

"Well, no, of course I don't think you're a child," Sarah replied, very much afraid she had talked herself into a corner. "And you do a wonderful job, but . . ."

"But what?"

Sarah was certain she had had many such conversations with her mother when she had been Maeve's age. Back then, her mother had always been able to think of valid arguments. Why couldn't Sarah remember just one of them?

Fortunately, the doorbell rang at that very moment, granting her a reprieve. For once, she fervently hoped it was a delivery so she'd have some time away to gather her thoughts.

Maeve followed her to the front door and hung back, waiting to see what might be required of her. Since darkness had fallen, Sarah couldn't see any hint of who might be waiting on her doorstep. "Who's there?" she called.

"Malloy," came the reply.

Sarah threw open the door to find Malloy and a woman she'd never seen before, and her welcoming smile froze on her lips. "Come in," she said, mystified. Malloy had said nothing about returning so soon, much less about returning with someone else. And who on earth was this woman?

The woman nodded politely as she passed Sarah, but she was already looking around, taking in her surroundings with a keen eye that, Sarah felt certain, missed no detail. Her gaze quickly found Maeve standing in the shadows of the front room that served as Sarah's office.

"That her?" she asked Malloy.

"Yeah," he replied. "Mrs. Brandt, this is Allie Shea. Allie, this is Maeve."

"Pleased to meet you," Sarah was saying, but this Mrs. Shea was paying her not the slightest attention. She'd already walked over to where Maeve stood and was looking the girl up and down with a critical eye.

"She's young," Mrs. Shea said to Malloy. "How old are you, girl?"

Maeve lifted her chin defensively. "Eighteen," she said to Sarah's surprise.

"Maybe you will be someday, but not today," Mrs. Shea replied with a knowing smile. "Where are you from?"

"Who wants to know?" Maeve snapped, not happy at being judged by someone she didn't even know.

Mrs. Shea raised her eyebrows and looked back at Malloy, who said, "I told you."

"What did you tell her about me?" Maeve demanded. "And who is she to be coming into Mrs. Brandt's house anyways?"

"She's a Pinkerton agent," Malloy said. "Do you know what that is, Maeve?"

Plainly, Maeve didn't want to admit she didn't. Sarah rescued her. "The Pinkertons are *private* detectives. People hire them to . . . to do things the police can't."

"Or won't," Mrs. Shea added with a slight smirk.

"Or because they don't want the police mixed up in it at all," Malloy said.

"And these Pinkertons, they let women be detectives, too?" Maeve asked in amazement.

"Yes, they do. Sometimes women can find out things men can't," Mrs. Shea said.

Maeve smiled knowingly. "Mrs. Brandt already knows that."

"And so does your Mr. Malloy," Mrs. Shea replied.

Sarah suddenly felt as if she'd been shut out of something happening right in front of her. "Why don't we go into the kitchen, and I'll make some coffee?" she suggested in an attempt to regain some control over the situation.

"Sounds like a fine idea," Mrs. Shea said.

Maeve led the way.

"Do you see patients here?" Mrs. Shea asked Mrs. Brandt as they moved through the office.

"Not very often. My husband was a doctor, so this was his office."

Mrs. Shea's sharp gaze settled back on Sarah, silently telling her she knew all about Dr. Brandt. This shouldn't have surprised her, but she did feel a slight resentment that this stranger knew so much about her.

They took seats at the kitchen table while Sarah stoked the fire and put the coffee on to boil.

"Why are you here?" Maeve asked Mrs. Shea bluntly when they were all seated.

"To meet you," Mrs. Shea replied just as bluntly. "Mr. Malloy says you want to be a female detective."

"I never said so," Maeve said, giving Malloy a reproachful look.

"You did it, though, didn't you?" Mrs. Shea said before he could reply.

"I . . . I was just trying to help Mrs. Brandt," Maeve said.

"Tell me what you did," Mrs. Shea said. "Start

from when you first decided to do it. What were you thinking?"

Maeve frowned. She didn't like this. "Mr. Malloy was telling us how he was trying to find out about each one of the three men he thinks might've killed Dr. Brandt."

"Go on," Mrs. Shea said when she hesitated, but Maeve was looking at Sarah.

"It's all right," Sarah assured her.

Maeve continued reluctantly. "He said the killer used a silver-headed cane, so I thought he should try to find out which of them had one. Mr. Malloy said the real killer would've thrown it away by now, but I didn't think so."

"Why not?" Mrs. Shea challenged.

"Because something like that, it costs a lot of money."

"But he'd used it to kill a man," Mrs. Shea reminded her.

"Well, maybe he'd feel funny about using it after that, but he'd think how much it cost him, so he wouldn't just throw it away. Most people wouldn't anyway."

Mrs. Shea and Malloy exchanged a glance, but Sarah had no idea what they were thinking.

"Tell me how you got into the house," Mrs. Shea said.

Maeve told her the story, adding details she hadn't mentioned when telling the story earlier. Mrs. Shea asked questions, too, leading her to

214

reveal even more. After a few minutes, Sarah realized what Mrs. Shea was doing. She was trying to find out just how clever and cunning Maeve really was.

"You tried to search the room too soon," Mrs. Shea told her.

"I already know that," Maeve said impatiently. "Didn't I say so?" she asked Malloy.

"Yes, you did," he replied.

"How'd you get caught?" Mrs. Shea asked.

"Mrs. Rossmann was out visiting, and Mr. Werner was at work. I thought the other two girls was busy doing the laundry, and I was supposed to be polishing the silver in the butler's pantry, but I sneaked up the back stairs. I didn't think it would take long. There's not many places to hide a cane. I guess it took longer than I thought, though, because Gert, she's one of the other maids, she come looking for me. She caught me with my head in a wardrobe and started screaming that I was stealing."

"What did you do then?" Mrs. Shea asked.

"I told her I wasn't doing no such thing, but by then the other servants had come running, and when they asked why was I in Mr. Werner's rooms, I decided I shouldn't answer. Mr. Malloy had said it could be dangerous if Mr. Werner was the killer and he thought somebody was looking for him, so I just kept my mouth shut. I figured it was better if they thought I was stealing than if they knew what I was really doing."

"So they sent for the police?" Mrs. Shea asked.

"Not right off. They waited for Mrs. Rossmann to get home. I was really scared they'd wait for Mr. Werner, too, but she said there was no reason to bother him. I didn't work for them, after all. He probably didn't even know I was in the house. So they just got the patrolman. He and another copper took me in."

"When did you tell them to take you to Malloy?"

"Not 'til we was out of the house. I didn't want anybody in there to hear me or know about Mr. Malloy. I told them I was doing some special work for Mr. Malloy."

Mrs. Shea raised her eyebrows again. "Did they believe you?"

Maeve made a face. "They said some nasty things at first, about what kind of special work I might do, but when I told them Mr. Malloy was doing a job for Mr. Roosevelt and I was helping, they decided to drop me off at Police Headquarters, so if it was true, they wouldn't get in trouble."

"Mrs. Shea," Sarah said, "how are you involved in all this?"

"I was hired to get into the Alberton house."

"That's the one in Yonkers," Malloy said, in case Sarah didn't remember.

Maeve leaned forward, intrigued. "How did you get in?"

Mrs. Shea smiled indulgently. "I didn't. I wasn't as clever as you."

Maeve's cheeks glowed at the compliment, but Sarah was more interested in her earlier remark.

"Who hired you?" she asked sharply, startling everyone.

"Pardon me?" Mrs. Shea asked in surprise.

"You heard me. Who hired you?" Pinkertons didn't come cheap, and she couldn't imagine Malloy involving the private agency, even if he'd had the means.

"I don't really know," Mrs. Shea said uneasily. "I just report to Mr. Malloy."

"We'll talk about that later," Malloy said to Sarah, a note of warning in his voice.

"We certainly will," Sarah informed him with a warning of her own. But she was pretty sure she already knew.

Maeve wasn't interested in that subject, however. "Why didn't you get into the Alberton house? What did you do wrong?"

Mrs. Shea was only too glad to change the subject. "I asked for a job as a maid, but they didn't need any help, so they turned me away."

Maeve fairly beamed. "I was afraid of that, which is why I came up with another story."

Mrs. Shea and Malloy exchanged another look, and Sarah found herself feeling unaccountably jealous of their silent communication. How long had they known each other? And how well? Malloy gave Mrs. Shea a slight nod, which was all she needed. She turned back to Maeve.

"I didn't get the job because they didn't need a maid, but they told me they were looking for somebody to take care of a little girl. They have another child, you see, and she's young enough to need a nursemaid. I tried to convince them I could do it, but they thought I was just saying so to get them to hire me, which was true, of course."

Maeve's eyes were enormous in her small face, and Sarah could see where her thoughts had led. Suddenly, Mrs. Shea's presence here made perfect sense.

"They'd hire *me*, wouldn't they?" Maeve said eagerly.

"Now wait," Sarah said in alarm. "I thought we'd decided it was too dangerous for Maeve to be involved in this."

"It was too dangerous for her to go off on her own," Malloy said. "She won't be alone this time."

"What do you mean?"

"Mrs. Shea here will go up to Yonkers with her. She'll take a room in the town, and Maeve will check in with her every day."

"How will she do that?" Sarah asked skeptically.

"We'll work out a system," Mrs. Shea said. "Find a place we can leave messages. We do it all the time."

"And if we think Maeve is in danger, Allie can just go to the door all upset and say Maeve's dear old grandmother is dying, and she needs to go home right away," Malloy said.

"But won't they remember Mrs. Shea?" Sarah asked, still far from convinced.

"Maeve is going to tell them Allie is her aunt, and she told her about the job," Malloy said. "That'll explain why she showed up so quick."

"All right, suppose Maeve is in danger and can't leave you a message in your secret place," Sarah asked. She was angry and not certain why. Was it because Malloy had made this whole plan with a strange woman, with whom he seemed to be on the closest of terms, and not involved her at all? Of course not, but she was still angry.

"We'll have a signal," Mrs. Shea said. "She'll put something in the window for me to see. I'll be keeping close watch on her, don't worry. We know how to keep our agents safe, Mrs. Brandt. We've been doing this since the war."

"She won't be there long anyway," Malloy said. "As a new servant, she'll have good reason to ask questions and want to find out what the family is like."

"And she won't do anything stupid, like trying to search the master's rooms, will she?" Mrs. Shea asked with a pointed look at Maeve.

"No, ma'am, I won't." Maeve turned to Mrs. Brandt. "Can I do it?"

Sarah stared at her in dismay. "It could be very dangerous," she warned.

"I'll be careful. I promise!"

"It's the only way of getting information on the

family, Mrs. Brandt," Mrs. Shea said. "Everything else we've tried has failed."

How could she refuse? Sarah turned to Mrs. Shea and gave her the sternest glare she could muster. "If anything happens to her, I'll hold you responsible."

"No need to threaten me, Mrs. Brandt," Mrs. Shea replied cheerfully. "Mr. Malloy has already taken care of that."

# 10

CATHERINE CRIED THE NEXT MORNING WHEN Maeve told her she was leaving again.

"I'll be back soon, I promise!" Maeve assured her over and over, but Catherine would not be consoled. Maeve rocked and crooned to her for a long time, and when the child had finally calmed down enough, Catherine was able to voice her true fear.

"Are you going to jail?"

The whoops from Maeve and Sarah frightened her all over again until she realized they were whoops of relieved laughter. Everyone was only too happy to reassure her that Maeve most definitely was not going to jail. By then Mrs. Shea had arrived to escort Maeve on her journey, and she also promised Catherine that she would return Maeve safe and sound. Catherine still wasn't happy to lose her beloved nursemaid, but she accepted the situation and gave Maeve a kiss good-bye.

Maeve was teary-eyed, too, but Sarah could see

how excited she was all the same. She only hoped that Malloy and Mrs. Shea were right and that Maeve would be completely safe.

"I hope my letter of recommendation is convincing," Mrs. Ellsworth said with a sigh as they watched Mrs. Shea and Maeve turn the corner at the end of Bank Street and disappear from view.

"I thought you did a lovely job with it," Sarah assured her. "And mentioning that you're leaving for Europe makes it difficult for them to check with you."

"That Mrs. Shea person must have had an interesting life," Mrs. Ellsworth mused as Sarah closed the front door.

"She's a 'tective," Catherine reported in her whispery voice.

"I know she is, dear," Mrs. Ellsworth said. "I'm certain I never expected to see a female detective in my entire life . . . Present company excepted, of course," she added with a wink.

Sarah didn't feel much like being teased. Her conscience had been bothering her all night, ever since she'd agreed to allow Maeve to assist in the investigation. So many things could go wrong, and Maeve was still so young. She wouldn't have the wisdom or experience to know how to handle a difficult situation. Sarah prayed she'd at least have the sense to run away if things got out of hand.

For now, Sarah needed a distraction. "Let's go upstairs and play," she said to Catherine. The child slipped her tiny hand into Sarah's and obediently led her to the stairway.

MAEVE FELT MORE NERVOUS THIS TIME THAN she had when she'd talked her way into the Werner house. Her mind was fairly buzzing with the instructions Allie had given her last night and on the train ride up this morning. The important thing was to keep her eyes and ears open, though. She was there to collect information. Mr. Malloy would decide if it was important or not.

The house sat far back from the road and had no near neighbors. Maeve thought the people here must get very lonely with nobody to see or talk to except those living in the house with them. A nice man had given her a ride on his wagon from the boardinghouse where Allie was staying and dropped her at the front gate. Even still, she'd had quite a hike to the house itself. If they didn't hire her, she'd sure have a long walk back.

Drawing a deep breath, she lifted her hand and knocked on the back door while a battalion of butterflies did battle in her stomach. An older woman in an enormous apron opened the door. She looked harried and annoyed.

"What do you want?" she demanded.

"I've come about the position," Maeve said, then cleared her throat and tried again. "The nursemaid position," she clarified.

The woman looked her over with disapproval,

222

and for a moment, Maeve was afraid she'd just slam the door in her face. Then the woman sighed and said, "I suppose you'd better come on in, then. I'll get Mrs. Tate."

Maeve took a seat at the kitchen table as directed and waited while the woman, whom Maeve took to be the cook, went in search of Mrs. Tate. Allie had told her Mrs. Tate was the housekeeper, the woman she'd need to impress. They'd practiced what Maeve would say to her all during the long train ride.

When Mrs. Tate came in with the cook at her heels, Maeve jumped to her feet and bobbed a little curtsey. Mrs. Tate was a woman well into middle age with a thickening waist and a darkening patch of hair on her upper lip. She wore a black serge dress with no adornment except a bunch of keys hanging at her waist. Her once-dark hair was streaked with gray and combed into a neat if unflattering bun. She also looked harried.

"You're a nursemaid?" she asked doubtfully, looking Maeve over even more critically than the cook had.

"Yes, ma'am. I've got a year of experience and a letter of reference." She'd already taken the letter out of the bundle of clothing she carried and tried to present it to Mrs. Tate, who made no move to accept it.

"How did you hear about the position?" Mrs. Tate asked suspiciously.

"My aunt Allie, she was here looking for work.

She's a maid, and you wouldn't give her the nurse-maid position, so she told me about it. I came right on."

"You say you have experience?" Mrs. Tate asked with a frown.

"Yes, ma'am, a year and a month." Maeve looked her straight in the eye as Allie had advised her to.

"How old was the child you took care of?"

"Four," Maeve said without hesitation. "At least, she's four now. She was three when I started with her."

"And why aren't you with her anymore?"

"Her family, they went to Europe. Mrs. Ellsworth, she's the mother, she's not well. They went for her health." Allie had made up the story for her.

Mrs. Tate didn't seem happy with the story. "Why didn't they take you with them then?"

Maeve hesitated the way Allie had coached her. "I . . . I didn't want to go. I was afraid of crossing all that water. They'll be on a boat for weeks, they said, and I . . . I can't swim."

Mrs. Tate gave a snort. Maeve couldn't tell if she sympathized or disapproved, but she waited patiently, still looking the woman straight in the eye.

"I have a letter of reference," she repeated after a moment of silence and offered it again.

This time Mrs. Tate took it, but she didn't look at it. "Wait here," she said and turned on her heel.

When she was gone, the cook sighed again. "Sit

down, girl. If they hire you, it might be your last chance to rest."

Maeve did as she was told and watched the cook as she sliced up vegetables for soup. She wanted to ask some questions, but she knew better than to appear too nosey at this early stage. The cook hadn't been instructed by Allie, however, so she started questioning Maeve.

"You come from the city?"

"Yes, I did."

"You won't like it here. Too quiet."

"It's very pretty here in the country, though," Maeve observed.

"Dull, too. Nobody to visit. Young girl like you, you'll get bored."

"Don't you have any other young girls here?" Maeve asked.

"Just Kerry," Cook said with a frown. "And she keeps busy with Miss Christina."

"She's a lady's maid, then," Maeve guessed with what she hoped was an innocent expression.

Cook snorted rudely. "Not hardly. A lady's *keeper* more likely."

They heard footsteps, and Cook suddenly decided she needed something from the pantry. Mrs. Tate came back in. "Mrs. Alberton wants to see you. Leave your bundle here and come with me."

Maeve felt her heart pounding in her chest as she followed Mrs. Tate down a hallway to the front part of the house, where the family lived. The house wasn't as fancy as Mrs. Decker's, but much nicer than Mrs. Brandt's or Mrs. Ellsworth's and even the Werners'. The family did pretty well for themselves, she decided.

Mrs. Tate led her into a parlor filled with over-stuffed furniture and lots of little tables sitting around and covered with glass figurines and vases and all sorts of bric-a-brac. She had to look hard to find the lady sitting in one of the chairs by the window. The lady was watching Maeve carefully. Maeve tried to look calm and competent but not too forward.

"Here she is," Mrs. Tate said without much enthusiasm.

"Come closer, girl," Mrs. Alberton said. Her voice was soft, a lady's voice.

Maeve walked over and stood before her. Mrs. Alberton looked like she'd never had to turn her hand to do anything. She was small, with womanly curves and a smooth face. Her blond hair had some silver threads that glinted in the sunlight, but it was perfectly arranged. Her soft little hands lay folded primly in her lap.

"Tell me about yourself," Mrs. Alberton invited.

Maeve took a fortifying breath. "I've been looking after a little girl for a year now—"

"No, no," Mrs. Alberton chided. "Tell me about *yourself*. Where are you from? Who is your family?"

Maeve felt a small twinge of relief that Allie had helped her make up a story for this, too. "I grew up in the city. My ma was a maid for the Ellsworths for a long time, and when they needed somebody to look after little Ethel, well, I'd been looking after little ones for as long as I can remember."

"You come from a large family, I suppose," Mrs. Alberton said.

"I don't have any brothers or sisters myself, but lots of cousins," Maeve said.

Mrs. Alberton picked up the letter of reference, which had been lying on a nearby table, and glanced at it. "Did your mother go to Europe with the family?"

"No, ma'am," Maeve said with a trace of sadness. "She died a few months ago."

Mrs. Alberton nodded slightly to acknowledge Maeve's loss. "Why have you come all the way out here looking for work?"

"My aunt Allie, she told me about the position. I thought I might like being in the country for a change."

"How did your aunt know about it?" Mrs. Alberton asked with a confused frown.

Mrs. Tate, who had been standing beside her chair, leaned down and whispered something to her. She nodded again.

Maeve waited, forcing herself not to fidget or say something to fill the silence. Allie had warned her to keep her mouth shut and only answer what was asked of her.

After what seemed an eternity, Mrs. Alberton

said, "We have a hard time keeping nursemaids. It's not that Iris is a difficult child," she added too quickly, not quite meeting Maeve's eye. "It's . . . You see, my daughter, Christina, is ill."

Maeve knew this perfectly well, but she gave no indication. She simply waited to hear what Mrs. Alberton would tell her.

"You wouldn't have to care for Christina, of course," she continued. "She has a servant of her own, but sometimes . . . Well, sometimes she's unruly. If you're easily frightened . . ." She let the question hang.

"Oh, no, ma'am, I'm not." Maeve wished she could tell some stories to prove it, but she stifled the urge.

Mrs. Alberton looked down at the letter again, and Maeve held her breath. "Well, I suppose we can give her a try," she said to Mrs. Tate.

That was when Maeve saw it, the infinite weariness behind Mrs. Alberton's smooth face. She was very tired of the burdens she'd been forced to bear, almost too tired to go on.

"Thank you, ma'am," Maeve said with unfeigned gratitude. A chance was all she needed.

Mrs. Tate looked as if she still had her doubts, but she wouldn't question the mistress. "Come with me, girl," she said with little enthusiasm. "I'll take you to the nursery."

They stopped in the kitchen so Maeve could get her bundle of clothing.

"She's staying, then?" the cook asked Mrs. Tate.

"For now," Mrs. Tate replied. The words held more meaning than Maeve could guess.

Then Mrs. Tate took her up the back stairs to the second floor and down a long hallway with closed doors on either side. Maeve could hear the screams long before she and Mrs. Tate reached the room from which they came. At first she thought it must be Christina being "unruly," but when Mrs. Tate pushed open the door and Maeve saw the knowing expression on her face, she realized that Miss Christina wasn't the only unruly one in the house.

When she stepped into the room, she saw a girl about Catherine's age lying on the floor in the middle of a large playroom. She was kicking her feet and flailing her hands and screaming as loudly as she could. A woman in a maid's uniform stood over her, wringing her hands and pleading with her in a shrill voice.

"Please stop, Miss Iris! Please! You'll hurt yourself, you will. Please stop!"

The child completely ignored her and continued her tantrum with even more enthusiasm. When Maeve stepped into the room, the maid looked up in alarm.

"I didn't do anything to her, I swear!" the woman cried piteously.

"Of course you didn't," Mrs. Tate said from the doorway. "You can leave now, Lizzie. This is the new nursemaid. What's your name again, girl?"

"Maeve," she said, having to shout to be heard over the ear-piercing racket.

Lizzie cast her a sympathetic glance and fled.

"You can put your things in there," Mrs. Tate shouted, pointing at a door on the far side of the room. "Somebody will bring your meals up to you."

She pulled the door closed behind her.

Maeve looked at the child still flailing away. Of course they brought the meals up. No one wanted to be around this. Maeve went over to the door Mrs. Tate had indicated and opened it. The room that was to be hers was small and contained a narrow bed, a wardrobe, and a washstand. Maeve set her bundle of clothes on the bed and went to the washstand. The pitcher had a little water in the bottom. Not much, but it would do. She carried the pitcher back out to the playroom and went straight to where the girl lay thrashing on the floor. Without a word, Maeve upended the pitcher and dumped the water right in the child's face.

The screaming and the flailing stopped instantly, replaced by sputtering and outrage. Iris scrambled to her feet, looking around frantically to see who had assaulted her. When she saw Maeve, her eyes widened in surprise. "Who are you?" she demanded.

"I'm Maeve. I'm your new nursemaid, and let me tell you right away, I don't like what you were doing just now. That's not the way a proper young lady acts."

230

"I'm not a proper young lady!" Iris informed her belligerently.

"I know you're not," Maeve agreed. "You're a rotten little brat, but you can change."

Iris lifted her chin and glared at Maeve. "I don't want to change."

"Yes, you do," Maeve assured her. "Because if you behave, I'll play with you, and we'll go outside in the garden and have lots of fun. But if you don't . . ." Maeve looked meaningfully at the pitcher she still held.

Iris considered her options. Then her small face grew cunning, and she said, "I can't behave. I'm crazy."

Maeve looked at her in surprise. "Who told you that?"

"Kerry. Other people, too. I hear them talk."

"What does crazy mean?" Maeve challenged.

Iris gave her a contemptuous look. "Crazy means like Christina."

WHEN MALLOY ARRIVED AT HEADQUARTERS that morning, another message awaited him. The desk sergeant gave him a knowing grin, but the handwriting wasn't Sarah's. He tore open the envelope, and this time he found a message from Mrs. Johanna Rossmann. She wanted to speak to him immediately.

He considered ignoring the message. He was fairly certain she wasn't summoning him so she could tell him her brother had killed Tom Brandt. She didn't even know he was investigating that case. She had no way of connecting him with Maeve either. Maeve had been careful not to mention his name until they'd taken her away from the house. So what could she possibly want?

In the end, he decided he couldn't afford to ignore her. At the very least, he might get some additional information out of her about her brother.

The maid had been expecting him and showed him into the parlor, where he had to wait for Mrs. Rossmann to come from wherever she had been. When she entered the room, he could see she was angry. She closed the door behind her and marched right up to him.

"Why did you send that girl here?" she demanded.

So much for not connecting him with Maeve. "What girl?" he asked, having decided that denial was the best tactic.

"You know perfectly well what girl."

"I don't know what you're talking about," he tried.

She gave him a disgusted look. "I inquired after her this morning from the patrolman who works in this neighborhood. He's the one who arrested her, and I was *concerned* about her," she admitted in disgust. "I started feeling guilty and thinking maybe I'd been too hasty in turning her over to the police. Now I just feel like a fool!"

"Mrs. Rossmann, I—"

"He told me he took her to Police Headquarters and that she was working for *you*." Her eyes shone with fury.

Frank hadn't considered that he'd be betrayed by his own. He'd have a word with the patrolman, as soon as he found out who it was. Meanwhile, he had a furious female on his hands. Frank rubbed his jaw, wishing Maeve was here to clean up the mess she'd made. "She doesn't work for me," he said.

"I said that I *felt* like a fool, Mr. Malloy, not that I *am* one!"

Frank only debated his reply for a few seconds. The truth couldn't do any harm now. "It's true, Mrs. Rossmann. She works for Dr. Brandt's wife."

"Dr. Brandt?" she echoed in confusion.

"Yes, you remember, the doctor who tried to help Miss Werner."

She frowned, even more confused. "You mean the one who upset her so much?"

"Yes, Maeve is the nursemaid to Mrs. Brandt's daughter."

She tried to make sense of it and failed. "Then what was she doing *here*?"

"She knew that I was investigating Dr. Brandt's death, so she decided to help."

"What do you mean, *investigating Dr. Brandt's death*?"

"Dr. Brandt was murdered not too long after he saw your niece. We have reason to believe that

233

his killer was the father of one of his patients."

"But . . ." Her voice trailed off as the truth slowly dawned on her. "You think *my brother* killed him?" she asked in amazement.

"He had a good reason to hate Dr. Brandt," Frank reminded her.

"My brother isn't a murderer!" she insisted, furious all over again.

"I didn't say he was," Frank said, speaking calmly in an attempt to calm her in return. "I said I was investigating, so I had to check on all the fathers who could have had a reason to want Dr. Brandt dead."

Her eyes blazed with fury. "So you sent a girl here to spy on us?"

"I didn't send her anyplace. Like I said, she knew I was investigating Dr. Brandt's death, so she decided to help."

"How was she planning to *help*?"

"She was trying to find a cane."

"A *cane*?" Now she was simply baffled. "What did she want with a cane?"

"Dr. Brandt was killed by being hit in the head with a cane that had a large silver head. She thought—"

"She thought she'd find this cane in *my brother's* room?" she interrupted him, outraged.

"She thought if she did find it, she could prove your brother is the killer."

"So that's what she was looking for!" she cried,

beginning to pace. "I simply couldn't figure out what she was doing in Oscar's room if she wanted to steal something. All the valuable things are downstairs!"

"She wasn't going to steal anything," he said.

"And she wasn't going to find a cane, either," Mrs. Rossmann informed him in disgust, still pacing back and forth in front of him, as if her anger compelled her to move. "My brother doesn't even own a cane!"

"I know. She found that out from the other servants."

She stopped in her tracks and looked up at him in triumph. "I told you, my brother isn't a killer."

"What about the time he beat that stable boy?" Frank tried.

"What?" she demanded. "What are you talking about?"

"I heard he'd beaten a stable boy almost to death."

"Who told you such a thing?" she cried, outraged again.

Frank shrugged, not willing to name his sources.

"Well, it's a lie! He struck the boy after he'd almost killed one of our horses, but the boy fought back, and Oscar was lucky to escape himself. He's not a killer, Mr. Malloy."

"But I couldn't take your word for it, Mrs. Rossmann," he said.

She glared at him, but she said, "No, I don't suppose you could. You'd expect me to defend him, but now you have your proof. Your little spy even searched his room, and she didn't find anything, did she?"

"No, she didn't, and I've made sure she won't do anything that foolish again." At least he hoped that was true.

"I'm glad to hear it, but you should warn her she'd better not show her face around here again."

"I promise you she won't."

Frank was ready to take his leave, but she didn't dismiss him. Instead she just stared at him for a long moment, as if she were considering something. "Dr. Brandt was murdered?" she asked finally.

"That's right. By a man whose daughter was one of his patients."

"And he was hit with a . . . with a cane?"

"Yes."

"That's horrible."

"Yes, it is."

She frowned. "You said that you're investigating *all* the fathers. Does that mean there are other men who . . . ?"

"Who could've killed Dr. Brandt?" he finished for her. "Yes, there are."

"Then one of *them* did it, Mr. Malloy, not my brother."

"I'm sorry Maeve bothered you, Mrs. Rossmann."

"Is she . . . all right?" she asked reluctantly, as if fighting her own concern.

"Yes, she's fine. I took her back home." That was true, as far as it went.

"Good. She seemed like a nice girl."

Malloy didn't want to contradict her.

Mrs. Rossmann sighed. "I hope you find the man who killed Dr. Brandt."

Frank did, too.

AFTER LUNCH, CATHERINE WENT UPSTAIRS TO play while Sarah cleaned up. Mrs. Ellsworth dropped in just as she finished with the dishes. She looked as worried as Sarah felt.

"How's Catherine doing?" Mrs. Ellsworth asked.

"She's trying to pretend nothing's wrong," Sarah reported. "And so am I. We're trying to make each other feel better, I guess."

"It doesn't seem to be working with you, anyway," Mrs. Ellsworth observed. "I knotted Maeve's handkerchief," she added, reminding Sarah of when this good luck charm had worked for her.

"Something keeps bothering me," Sarah confessed, pouring coffee for both of them, then setting the cups on the table.

"Just *one* thing?" Mrs. Ellsworth asked with a slight smile.

"Well, one thing in particular, at least," Sarah clarified. "Did you think it was odd that Malloy's been working with a Pinkerton detective?"

Mrs. Ellsworth picked up her cup and took a sip

to test the temperature, then set it back down to cool some more. "I don't know much about how the police work," she admitted, "or the Pinkertons either, for that matter."

"They're private investigators. People hire them when they don't want the police involved or when they don't trust the police to help them."

"I remember reading about Allan Pinkerton's adventures during the war," Mrs. Ellsworth recalled. "Didn't President Lincoln rely on him and his agents to spy on the South?"

"Yes, but I don't suppose they do much spying now."

"No, I think they just do things like find people who go missing or solve crimes discreetly, that sort of thing."

"But someone has to pay them to do it," Mrs. Ellsworth said with a frown.

"Not unlike the police," Sarah reminded her, "at least if you want them to really work hard."

"But I'm guessing the Pinkertons would be much more expensive than just paying a reward to the police."

"I think so, too, which brings us back to how Malloy happens to be working with one of their agents. Do you think he was paying for her services?"

"Her *services*?" Mrs. Ellsworth repeated suggestively.

Sarah felt the heat rising in her cheeks and hated

what that betrayed. "For her *detective* services," she clarified.

Mrs. Ellsworth shook her head. "I can't even imagine him working with another police detective on this case. He's so determined to solve it himself."

"I know. For a long time I've been angry with my father for not offering a reward back when Tom died. If he had, we might have found the killer then. At first, I thought he just didn't know that was required, but now I realize he must have."

"So if he didn't pay back then, he had a reason," Mrs. Ellsworth guessed. "Do you know what it was?"

"At first I thought he just didn't care, but since then, Malloy told me my father had received a letter from someone just before Tom died, accusing him of seducing young women who were his patients."

"How awful!" Mrs. Ellsworth reached out and laid her hand comfortingly on Sarah's arm.

"Yes, it was. Now we know it probably had something to do with the sickness these women have, but my father wouldn't have known that. He would have believed it."

"If so, he must have been relieved when your husband was killed," Mrs. Ellsworth said.

"I'm sure he was. I think he was afraid to find out who killed him because everyone would have known what kind of man Tom was, or rather what kind of man he thought Tom was."

"More importantly, *you* would have found out."

"But now, for some reason, my father has decided to help Malloy find Tom's killer."

"What makes you think so? Did Mr. Malloy say something?"

"Oh, no. I'm sure my father doesn't want me to know he's involved. That would be just like him. But when Malloy let it slip about the letter, I realized my father had to be involved. How else would Malloy have known about it? And now . . ."

"Now?"

"Now, who else would have hired a Pinkerton to help?"

"You're right," Mrs. Ellsworth agreed. "That sounds like exactly what a man like your father would do. He'd never trust the police."

Sarah took a sip of her coffee and fiddled with the cup.

"What's the matter?" Mrs. Ellsworth asked.

"I don't know," Sarah admitted. "When I think about my father being involved . . ." She shrugged helplessly.

"You should be happy your father is involved," Mrs. Ellsworth said. "Mr. Malloy is an excellent detective, but this is a big job, and he can't be everywhere. He certainly can't sneak into people's houses to find out more about them the way Maeve and that Pinkerton woman can."

"But I never would have expected Malloy to accept any help at all, yet he seemed almost happy to be sending Maeve off with that woman."

"I don't think he looked *happy*," Mrs. Ellsworth corrected her. "More like resigned."

"Resigned, then, but he did bring her here in the first place. Would you have believed that was even possible?"

"No," Mrs. Ellsworth admitted. "I think it proves just how determined Mr. Malloy is to solve Dr. Brandt's death. He's doing this for you, after all."

"I know," Sarah said. "I understand why he's doing it. What I don't understand is why, after all this time, my *father* has decided to help."

"Could Mr. Malloy have asked him to?" Mrs. Ellsworth asked.

Sarah looked at her in surprise. "I can't imagine him doing such a thing, can you?"

"Well, no, not really," she admitted. "I can't imagine him doing Mr. Malloy a favor either."

"Especially because he didn't want Tom's killer found in the first place."

Mrs. Ellsworth considered this. "Could he have changed his mind since then? About finding Dr. Brandt's killer, I mean?"

"I suppose he could have," Sarah allowed, "but why would he? What's different now?"

Mrs. Ellsworth looked at her. "You're different."

"What do you mean?"

"I mean you've involved yourself in solving murders. You've shocked people who know you, and you've probably caused a lot of gossip among your parents' friends."

"Oh, my goodness, I'm sure I have," Sarah said. "I hadn't really considered that. My father has wanted me to return home ever since Tom died, too, even before I started causing a scandal by my behavior. Now . . . Well, now he has an even bigger reason to want me living under his roof again."

"So he can keep you out of danger," Mrs. Ellsworth said.

"More likely so he can keep me out of trouble," Sarah corrected her. "I'm sure life in the Decker household would be very dull indeed. I don't know how solving Tom's murder would motivate me to move back to my parents' house, though."

"I don't either, unless . . ."

"Unless what?"

"I don't know. I was just thinking out loud. You said your father thought Dr. Brandt was doing terrible things to his young female patients, and he didn't want the murder investigated because he didn't want you to find out about it."

"That's my theory, at least," Sarah admitted.

"But now, all of a sudden, your father is hiring Pinkerton detectives to help Mr. Malloy find the killer."

"And even more peculiar, Malloy is accepting this help," Sarah added.

"As if they had formed some sort of partnership."

"An unholy alliance, more likely," Sarah said, shaking her head. "But you're right. Two men who have nothing in common—"

"Except you," Mrs. Ellsworth reminded her.

"Except me," she agreed. "Those two men have decided to work together."

"Maybe you've underestimated your father," Mrs. Ellsworth suggested.

"I'm afraid not," Sarah said with a sigh. "Solving Tom's murder will do one of two things—punish the killer of an innocent man or prove to the world that Tom deserved to be killed. Proving Tom an innocent man would gain my father nothing."

"But what would exposing Dr. Brandt accomplish?"

Sarah had finally figured out the answer to this, and she didn't like it one bit. "It would break my heart and perhaps my spirit as well," Sarah said.

"Why would your father want to do that?" Mrs. Ellsworth asked in dismay.

"He probably thinks that would drive me back to him."

"Oh, my," Mrs. Ellsworth said. "He doesn't know you at all!"

# 11

IRIS ALBERTON WAS FAST ASLEEP. MAEVE FELT a sense of relief that she had not done the child any physical harm this first day, in spite of numerous provocations. Iris had felt compelled at every opportunity to test Maeve's resolve to make her behave. Meals had involved spilled food and smashed dishes. Playtime gave occasion for toys to be thrown or broken. Naptime caused another tantrum, which Maeve ignored until Iris finally gave up in exhaustion and fell asleep. Bedtime was another battle, with Maeve promising stories from one of the gorgeously bound books on the shelf in the nursery if Iris cooperated. When Iris misbehaved instead, Maeve refused to read, and this time, Iris attacked her, screaming and punching and kicking, until Maeve managed to use her greater size and strength to pin the child to the floor, her knees on Iris's ankles and her hands gripping the child's small wrists. But when Maeve looked down into her eyes, this time she saw not defiance but sheer terror.

"Are you going to hurt me like they hurt Christina?" Iris asked in a tiny voice.

"I'm not going to hurt you at all," Maeve replied in surprise. "I just want you to stop hitting me."

"I will!" she promised desperately. "Just let me go!"

Maeve rocked back, releasing the child, who scrambled up and ran to the far side of the room and huddled there. The change in her was so drastic, Maeve could hardly believe it. "If you get into bed without any more fussing, I'll read you one story, but only one," she relented.

Iris's eyes grew wide, and she darted over to the bed and dove under the covers. She lay as meek as a lamb until Maeve had read the story of Cinderella from one of the storybooks. By then, Iris's eyelids were drooping. She looked almost angelic with her golden curls framing her small face. Maeve thought of Catherine and missed her with a stab of real pain.

"Would you like a kiss good night?" she asked impulsively, even though she felt no affection at all for Iris. She was simply missing Catherine too much.

"Yes," Iris whispered in surprise.

Maeve leaned down and kissed her cheek, half expecting Iris to pull her hair or punch her in the eye. But the child lay still, and when Maeve pulled away, she saw an expression in the child's eyes she didn't understand.

"Will you stay until I fall asleep?" she asked.

"Yes," Maeve agreed, happy to see some sign that Iris was accepting her. She didn't have to wait long after she'd turned down the gas jet on the wall. Iris drifted off within a few moments, and Maeve slipped out quietly.

This was the first opportunity she'd had to unpack and get settled into her room. The process wouldn't take long, since she'd brought so little with her. She was grateful for that, since her many battles of will with Iris had left her exhausted and somewhat bruised and very anxious for bed herself.

The bed in her small room had already been made up when she arrived. When she opened the wardrobe, she found a black skirt and shirtwaist like the other maids wore. She hoped they fit. If not, someone in the house would probably be handy with a needle and make adjustments. Hanging up her own things was the work of only a few minutes. Then she took the pitcher and towel from her washstand and carried them out into the hallway, where one of the maids had shown her a bathroom she could use. She washed quickly and filled her pitcher, in case Iris woke early and didn't give her a chance to make this trip in the morning.

She made her way back to the nursery and her room and was just unbuttoning her shirtwaist to change into her nightdress when she heard a sound that made the hairs on her arms stand on end. At first she thought it must be the wind playing some tricks in the eaves of the house, but after a few seconds, she recognized it as a human voice. A human voice raised in a sound so plaintive and sad, it brought tears to Maeve's eyes. In a few more seconds, she recognized it as a song. Someone was singing, and she had the voice of an angel.

Maeve hurried out of her room and across the darkened nursery to make sure the sound had not disturbed Iris, but she lay still, peacefully sleeping. Closing the door softly, Maeve hurried back to the door that led to the hallway and stepped out to find out who was singing.

She had already learned that Mr. and Mrs. Alberton slept on the other side of the house. Maeve had guessed they wanted to be as far as possible from Iris and her tantrums. The singing came from the room across the hallway, though, so she knew it couldn't be Mrs. Alberton. Unless one of the servants was singing, which seemed doubtful, Maeve could guess who it must be. She walked across the hall and put her ear to the door so she could hear more clearly.

The song was a hymn of some kind. She'd learned some hymns since seeking refuge at the Prodigal Son Mission and in subsequent visits to church with Mrs. Brandt and Mrs. Ellsworth, so she knew the difference between the songs they sang in church and the ones they sang in saloons and music halls. She'd never heard this one before, though, and she couldn't quite make out the words.

The woman hit every note truly and sweetly, and Maeve was so caught up in trying to understand the words that she never heard another thing until the door opened abruptly, nearly sending her staggering into the room. On the other side of the door stood a pert Irish girl with glossy black curls and bright blue eyes that stared at her shrewdly.

Before Maeve could decide if she should apologize or not, the girl said, "You're the new one."

Maeve straightened, trying to reclaim some dignity. "I'm the new nursemaid."

"What's your name, nursemaid?" she asked with a sly grin.

"Maeve Smith. What's yours?"

"Kerry Murphy," she replied, looking Maeve up and down. "I guess you're curious about the lunatic."

"Nobody said she was a lunatic," Maeve protested. "They just said she was sick."

"Sick in the head," Kerry said, taking Maeve's measure again. "You scared of crazy people?"

"No," Maeve said, although she'd never been around anyone who was truly crazy before, so she didn't really know.

The singing stopped suddenly, and a plaintive voice called from an adjoining room, "Who's there? Who are you talking to, Kerry?"

"Nobody, just one of the girls," Kerry called back. "Keep singing."

Kerry waited until the singing started again. Maeve could hear the words clearly now. They were about God and heaven. A hymn, she'd been right. Kerry turned back to her. "Singing keeps her calm. I guess we're lucky she's good at it."

Maeve tried to imagine what Allie would do in this situation. Ask Kerry as many questions as possible or just play dumb and see what Kerry would volunteer? A question or two would probably be all right. She'd probably think it strange if Maeve didn't ask anything at all.

"Is she dangerous?"

"Her?" she asked, jerking her head in the direction of the singing. "No, not hardly."

Maeve remembered Iris's reaction to being held down. She'd seen someone holding Christina down. "Mrs. Alberton said she gets unruly."

"*Unruly*, is it? That's new. She screams sometimes, gets all scared of things nobody sees but her. Imagines things, she does." Kerry watched Maeve for a reaction. When she saw none, she said, "You want to see her?"

Maeve wanted nothing more, but she didn't want to seem too eager. "I shouldn't."

"Why not?" Kerry scoffed. "Come on. She won't care."

Maeve stepped into the room and found it was a twin suite to the nursery across the hall. The large center room was furnished as a sitting room on this side, though. Christina would have the larger bedroom, as Iris did, and Kerry would have the small one.

Kerry led her into the larger bedroom. It was filled with dainty, feminine furniture and a large canopied bed. The gas jets burned low, but Maeve could see the young woman sitting up among the bedclothes, still singing to herself. When she heard them, she started, pulling the covers up to her chin and cowering.

"Is he here?" she demanded shrilly. "Is the doctor here?"

"No, he's not here," Kerry said. "This is the new girl, Maeve. She's taking care of Iris."

"Pleased to meet you, miss," Maeve said. "I heard your singing. It was real pretty."

"Is the doctor here?" Christina asked again. She seemed afraid.

"No, just me and Maeve," Kerry said in a perfectly normal tone of voice. Maeve was surprised. She'd supposed you had to talk to crazy people differently. "Say hello to Maeve, Miss Christina."

"Hello, Maeve," she said obediently, letting the bedclothes fall again. She wore a nightdress trimmed with lace and tied with satin ribbons. Her hair, which was even lighter than Iris's, was braided down her back. "Who are you?"

Maeve looked at Kerry, who nodded that she should reply. "I'm taking care of Miss Iris."

"Iris," she repeated vaguely, as if she'd never heard of the girl. "She's little, isn't she?"

"That's right," Kerry said. "She's a little girl, and you're a big girl. You need to go to sleep now, Miss Christina. Lay down so I can put out the light."

"Is Iris sleeping?" she asked.

"Yes," Maeve said.

"Good," Christina replied. "She wakes me up with her screaming sometimes."

"She won't wake you up tonight," Kerry said, going over and helping her arrange the covers when she was lying down. "That's a good girl. You sleep now."

Kerry went to the wall and turned off the gas jet. Maeve went out the door with Kerry behind her. Just as she was about to close it, Christina's voice came drifting through the darkness. "Is the doctor coming tonight?"

"No, he's not," Kerry said. "You can go to sleep."

250

When the door was closed, Maeve asked, "Does she have a doctor who visits her?"

"No, not anymore," Kerry said. Her smooth forehead creased as she frowned. "I shouldn't tell you, but . . . Well, she talks about it a lot so you should know. Something happened to her."

"You mean what made her crazy," Maeve guessed.

"No, she was like this already when it happened." She motioned for Maeve to sit on the sofa. Maeve felt funny doing so. Servants didn't sit on the furniture the family used, but Kerry went over and sat down as if she did it every day, so Maeve joined her. "From what they tell me, she was normal until her brother died. That was almost six years now, I guess."

"How did he die?" Maeve asked, although she knew perfectly well.

"He was killed riding one of them bicycles. Fool thing to do, if you ask me. You'll never catch me on one of them things."

"Me either," Maeve agreed fervently. "That must've been a shock, though."

"It was," Kerry confirmed. "To everybody, but Miss Christina was his twin, so she took it real hard. That was when she first started acting strange. She'd hear voices and see things that weren't there. She'd run outside in her nightdress."

Maeve looked appropriately shocked.

"I only heard all this, mind you. I didn't work for

them then. I came later, after the doctors told them what to do for her."

"What did they say to do?"

"To keep her quiet mostly, and in the dark. She does fine most of the time. We keep the windows covered." She nodded at the window, which was completely draped in heavy maroon velvet. "It was hard to keep it quiet in the city, but here it's easy. Nobody ever comes here."

Maeve nodded. When Kerry stopped talking, they could almost hear themselves breathe.

"You said something happened to her," Maeve reminded her.

Kerry frowned again. "Yeah, with the doctor. The Albertons, they'd had a lot of doctors to see her in the beginning. They wanted somebody to cure her, but nobody could. The best they could do was say she might get better but she might not. They'd almost given up hope when one more doctor came to see her." Kerry paused dramatically, making Maeve beg for the information.

"What did he say?"

"It wasn't what he said so much. Oh, he did tell them he thought he might be able to help her, so they let him see her. They even let him see her alone. He was in with her for a long time, but when he came out, he told them he didn't think he could help her after all, and he left."

"That's all?" Maeve asked, not having to feign her disappointment.

"That was all at first," Kerry said ominously. "Until we found out that . . . well, that he'd had his way with her."

Maeve was genuinely shocked, even though she'd known Dr. Brandt had been accused of this. "That's awful! But . . . but how did you find out?"

"We just . . . Well, she told us," Kerry admitted reluctantly. "She told me first, and then, well, she told anybody who would listen."

It was just like the others, Maeve thought. The other women had claimed to have relations with their doctors, too, but those men had been innocent, just like Dr. Brandt was innocent. Christina had imagined the whole thing. "But you said she hears voices and things that aren't there. Maybe she imagined that, too," Maeve suggested.

Kerry gave her a condescending look. "Don't you think we hoped that was true? We even told her it never happened, but then . . ."

"Then what?" Maeve prompted when Kerry hesitated.

"Then we just found out it was true, that's all," she said dismissively. "And Miss Christina wasn't the only one he'd done it to either."

Maeve wanted to argue with her. She wanted to convince Kerry she was wrong, that Dr. Brandt would never do anything so wicked. She couldn't do that without giving herself away, though, so she bit back her anger. "What a terrible man!" she said instead.

"I hope he rots in hell," Kerry agreed. "Taking advantage of a poor, crazy girl what can't defend herself."

Maeve shook her head, unable to think of anything she wanted to say about poor Dr. Brandt.

"So you see," Kerry continued after a moment, "that's why she's always asking about the doctor. She's afraid he'll come back and hurt her again."

"Oh," Maeve said, as if it all made sense now. Of course it made no sense at all, but she couldn't say so. "How long has it been now, since it happened?"

"Over four years, almost five maybe."

"And she's still talking about it?" Maeve asked in wonder.

"She's crazy," Kerry reminded her patiently. "Sometimes she talks about things that happened when she was a little girl like they happened yesterday. Sometimes she thinks her brother, Sam, is still alive, and sometimes she talks about things that never happened at all."

Maeve looked at Kerry with new eyes. "Don't that make you mad? To not be able to make her talk sense, I mean?"

Kerry shrugged. "You get used to it. I just ignore it or play along with her."

"I don't know how you stand it," Maeve said quite truthfully.

"They pay me a pretty penny," Kerry said grimly. "They have to."

"Do you need the money that bad?"

Kerry gave her a condescending look. "I'm saving up so I can make something of myself. I don't want to be taking care of a crazy girl all my life."

"Oh," was all Maeve could think to say.

"So," Kerry continued, "that's why Miss Christina is so scared of doctors. And what about you? How did you do with Miss Iris today?"

Maeve made a face, and Kerry grinned knowingly.

"Somebody should drown that brat!" Kerry said.

"Oh, she's not so bad," Maeve said, feeling compelled to defend the child after she'd semidrowned her herself. "She's just spoiled."

"Spoiled rotten," Kerry confirmed. "Too bad you got stuck with her. I like you, but you won't be around long. Nobody ever lasts more than a week with her."

Maeve probably wouldn't last more than a week either, but it would have nothing to do with Iris and her behavior. "She just needs a firm hand," Maeve said.

Kerry snorted in disgust. "She won't get it here. Nobody cares what she does, just so long as she doesn't do it in the parlor."

"I care," Maeve said. "And she won't do it in the nursery either."

Kerry raised her eyebrows and gave her a skeptical grin. "We'll see, Miss Maeve. We'll see."

• • •

SARAH HADN'T REALLY EXPECTED MALLOY TO come by that evening, but she'd been hoping. She knew he couldn't give her any information about Maeve yet, but he could at least answer some questions. She wasn't going to let him out of her house until he did, either.

She'd removed her apron on the way to answer the door and patted her hair back into place. She wasn't being vain, she told herself. She just wanted to look serious so Malloy would take her seriously. Catherine was already in bed. At least Malloy had timed his visit so they could speak openly.

She opened the door and motioned for him to enter, skipping her usual greeting.

He looked at her askance as he stepped past her into the foyer. "You're mad," he said.

"Of course I'm mad," she confirmed. "You bring a strange woman into my house and she takes my nursemaid away."

"You said it was all right," he reminded her.

"I said she could do it," Sarah corrected him. "I never said it was all right."

He pulled off his hat and hung it up. Then he ran his fingers through his thick, dark hair and sighed. Only then did she notice how tired he looked, and her conscience pricked her.

"Are you hungry?"

"If Mrs. Ellsworth has been baking, I'm starving," he replied with a small grin.

256

"I think there's some cake left," she allowed. "Come on into the kitchen."

He followed her, and she found the cake and cut a piece for him. Then she put the coffeepot on to boil and sat down at the table opposite him. She let him eat. He made short work of the cake, and when it was gone, he looked up warily. "You can start now," he said.

"Start what?" she asked.

"Start lighting into me about whatever you're mad about."

Sarah didn't like his attitude. She wanted him to be more defensive. She wanted him to be worried about *her* attitude. He didn't seem to be either, but this would have to do. "Who is this Allie woman?"

"I told you, she's a Pinkerton detective."

"How long have you known her?"

"A few days."

*"A few days!"* she echoed in outrage. "You trusted her to look after Maeve, and you've only known her a few days?"

"You met her," he pointed out. "Besides, I'm not worried about Maeve."

"Of course you're not," Sarah said angrily. "She's not your responsibility!"

"No, she's not," he replied, as angry as she was now. "But that doesn't mean I don't care what happens to her! I wouldn't have let her go if I didn't think Allie could take care of her."

"And that's another thing," Sarah said. "Why

are you suddenly hiring Pinkerton detectives?"

"What?" Malloy asked, confused by the sudden change in subject.

"Why are you hiring Pinkertons?" she repeated. "I've never known you to need that kind of help with a case before."

"I never worked on a case like this before," he countered.

"What does that mean?"

"It means I've never worked on a case this old and where I couldn't just barge in and question the suspects and the witnesses whenever I need to."

"How are you paying for them?" she demanded.

"Paying for who?" he asked with a frown.

"You know who," she snapped. "The Pinkertons. They don't work for free. Someone has to pay their fees."

"That's none of your concern," he tried.

"Maybe not, but I don't want you spending your own money on something like that," Sarah said, testing him.

He stiffened, as if she'd surprised him. "I told you, it's not your worry."

"Is it my father's worry?" she asked.

This time he really was surprised. "What makes you think that?"

"Because my father is the kind of man who'd hire a Pinkerton instead of going to the police. He's the kind of man who would refuse to pay a reward to the police to find Tom's killer but who would think nothing of hiring a detective to do the same thing."

"If you think your father hired Allie, why not just ask him?" Malloy asked reasonably.

"Because he wouldn't tell me," she said.

"Why not?"

Sarah had to think about that. "I don't know," she finally decided. "I just know he wouldn't. He would probably consider it something I didn't need to know."

"Maybe he's just a private man," Malloy suggested. "Doesn't like people to know his business."

"I'm not 'people,'" she reminded him. "I'm his daughter."

"All the more reason to protect you."

"Protect me from what?" she asked in exasperation. "I already know Tom is dead. What can be worse than that?"

"Lots of things can be worse than that," Malloy said grimly.

"Like what?" she challenged.

The coffeepot started to hiss as it boiled over and the liquid hit the hot stovetop. Sarah jumped up to rescue it and then poured them each a cup. When she was seated again, she said, "What could be worse than dying?"

"You've got his memory, Sarah," he said softly and so kindly that her eyes flooded with tears.

"What do you mean by that?" she asked, angrily dashing away the moisture.

"I mean you've got your memory of the way he

259

was." He paused, then said, "The way you thought he was."

"The way I *thought* he was? What does that mean?"

"It means people aren't always what we think they are."

"Tom was *exactly* the way I thought he was," she argued.

"People said some evil things about him," he reminded her.

"None of that was true, though. Those women are insane," she reminded him.

"Somebody thought it was the truth and killed Tom," Malloy reminded her right back.

"That doesn't mean it was!"

"That doesn't mean it wasn't."

Sarah stared at him as if seeing him for the first time. His familiar features stared back at her, silently challenging her to consider the unthinkable. "Do *you* think it was true?" she asked.

"No," he said, but before she could even feel relief, he added, "but I could be wrong. You need to be ready, Sarah. You need to be ready for anything."

"I knew Tom, Malloy. I knew him better than anyone. He could never have done those things they accused him of."

He picked up his cup and blew on it, then took a sip, very obviously avoiding a reply.

"Don't worry about my feelings," she told him. "I

don't care what lies they tell. I just want you to find Tom's killer once and for all."

"Then don't worry about Maeve," he said. "She can take care of herself. She's a grifter."

"A what?" Sarah asked in surprise.

"A grifter. A con artist."

"What does that mean?"

"It means she used to cheat people for a living. Her family probably trained her to do it from birth. That's usually how it happens. They pass the skills down through families, because they can't trust anyone else."

"She was a thief?"

"I said she was a cheat, not a thief. Usually, they trick people who think they're going to get something for nothing. Their marks—their victims—aren't completely honest either, so they don't usually call the police when they get cheated."

"How do you know all this? Did she tell you?"

"I figured it out from what she did at the Werner house. A sweet, innocent girl wouldn't have known how to talk her way in there like she did. Or how to convince the cops who arrested her to take her to me. That's why I decided she'd be able to go into the Alberton house. And Allie agreed."

"That's horrible! And her family taught her how to do it?"

"Her family or whoever raised her. It could be worse, Sarah. She could have had to sell herself."

Sarah rubbed her eyes, which were moist again.

261

"I thought that's what she'd done," she admitted. "Most of the girls at the Mission did. It was the only way they could survive."

"Maeve was lucky, then."

She looked up in surprise. "Lucky?"

"She had other skills. And then she found you."

Sarah had an uneasy feeling. "Do you think she was lying to me all this time? About wanting to work here and learn how to be a nursemaid?"

"I don't think so. I can't be sure, of course, but she takes good care of Catherine, doesn't she?"

"Yes, of course. And you can't fool a child. They always know who cares and who doesn't."

"Catherine is nobody's fool either," Malloy reminded her.

"You're right," Sarah said with a relieved smile. "She couldn't have fooled Catherine."

"And she really does want to help you," Malloy said. "She's grateful for all you've done for her, and she wants to pay you back."

"What did you call her?"

"A grifter."

Sarah shook her head in wonder.

"She'll be fine," he said. "Worry about yourself."

"I don't have to worry about myself, Malloy," she said. "I know my husband. You won't find out anything about him I don't already know."

THE NEXT MORNING, MAEVE TRIED TAKING Iris out into the yard. She needed to find the place

Allie had described, where she was to leave her daily reports, so taking Iris for an outing seemed the most logical way to get out of the house. But Iris wouldn't listen to her and ran away, headlong down the path, until she fell and tore her stockings. Maeve picked her up, kicking and screaming, and took her back into the house.

"I told you," she reminded the screaming, thrashing child. "If you don't listen to me, you can't play outside."

Iris tried another tantrum when they got back to the nursery, but Maeve splashed some water in her face again and Iris settled down in a hurry. By noontime, the girl was much more obedient, and they got through the meal without incident.

"If you go to sleep without a fuss for your nap, we'll go outside when you wake up," Maeve promised, knowing she had to give the child another chance because she still hadn't found the drop-off place for her messages to Allie. "And if you're good while we're outside, you can even stay for a while."

"I'll be good," Iris promised solemnly. And to Maeve's surprise, this time she was.

That afternoon, Maeve had to ask Iris if she knew the way to the creek, where Allie had told her the pickup spot was. She did, and she led Maeve out the garden gate and down a path and into some woods.

Maeve had never seen so many trees all together

in one spot before. They had trees in the city parks, of course, but no matter how many grew together, you could still see what was on the other side of them. These trees were too thick, and once they were inside the woods, she couldn't hear anything at all except the wind rustling in the leaves and other sounds that she couldn't identify. She thought of bears and lions. She didn't think they had lions in New York, but she wasn't sure about bears. She'd seen one once, in the city. A trainer had it on a chain and was making it do tricks. It was huge and had teeth as long as her fingers. She didn't want to meet one out here.

"What's the matter?" Iris asked suddenly.

Maeve didn't want to admit she was frightened. "Are there any animals in these woods?"

Iris nodded.

"What kind?" Maeve asked in alarm.

"Squirrels. Chipmunks, too. They're little. And mice."

"No big animals?" Maeve asked, still suspicious.

"Squirrels are big," Iris said.

Maeve supposed they were, to Iris. She drew a fortifying breath and forced herself not to hear the strange sounds coming from the trees around her. After only a few minutes, they reached a lovely little creek that flowed through the trees.

Maeve easily found the rock beneath which she was to leave her report for Allie, and while Iris was busy trying to catch a frog whom they had disturbed, she slipped the folded paper she'd brought beneath it.

Maeve and Iris threw rocks and explored and watched some tiny fish swimming in the clear water. Iris pretended to tell her a story. From what Maeve could make of it, Iris used to be a beautiful princess but an evil pirate kidnapped her and brought her to this awful place where they kept her prisoner.

"Someday my father the king is going to come and take me home," she informed Maeve quite seriously.

Maeve didn't laugh at the childish fantasies. She'd had the same ones when she'd been growing up in the teeming tenements on the Lower East Side of Manhattan, moving from one cheap lodging to the next every few months, one step ahead of the rent collector and two steps ahead of the police.

On the way back to the house, they encountered Mrs. Alberton, who was trimming her rosebushes for their spring growth. She was wearing a broad-brimmed bonnet, a duster to protect her clothes, and heavy canvas gloves, and wielding a large pair of clippers.

"There's your mother," Maeve told Iris, and she watched the girl stiffen as if in alarm at the sight of her. Her small hand tightened in Maeve's.

"What's the matter?" she asked, but Mrs. Alberton had heard them, and she looked up in surprise.

The frightened look she gave Iris startled Maeve, but it lasted for only an instant. Then she stretched her lips into a tight smile that would have fooled no one.

"Good afternoon," she said.

"Good afternoon, Mrs. Alberton," Maeve replied.

Iris didn't speak. She was watching Mrs. Alberton warily.

"Where have you girls been?" she asked with forced cheerfulness.

Maeve waited for Iris to reply, but she didn't speak. She just stared solemnly back at Mrs. Alberton, whose smile was starting to look a little crooked. "Down to the creek," Maeve said after a few moments. "It's real pretty down there, isn't it, Iris?"

Iris didn't appear to have heard her. She just kept watching Mrs. Alberton, who kept watching her right back, like two stray dogs trying to decide if they were going to fight or not and waiting for the other to make the first move.

"Iris was a very good girl today," Maeve reported. "That's why she got to go down to the creek."

Mrs. Alberton's smile had vanished, and she was staring at Maeve as if she'd suddenly started speaking a foreign language. "That's . . . very nice," she said, as if she didn't think it was nice at all. As if she didn't even believe Maeve.

"I *was* a good girl," Iris insisted with a trace of defiance. "I really was!"

Mrs. Alberton's smile reappeared. "I'm sure you were, dear. You must like Mary very much."

"*Maeve,*" Iris said as if correcting someone slow-witted. "Her name is Maeve. Mary left a long time ago."

"Oh, yes, of course," Mrs. Alberton said vaguely. "There's been so many, it's hard to keep track."

Maeve wanted to end this uncomfortable exchange as quickly as possible. "Let's go inside and see if Cook has any cookies," she suggested.

Iris hardly seemed to hear her. She was still watching Mrs. Alberton, but when Maeve gave her hand a little tug, she seemed to snap out of her trance and walked obediently away from where her mother still stood, staring after them.

Cook looked just as surprised to see them as Mrs. Alberton had, and she was equally wary of Iris, but the girl seemed to take a perverse pleasure in shocking the older woman with her good behavior. Cook didn't have any cookies, but she found them some cake left over from last night's supper and suggested they take it up to the nursery. Apparently, she didn't expect Iris's good humor to last long.

It did, though. The girl was a perfect angel the rest of the afternoon, and she followed Maeve's instructions about sitting up properly to eat the supper that was laid for them on the small table in the corner of the nursery. They were just about finished with their meal when a loud crash startled them. Immediately, someone started to wail in anguish.

Maeve looked in the direction of the sound and realized it must be coming from Christina's rooms. Before she could think what to do, Iris had jumped up from her chair and climbed into her lap. When Maeve looked down into her face, she saw the child was terrified.

"It's all right," Maeve assured her, although she had no idea if it was or not. "Don't be scared."

"It's Christina," Iris said, as if Maeve couldn't have figured that out for herself.

Maeve wondered if Kerry might need some help, but she couldn't leave Iris alone. Her little body was trembling. The wailing *was* frightening. Maeve wrapped her arms around her and kissed her forehead. "Does she do this much?" Maeve asked.

Iris nodded against Maeve's bosom.

"She doesn't hurt anybody, though," Maeve pointed out. "She's just unhappy."

"She's crazy," Iris whispered, just as she'd warned Maeve yesterday.

Maeve instinctively started to rock back and forth, offering silent comfort, and after a few minutes, the wailing stopped. The silence felt oppressive and tentative, since Maeve didn't know if the cries might start up again at any moment. Still Maeve held her close, as much to comfort herself as to comfort Iris. Soon Iris stopped trembling, but she made no move to get down. Maeve suspected she was seldom cuddled and wanted to make it last as long as possible.

Maeve's conscience pricked her. What would become of the poor child when her task here was complete? Who would care about her after this? And even worse, why did no one seem to care about her now? The only time Mrs. Alberton had even seen Iris since Maeve's arrival was when they'd happened upon her in the garden. Hadn't Allie told her they doted on the child? Maeve couldn't help wondering how she'd come to that conclusion. From the look on Mrs. Alberton's face when she did see Iris, she never wanted to see her again.

The setting sun had cast long shadows in the room. Soon she would need to turn on the gas jets. Then they would go back to eating their supper. But not just yet. The silence enveloped them, and Maeve could feel the tension she'd held inside her since she'd arrived here easing somewhat. She could do this. She could bide her time and wait for the information she needed, and she would find out the truth so Mrs. Brandt didn't have to worry anymore about who had killed Dr. Brandt.

"I know a secret," Iris said, rousing Maeve from her reveries.

"You do?" she asked, humoring her.

"About Christina," she said.

Maeve didn't think she wanted to know any more about Christina. "If it's a secret, you don't have to tell me."

"I want to."

Maeve bit back a smile. "All right. What's the secret?"

Iris drew a deep breath, as if she need more air to say it.

"Christina is my mother."

# 12

FRANK KNEW IT WAS LATE FOR A SOCIAL CALL. He'd purposely waited until Amelia Goodwin's father had gotten home from work and had time to eat his supper. He'd be settling in for the evening, probably reading the newspaper by now. Frank hammered the door knocker with all the authority of his office.

The girl who opened the door stared at him in surprise. He'd been here once before, but that was months ago, and she didn't remember him.

"I need to see Mr. Goodwin," he told her in a voice that brooked no argument.

"He's . . ." she started to say, then caught herself. "Who's calling, please?"

"Detective Sergeant Frank Malloy from the New York City Police," he said, shocking her completely. While he had her off guard, he managed to push the door open far enough so he could step inside.

The maid made a small sound of protest and backed up a step in alarm.

"Go tell him I'm here," Frank advised her, handing her his card.

She took it with two fingers, as if it were on fire, and scurried away in alarm, leaving the front door hanging open. Frank pushed it closed and waited. He remembered the house. The front hallway was tastefully furnished if somewhat dark in the fading twilight. He wondered idly if Amelia Goodwin still lived here or if her family had finally sent her away someplace where she couldn't embarrass them again.

He heard a door open down the hallway, and a man appeared. He came forward from the shadows, and when the light from the single hallway fixture touched him, Frank saw he was wearing a smoking jacket. He'd removed his shirt collar and tie and replaced his shoes with comfortably worn slippers. His face was contorted with an emotion somewhere between anger and alarm. Plainly, he wasn't accustomed to having the police visit his home.

"What's this all about?" he demanded when he was close enough for conversation. Only then did Frank notice another figure had followed him out into the hallway but stopped a good ten feet back. A woman's silhouette was all he could see, but she stood very still, obviously listening.

"Maybe we should speak privately, Mr. Goodwin," he suggested, with a meaningful glance at the shadowy figure.

Goodwin looked as if he might argue the point, but then he glanced over his shoulder and quickly changed his mind. "In here," he said, stepping to a nearby door. He pushed it open and waited for Frank to follow him inside, then closed the door behind them. The light from the streetlamp filtering in the front window was enough to allow Goodwin to cross to the desk on the far side of the room, find a match, and light a lamp sitting there. The puddle of light it produced revealed a comfortably furnished, decidedly masculine room that smelled of pipe tobacco. "Now, what's this about?" he asked again, still none too civil.

"A murder, Mr. Goodwin. Why don't we sit down?"

"You won't be here that long, Mr. . . ." Goodwin reached into the patch pocket of his smoking jacket and withdrew Frank's card. "Mr. Malloy. Who's been murdered?"

Frank took a small step to one side so he could see Goodwin's face more clearly in the dim light. "Dr. Tom Brandt."

Goodwin's face registered no reaction at all. "Never heard of him."

"Oh, I think you have, Mr. Goodwin. He treated your daughter."

"My daught—" he began, but caught himself. His eyes narrowed as he looked at Frank with a new appreciation. "What does my daughter have to do with a murder?"

"Maybe you'd like to reconsider sitting down," Frank suggested mildly.

Goodwin's face tightened with suppressed anger.

272

He had been a handsome man but was going flabby in his middle age. His dark hair had receded to a deep widow's peak in front, and his mustache was starting to gray. "Maybe I should throw you out into the street," Goodwin replied.

"Then I'd have to come back with some uniformed patrolmen who would be happy to thoroughly search your house."

"For what?" he scoffed.

"For anything they could find," Frank replied mildly.

Now he was openly furious. "I'd have your job!"

"And your house would be wrecked," Frank said. "So why don't we sit down and discuss this instead."

Goodwin was beaten and he hated it. He turned and strode over to where two leather wing-backed chairs sat on either side of a smoking stand. He lowered himself into one with all the enthusiasm of one sitting down on a bed of hot coals. Frank strolled over and sat down in the other chair.

"I told you, I never heard of this doctor who was murdered," Goodwin reminded him testily.

"And I told you, he treated your daughter. Your daughter *is* Amelia Goodwin, isn't she?"

He flinched when Frank said her name. Amelia was obviously a painful subject. "My daughter hasn't seen a doctor in years," Goodwin said.

"I know," Frank said. "Ever since she developed an embarrassing obsession for Dr. Unger."

"How did you . . . ?" he began, leaning forward in his chair and gripping the armrests as if he were going to jump to his feet again. "Is Unger behind this? Did he send you here?"

"No, he didn't," Frank said. "Why would he?"

"Because . . . we had a misunderstanding," Goodwin admitted reluctantly. "But it was years ago, and I thought we'd settled it like gentlemen."

"You did. He didn't send me here. Tell me, Mr. Goodwin, do you use a walking stick?"

"A what?" he asked, confused by the sudden change of topic.

"A walking stick. A cane."

"I don't need a cane!" he protested indignantly.

"Many gentlemen carry one whether they need it or not. Do you?"

"No, I don't, not that it's any of your business."

"Have you ever carried one?"

"What difference does it make if I did or not?"

"It might make a lot of difference," Frank said, still speaking mildly. "Do you remember Dr. Tom Brandt?"

"I already told you, I never heard of the man."

"He's the young doctor who came to see your daughter after the unfortunate situation with Dr. Unger," Frank reminded him. "He thought he could help her."

Frank watched as Goodwin searched his memory, and he knew the instant Goodwin made the proper connection. "That bastard!"

274

"Then you do remember him?"

"Of course I remember him," he said, outraged all over again. "He claimed he could help her, and he made her hysterical!"

"Is that all he did?"

"All? Wasn't that enough? We had to tie her to her bed and dose her with laudanum for days until she calmed down again."

"Didn't your daughter make up stories about what he'd done to her, like she did with Dr. Unger?"

This time, Goodwin looked embarrassed. "What are you talking about?" he tried.

"You know what I'm talking about. Your daughter had made up stories about Dr. Unger being her lover. Did she make up the same stories about Dr. Brandt?"

"No!" he said indignantly. "She never mentioned him again after he left here. She's remained remarkably faithful to Dr. Unger," he added acidly, although Frank could see the admission pained him. "She still talks about him after all this time. Why are you asking me these questions?"

"Because someone murdered Dr. Brandt."

"And you think Amelia did it?" he asked incredulously. "I can assure you, she hasn't left this house since the day he was here."

"A *man* killed Dr. Brandt," Frank informed him. "A man whose daughter was a patient of his."

"Then I can't imagine why you've come here,"

Goodwin told him. "Amelia was never his patient. He only saw her once, and that was long ago."

"Dr. Brandt was killed shortly after he visited your daughter," Frank told him. "And as I said, he was killed by the father of one of his patients."

Again, he watched as understanding dawned on Goodwin. His face flushed crimson. "And let me guess, the killer carried a walking stick." This time Goodwin did push himself to his feet. "Are you accusing me of murder, Malloy?"

Frank rose to his feet, too. "I told you, I'm *investigating* a murder, Mr. Goodwin. I have to question everyone associated with Dr. Brandt in the months before he died."

"You could have saved yourself this trip, then. I was never *associated* with Dr. Brandt, and I certainly didn't kill him."

"Like I said, Mr. Goodwin, I'm investigating."

"Then get out of here and get on with it." He strode purposefully back to the door and threw it open, then crossed his arms and waited for Frank to take his leave.

"I'm sorry to have bothered you, Mr. Goodwin."

"Not as sorry as I am," Goodwin muttered.

"MAEVE IS DOING WHAT?" MRS. DECKER exclaimed.

"It's a long story," Sarah said as she quickly changed her clothes. The two women were in Sarah's bedroom while Mrs. Ellsworth kept

Catherine busy upstairs. Mrs. Decker had arrived that morning just moments after a young man had come to fetch Sarah to a delivery. "Mrs. Ellsworth can explain everything."

"Tell me the beginning of it, at least," Mrs. Decker begged.

Sarah sighed as she shrugged into her oldest shirtwaist and began to button it. "Well, you know she was trying to help, so she'd gone to the Werners' house, trying to get hired as a servant. Malloy brought her back here after she got thrown out—"

"Thrown out? Whatever for?"

"Stealing, although she wasn't really stealing," Sarah added quickly when her mother gasped. "She was just trying to find out if Mr. Werner had a cane hidden someplace in his room, and they thought she must be looking for something to steal."

"Did she find one?"

"No. It seems Mr. Werner never owned a cane of any kind."

"How convenient."

"But Malloy got the idea from her experience there that she could go to the Alberton house to see what she could find out."

"What gave him an idea like that?"

"He thought . . . Well, he just thought she showed an aptitude for that kind of thing," Sarah hedged. No sense in explaining Maeve's criminal background. Her mother would keep her here all day. "So the female Pinkerton agent took her—"

"The *what*?" Mrs. Decker cried.

Sarah sighed again. The story was getting longer and longer. "The female Pinkerton agent. Her name is Allie Shea."

"How did a Pinkerton agent get involved?"

"Do you know what a Pinkerton agent does?" Sarah asked.

"Of course," Mrs. Decker said. "They were spies during the war. Who on earth do they spy on now?"

"They don't spy anymore," Sarah explained as patiently as she could while knowing that somewhere in the city a baby was going to arrive, with or without her help. "They work as private detectives, investigating things people don't want the police involved with."

"Do they work with the police?"

"Not usually."

"Then how does Mr. Malloy come to have one—and a female one, at that—working with him?"

"That's a question you should ask Father," Sarah said, checking her hair in the mirror to make sure she looked at least presentable.

"Your father? Why would he know?"

"Because I'm fairly certain he's the one who hired this woman. Or at least who's paying for the Pinkertons to help Malloy in this."

"Why would he do that?"

"I have no idea, Mother. You'll have to ask him. Now I'm afraid I must go."

"But how do you know he's involved in this?"

278

her mother demanded when Sarah opened her bedroom door.

"I just guessed, but it's the only explanation that makes any sense. Malloy can't afford to pay Pinkertons, even if he wanted their help. I didn't hire them, and you didn't either. Who else would do it?"

Sarah left her mother staring after her, openmouthed.

She found the young man still standing in the foyer, nervously mangling his cap as he waited impatiently for her return.

"Can we go now?" he asked almost desperately.

"Just a moment," Sarah said with a smile meant to reassure him. It failed. She opened her medical bag and gave it one last check to make sure all her supplies were in place. She'd replenished it after the last delivery, but she always checked, in case she'd overlooked something. Seeing everything in readiness, she went to the coat rack in the hallway and retrieved her cloak. The sky was clouding up, and there was no telling what the fickle spring weather would be like by the time she returned.

"Catherine, I'm leaving!" she called up the stairs.

Mrs. Decker had followed her and stood in the middle of the office, watching her with growing apprehension. "What are you going to do about Maeve?" she asked while Sarah waited for the child to race down the stairs.

"Wait for her to come back," Sarah said simply.

"Mrs. Ellsworth has offered to watch Catherine for me, and of course you're welcome to stay as long as you like. I'm sorry I won't be here."

Catherine had reached the bottom of the stairs and threw herself against Sarah's legs. She leaned over and kissed the small, upturned face.

"I'll be back as soon as I can. You be a good girl."

Catherine nodded solemnly.

"Catherine," Mrs. Decker said with forced brightness, "would you like to go to my house for a visit? You can stay overnight and sleep in your mama's old bedroom."

Catherine's eyes lit up, and she looked to Sarah for permission.

"Oh, Mother, how very sweet of you," Sarah said, giving Mrs. Ellsworth an apologetic glance.

"Yes, it is very sweet," Mrs. Ellsworth said graciously, even though Sarah knew she would have been thrilled to watch Catherine for as long as necessary. "I'll miss you, of course, Miss Catherine, but I get to see you every day, and Mrs. Decker doesn't."

"Come along, then," Mrs. Decker said as cheerfully as she could. "Let's pack some clothes for you."

Sarah watched with mixed emotions as Catherine and her mother disappeared up the stairs. "Thank you," Sarah whispered to Mrs. Ellsworth, who waved away her gratitude.

"Mrs. Brandt?" the young man pleaded,

reminding Sarah of her duty. "Can I carry that bag for you?"

Sarah relinquished it gratefully and followed him out the door.

"WOULD YOU LIKE TO GO DOWN TO THE CREEK this morning?" Maeve asked Iris. She'd been watching the sky and was afraid if they didn't go now, the rain would prevent them from going this afternoon. Maeve needed to get her latest report to Allie as soon as possible, and once the rain started, she'd have a difficult time explaining why she wanted to go for a walk, much less take Iris with her.

"Yes, yes!" Iris exclaimed, jumping up and down.

"Is that the right way to answer?" Maeve asked with mock sternness.

Iris stopped jumping instantly and stood very straight and folded her hands demurely in front of her. "Yes, please, Miss Maeve," she said. "I should love to go outside for a walk."

Maeve clapped her hands in approval, and Iris beamed. Maeve could hardly believe she was the same hellion she'd seen that first morning. Two short days later and she was a perfect angel. Oh, every few hours, she'd pretend she was going to do something naughty, but first she'd check to see if Maeve was paying attention. A stern look was all it took to ward off a rebellion. Iris just wanted to make sure Maeve still cared what she did.

As she tied Iris's pretty bonnet over the girl's blond curls, she remembered the secret the child had shared with her last night. If Maeve had wondered why Mrs. Alberton had behaved so oddly out in the garden yesterday, she could now guess the reason. Iris was mad Christina's bastard child. As such, she carried the double taint of Christina's illness and her shame. Maeve could guess the rest of the story as well, piecing it together from what Kerry Murphy had told her that first night. Dr. Brandt had raped Christina, or at least the family believed he was the one. In any event, *some* man had raped her and gotten her with child. Now Maeve understood why Kerry had hedged when she'd asked how they had known Christina had been attacked. They wouldn't want anyone to know Iris's origins.

Maeve smiled at Iris and took her hand as they made their way down the hall to the back staircase. Iris held on tightly, as if afraid Maeve would abandon her. Iris was actually humming by the time they reached the back door and stepped into the garden. Maeve wouldn't allow her to run, at least not in sight of the house, but they skipped happily through the rows of neatly trimmed rosebushes until they'd passed through the gate. The sky was gunmetal gray, and Maeve hoped they could make it to the creek and back without getting soaked. Of course, she doubted anyone would care if Iris got wet or chilled. They might not even care if she got sick and died.

Shaking off that awful thought, Maeve started running, and Iris squealed with joy as they tore down the path through the trees, hand in hand, so fast that Maeve didn't even have time to worry about lions and bears lurking in the shadows. They were both laughing by the time they reached the creek bank. Maeve had to stop to catch her breath, but Iris darted along the bank, peering over the edge to see if she could catch a glimpse of the tiny fish they'd seen yesterday. While she was busy, Maeve stepped over the rock and lifted it. Although she had expected it, she was still surprised to see that the note she'd left yesterday was gone. Allie had been there, just as they'd planned. For some reason, the knowledge thrilled her. She quickly placed her new message, the one she knew would shock Allie as much as it had shocked her, beneath the rock and let it fall back into place.

"What are you doing?" Iris called from where she had paused in her quest to find fish.

"Resting," Maeve called back. "Look, there's some flowers," she said, pointing to some wild-flowers growing in a clump. "Let's pick some."

"Why?" Iris asked.

"We'll take them back to the house and put them in some water. We'll have flowers on our table the way they do downstairs in the dining room."

Iris clapped her hands in delight and raced over to the clump of flowers. At first she tried to pull them up by the roots, but Maeve showed her how to break off the stems, and soon she had a fistful of the pretty weeds.

"That's a lot of flowers," Maeve said when Iris had picked every one they could find. "Maybe we could share them."

"With who?"

"With Christina," Maeve suggested. "Does she like flowers?"

Iris frowned thoughtfully. "I think she does," she finally decided.

"I think she does, too."

By then the sky had darkened even more, and Maeve decided they should get back to the house as quickly as possible. Once inside the garden gate, Iris ran ahead, dodging the raindrops that had started to fall. Maeve looked up as she hurried through the garden. She hadn't paid much attention to the back of the house before, and she was surprised to see that a balcony ran across the second floor. She easily picked out Christina's windows from the heavy drapes covering them to block out any sunlight. The one in the middle was actually a set of French doors that opened onto the balcony. What a pity Christina couldn't tolerate the light. She could have at least sat out there for some fresh air. She would have been safe from escaping, too, since Maeve could see no way to get to the balcony except from inside the house.

"Hurry, Miss Maeve!" Iris called from the shelter of the doorway, so Maeve did, reaching it just as the heavens opened up with a drenching rain. Both girls were giggling with excitement from the narrow escape when they stepped into the back hallway.

"You got wet," Iris cried happily, pointing at the rain spots on Maeve's dark uniform.

"And you didn't," Maeve replied. "You were too fast!"

"I'm very fast!" Iris said proudly as she turned toward the back staircase, but she stopped dead when she saw a man's figure in the shadows of the hallway.

Maeve sensed the instant tension in the child, and Iris instinctively drew back until she bumped into Maeve, as if she needed the safety of her presence.

"Who's this?" the man asked, stepping forward into the light. His voice was kindly, and his face betrayed not the slightest hint of malice to cause Iris to recoil. His suit was tailor-made, and his shirt spotless and stiff with starch. Obviously, he was the master of the house, home today because men like him didn't work on Saturday, and Maeve felt a chill at the thought he might have killed Dr. Brandt. "Oh, you must be the new girl," he said when he'd gotten a better look at Maeve.

"Yes, sir."

"What's your name?"

"Her name is Miss Maeve," Iris informed him before Maeve could.

"Miss Maeve, is it?" he asked with slight surprise, as if the family pet had answered his question.

"Maeve Smith, sir," Maeve clarified. She put her hand on Iris's small shoulder to reassure her.

"Mrs. Alberton told me she'd hired a new nurse-maid. You're very young."

"I'm eighteen, sir," Maeve lied. "I have a lot of experience with children."

"She's nice," Iris offered.

"Is she?" He looked at Iris for a long moment, as if he hadn't seen her in a long time. Maeve took the opportunity to study him. He wasn't a large man, but he had that air of power she'd noticed in men who had been successful. He was used to having other people do what he told them. His blond hair was faded, and he'd started to thicken through the middle. His gold watch chain stretched across a rounded stomach. "I heard you laughing," he marveled.

"I'm sorry, sir. We didn't mean to disturb anybody," Maeve said.

"Nothing to be sorry about," he said. "Nothing wrong with laughing." He was still looking at Iris, and Maeve couldn't help wondering what he was looking for. Some trace of madness, maybe? Some hint that she'd start hearing voices and need to be locked away in a dark room like Christina?

Iris was looking back at him, but Maeve couldn't see her face from this angle. She could feel the stiffness in the child's shoulder, though. She tried to think of something to say to ease Iris's tension and make the man think well of the child.

"Iris picked some flowers," she said lamely.

"I see," he said. "They're very pretty."

"They're for Christina," Iris said in a voice Maeve hadn't heard since that first day, a voice filled with anger and defiance.

The man flinched, and Maeve could actually feel his goodwill evaporate.

"Christina likes flowers," Iris added belligerently.

His shoulders actually sagged, as if under an invisible burden. "She used to," he said softly and turned away, as if unable to face the subject of his daughter anymore.

"She does!" Iris called after him, but he didn't stop. In another moment, he disappeared into the shadows. Iris turned, her young face flushed with fury. "I don't like these anymore." She threw the flowers on the floor and turned and raced up the stairs.

Maeve took a minute to salvage the ragged bouquet, and then followed her at a more respectable pace. As she'd suspected, the child had run into the sanctuary of the nursery. Maeve found her huddled on her bed. She laid the flowers on the dresser and went over to where Iris lay. She was curled up with her knees to her chest and had her thumb in her mouth.

"Why did you get so mad at him?" Maeve asked.

Iris looked up in surprise and pulled out her thumb. "He doesn't like Christina."

"How do you know?"

"He just doesn't."

Maeve gently stroked the blond curls away from her face.

"He doesn't like me either," Iris added after a moment.

Maeve suspected this might be true, but she certainly wasn't going to let Iris know it. "Maybe he just doesn't like the way you act."

Iris looked at her in surprise.

"I don't like the way you act when you get angry," Maeve confessed. "That's why I'm trying to teach you to act like a lady."

"Will he like me if I act like a lady?"

"Everyone will like you more if you act like a lady."

"Will Christina?"

"I'm sure she will."

"She doesn't like it when I scream," Iris confided.

"It probably scares her."

"Everything scares her."

"Let's see if the flowers scare her," Maeve suggested.

Iris sat up, intrigued at the thought. She took Maeve's hand, slid off the bed, and went with her out of the room. Maeve stopped to retrieve the wilted bouquet on the way. They could hear the murmur of conversation as they crossed the hall. Maeve would have knocked on Christina's door, but Iris just opened it and walked right in. They surprised Christina, who was sitting quietly on the sofa. To Maeve's surprise, the voice had been Christina's. She had been reading aloud from a book that looked suspiciously like a novel. The ladies at the Prodigal Son Mission had warned her about the dangers of reading novels.

Christina looked up in alarm.

"Didn't mean to startle you," Maeve said, hoping the shock wouldn't set her off. She looked around anxiously. "Where's Kerry?"

Christina looked around, too, as if she hadn't missed Kerry until Maeve had asked about her. Then she said, "She's outside."

"Outside?" Maeve echoed, and then she noticed that the heavy draperies covering the French doors had been disturbed. "You mean on the balcony?"

Christina didn't answer, but that seemed the logical explanation. Maybe she'd gone out for some air. Being cooped up with a crazy woman all the time had to be stifling. Maeve didn't want to visit Christina without Kerry's guidance, though. She walked over and pushed the drapery back to find the door was ajar. She pushed it farther open and called out, "Kerry?"

She heard the patter of footsteps and what sounded like a door slamming farther down and looked out to see Kerry hurrying toward her from the far end of the balcony.

Maeve stepped back as Kerry bustled into the room, breathless and not at all pleased. "What are you doing here?" she asked with a frown.

Kerry looked embarrassed beneath her anger, like she'd been caught doing something she shouldn't. The sound of the slamming door—she was sure now that's what she'd heard—told Maeve what it was, too. Kerry had a sweetheart who had somehow figured out how to get up onto the balcony to see her. She didn't need to worry about Maeve betraying her secret, though. She wasn't even going to let on that she knew.

"Iris brought something," Maeve explained innocently. She offered the bouquet to the child, who took it using great care not to drop a single bud. When she had it securely gripped in both of her small fists, she carried it over to Christina and held it out for her inspection.

"It's flowers," she said, in case Christina didn't recognize them.

Christina still looked a bit alarmed, although Maeve couldn't tell if she was just surprised to have company, if she was afraid of Iris, or if she was suspicious of the flowers.

"They're just weeds," Kerry said dismissively.

"They're *flower* weeds," Iris argued with childish wisdom.

To Maeve's amazement, Christina reached out and took them. "Thank you," she said softly.

"They're for the table where you eat," Iris informed her.

Kerry still looked unhappy, but Maeve didn't particularly care. She wanted Iris to feel good about her gift. "You need to put them in some water," Maeve said.

Kerry shot her a black look, but she went to a cabinet and found a glass. Then she disappeared into her bedroom, and when she returned, the glass was filled with water. She held it out to Christina, who placed the stems into the glass with the same elaborate care Iris had used to handle them earlier.

"Iris, why don't you put them on the table for Christina?" Maeve said. "Be careful so you don't spill the water."

Iris took the glass from Kerry, carried it reverently to the small table where Christina and Kerry obviously took their meals, and set it down in the center. "There," she said with satisfaction, then turned to look at Christina. "Are you scared of the flowers?"

"No," Christina said. "They're pretty." She was looking at Iris the same way Mr. Alberton had been looking at her, as if she hadn't seen her in a long time.

"What were you reading when we came in?" Maeve asked.

Christina looked down, as if surprised to find a book in her lap. "A story. Kerry likes for me to read stories."

"It keeps her calm," Kerry said in an attempt to remind Maeve who was in authority here.

"Miss Maeve reads me stories, too," Iris offered.

Kerry looked at Maeve in surprise. Not many Irish

291

girls could read, but Maeve's family had thought it would help her con a better class of people. Maeve didn't see any reason to explain this to Kerry, though. "Maybe Miss Christina would read you stories sometimes, too," Maeve suggested to Iris.

"They don't like her to come in here," Kerry said.

Maeve looked at her in surprise. "Why not?"

Kerry crossed her arms over her chest, silently telling Maeve she shouldn't challenge Kerry's pronouncements. "They're afraid she'll get crazy, too."

"I'm not crazy," Iris informed her defiantly.

Kerry glared at the child. "Not yet," she said.

Maeve wanted to slap her. "Come on, Iris." She took the girl's hand and led her from the room, biting her tongue to keep from saying what she wanted to say to Kerry. That could wait until later.

"Iris."

Both Maeve and the girl turned back at the soft call. Christina was staring at the child with that same intensity.

"Thank you for the flowers," Christina said.

"What do you say?" Maeve prompted when Iris just stared back.

"You're welcome," she said obediently.

To Maeve's surprise, Christina smiled, and for the first time since she'd come here, Maeve caught a glimpse of the girl she had once been.

"You should go," Kerry said sharply, "before she gets upset."

Maeve didn't think Christina would get upset, but she did want to get Iris away from here before *Kerry* said anything to upset the child. She led Iris out into the hallway and closed the door behind them. She didn't say anything until they were safely back in the nursery.

"I think Miss Christina liked the flowers," she tried.

"She wasn't scared of them," Iris said.

"I didn't think she would be, did you?"

"No," Iris said. She wandered over to where one of her dolls sat in a toy baby buggy and idly began to push the buggy back and forth.

Maeve went to one of the adult-sized chairs in the room and sat down. They could hear the rain outside hitting the windowpane. Maeve hoped the rock would protect her note until Allie could find it. She also hoped Allie would have some advice on what to do with the information about Iris's parentage.

She hadn't been paying much attention to Iris, so she was a little surprised when the girl started to climb into her lap. Maeve helped her up and wrapped her arms around her, and Iris leaned her head on Maeve's shoulder. They sat like that for a few minutes until Iris finally broke the silence.

"Will I get crazy like Christina?"

"No," Maeve said. She had no idea if this was true or not, but she fervently hoped it was, and she knew it was what Iris needed to hear.

"Kerry said so," Iris reminded her.

"She doesn't know anything," Maeve said. "And

you can't get crazy from just visiting Christina. If you could, Kerry would be crazy by now."

She wasn't sure if Iris understood that logic, but she seemed comforted. They sat in silent companionship for a few more minutes until someone knocked on the door.

"Come in," Maeve called, thinking it was early for someone to be bringing their lunch.

One of the maids came in. She seemed surprised to see her holding Iris, but she recovered quickly. "Mrs. Alberton wants to see you," she said ominously. "Right away."

# 13

MAEVE LEFT THE MAID TO WATCH IRIS WHILE she made her way downstairs. The child had sensed Maeve's apprehension, so maybe that would keep her on her good behavior. She didn't want the maid carrying tales of how Iris had thrown one of her customary fits as soon as Maeve was out of sight.

She nervously smoothed her uniform as she hurried down the back stairs and made her way to the back parlor, where Mrs. Alberton was waiting for her. Surely, they couldn't have discovered why she was really here. She'd done nothing to give herself away, unless somebody had found the notes she'd left for Allie. The thought horrified her, but she knew better than to let anyone see her apprehension. When she reached the parlor door, she stopped and drew a calming breath and schooled her features before raising her hand to knock. No one else needed to know her heart was pounding like a drum in her chest.

Mrs. Alberton's voice bade her enter. This room was smaller and more informal than the one where Mrs. Alberton had interviewed her. The furniture here showed signs of wear and a chess board had been set up in one corner, the game half-finished. A newspaper lay on the table by the sofa, and a ladies' magazine was beside it.

"You wanted to see me, Mrs. Alberton?" Maeve said, glad to hear her voice sounded confident.

"Yes," she said. She was sitting on the sofa, and Maeve had stopped to stand in front of her.

Maeve waited, folding her hands so the older woman wouldn't see they were shaking. And she waited some more as the silence stretched, the only sound the patter of the rain on the windows.

Oddly, Mrs. Alberton seemed even more ill at ease than Maeve felt. Maeve tried tilting her head slightly to the side, a trick that often prompted people to speak, even when they didn't want to.

Finally, Mrs. Alberton blurted out, "What have you done to Iris?"

Maeve blinked in surprise. "I beg your pardon, ma'am, but I haven't done anything to her." Except throw a little water in her face to get her attention, she thought, but nobody could be mad about that, could they?

"Come, come," a male voice said, and Maeve jumped in surprise. She hadn't realized anyone else was in the room. She looked over her shoulder to see that Mr. Alberton had been standing in the shadows by the far window. "You must have done something to her. She hasn't thrown a tantrum in two days."

Maeve felt the tension drain out of her as Mr. Alberton came over to stand beside where his wife sat. Both of them were looking at her expectantly, but Maeve didn't dare answer their question for fear of saying the wrong thing.

"Did you . . . beat her?" Mrs. Alberton finally asked with a small shudder.

"Oh, no, ma'am," Maeve said quickly. "I never laid a hand on her. You can ask her if you don't believe me."

Mrs. Alberton just stared back at Maeve as if she were speaking a foreign language. Then she looked up at her husband. "You said you heard her laughing this morning."

"Yes," he confirmed in a tone of wonder. "They were both laughing when they came in from outside."

"I hope we didn't disturb anyone," Maeve said apologetically, although she recalled distinctly that Mr. Alberton had assured her there was no harm in laughing.

"Not at all," Mr. Alberton said. "It's just . . . We have seldom heard Iris laugh."

Maeve could think of no suitable reply to that, so she held her tongue and waited, still trying to figure out why they had summoned her here. If they wanted to dismiss her, why didn't they just get on with it?

"Iris is not a happy child," Mrs. Alberton said at last.

Maeve could agree with that, or at least she could agree that Iris hadn't been happy when Maeve arrived.

"No one would dare take her outside before this," Mr. Alberton added. "She would run off and get lost. Sometimes it took the whole household to find her."

Maeve felt certain that was true.

"Why didn't she run away from you?" Mrs. Alberton asked, her plump little face scrunched into a puzzled frown.

"She tried to, the first time," Maeve said.

"And what did you do?"

"I caught her and took her back inside and told her she wouldn't be able to go back outside unless she behaved herself."

"Didn't she throw a tantrum?" Mr. Alberton asked in amazement.

"Yes, sir, she did," Maeve admitted.

"And what did you do then?" Mrs. Alberton asked, leaning forward eagerly, as if Maeve were going to solve a great mystery for her.

"I . . ." Maeve bit her lip, loathe to admit her sins.

But Mr. Alberton leaned forward, too, eager to hear her secret.

"I splashed a little bit of water in her face," she said reluctantly, then quickly added, "It don't hurt her none. Just gets her attention focused on something else. You can't talk sense to her when she's screaming."

They stared at her as if she'd just pulled a live rabbit from a hat.

"She's not a bad girl," Maeve went on eagerly when they didn't seem shocked by her methods. "She just needed somebody to pay attention to her, somebody who really cares about her. But before I came, the only time anybody noticed her was when she was screaming, so that's what she did."

They just kept staring at her, so she decided to use the opportunity to best advantage.

"Kerry said you don't want her to visit Miss Christina."

They both flinched as if she'd struck them, and she instantly regretted her boldness.

She hurried on, figuring she could hardly do any more harm. "She took Miss Christina some flowers that she picked today. Miss Christina seemed very pleased."

"We . . . we don't think . . ." Mrs. Alberton began, then looked up at her husband helplessly.

"We think seeing Christina would not be good for Iris," he said.

Maeve didn't think it would be proper to argue, but

she knew Mrs. Brandt wouldn't hesitate in a situation like this. "She knows all about Miss Christina. She can't help it. We can hear her and . . ."

"And what?" Mr. Alberton asked sharply when she hesitated.

"And it scares Iris when she screams or moans. Scares me, too, come to that, but seeing her when she's calm, that sort of makes it not so bad when we do hear her."

"She wasn't always like that," Mrs. Alberton said, her pale eyes filling with tears. "She was such a happy girl until . . ."

"Her brother died," Mr. Alberton said gruffly, as if he was afraid he might cry himself. "She's never been the same since."

"Kerry told me," Maeve confirmed. She needed to know one more thing but wasn't sure if she should ask. They might get mad and throw her out into the rain. For a second she imagined trudging back into town, looking like a drowned rat, to find Allie. Then she lifted her chin and said, "She told me something else, and I'm wondering if it's true."

Both of the Albertons stiffened, and their eyes grew instantly wary. They didn't ask her what it was, but maybe they didn't have to because they already knew.

"Is Christina Iris's mother?" she asked.

Mrs. Alberton made a strangled sound and raised a hand to cover her mouth. Mr. Alberton's face flooded with color as he silently fought the rage he must feel.

Maeve stood perfectly still, knowing that if she didn't speak, one of them soon would. Humans felt compelled to fill the silence, even if that meant speaking of something that caused them unbelievable pain.

"An evil man took advantage of her," Mr. Alberton finally said.

"After she became sick," Mrs. Alberton added quickly. "She didn't even understand what he was doing."

Maeve gave them a moment to recover before handing them another shock. "She knows."

"Who knows what?" Mr. Alberton asked, confused.

"Iris knows," Maeve said. "She told me Christina is her mother."

This time Mrs. Alberton didn't even try to hold back her cry of anguish.

"Good God," Mr. Alberton said. "She's just a baby! How could she know that?"

"Children don't miss much," Maeve said. "She probably heard somebody talking."

"We never discuss it," Mrs. Alberton insisted.

"The servants know," Maeve reminded her. "People forget children are around. They say things."

Mrs. Alberton was weeping now, and Maeve's conscience pricked her. "I'm sorry, ma'am," she said quite sincerely. "I never meant to upset you."

Mr. Alberton put his hand on his wife's shoulder as she pulled a handkerchief from her sleeve and tried to dab at her eyes. "You can go now, Maeve," he said.

Maeve was only too glad to escape. She headed for the door, but when she realized this might be her last opportunity to speak to them, she decided she needed to say one more thing. She stopped at the door, with her hand on the knob, and turned back to face them. "Iris isn't crazy, Mr. Alberton. She just needs somebody to love her."

Before they could reply, she pulled open the door and fled, half expecting to hear a roar of rage at such presumption. But she heard nothing except the sound of her own footsteps as she hurried to the back staircase and raced back up to rescue Iris from the maid . . . or rescue the poor maid from Iris.

FRANK HAD SPENT MOST OF THE DAY WITH HIS son, Brian, but he'd been unable to forget Sarah's accusations that he didn't care about Maeve's safety. Truth to tell, he cared more than he wanted to admit, even to himself. Late that afternoon, when the rain had finally let up, he'd told his mother that he had some business to attend to and left for Grand Central Station. There he'd boarded a train that let him off at the country station closest to where the Alberton family lived. His mother had convinced him to take an umbrella, and although he had grumbled, he was now glad that he had. The rain had started falling again from the leaden sky, and he turned up his collar against the damp chill.

Allie had told him she'd be staying in a boarding-house near the station, and he found it easily after making inquiries of the stationmaster.

The house had once been a fine one, but the owners had fallen on hard times. Now the paint was weathered, and one shutter hung crooked from a hinge that had rusted through. The wood on the broad front porch gave gently, as if undecided whether to collapse or hold firm, as Frank walked across it. An outline in the paint on the front door told him a brass knocker had once adorned it. Someone had probably sold it. He knocked loudly after lowering his umbrella and shaking the water from it.

A woman with iron gray hair and a disposition to match answered.

"I'm looking for Allie Shea," he told her.

"There's no gentleman callers allowed," she informed him, looking him over disapprovingly.

"I'm her brother," Frank said.

"A likely story," the woman scoffed. "I run a decent house here."

"I wouldn't want Allie staying in any other kind," Frank assured her. "Maybe if you tell her I'm here . . ."

"Frank," Allie exclaimed from behind the land-lady. "What're you doing here? Is Ma all right?"

"Is this really your brother?" the landlady asked skeptically.

Allie gave her a pitying look. "Do you think I'd take up with anybody that ugly?"

"Ugly?" Frank echoed in outrage.

"Don't act surprised," Allie said sweetly. "Haven't I been telling you that all your life, Frankie, dear?"

The old woman snorted. "I guess he is your brother, but I still don't allow men in the house. You have to sit out on the porch."

"It's freezing out there," Allie protested.

"Then get a shawl," the landlady advised.

Allie gave her a black look, but she pushed past her out onto the porch and led the way to where the porch wrapped around the side of the house where the rain wasn't blowing in.

Frank stopped short at the sight of the metal contraption sitting there, leaning up against the house. "What's that?"

"My bicycle," Allie said. "I need to be able to get out to the Alberton house quickly."

Frank eyed it doubtfully. "You ride that thing?"

"I certainly do."

"You know the Albertons' son got killed riding one of those?"

"I'm very careful," she assured him with amusement. "Now why are you here?"

Frank shook off his fascination with the bicycle. "Have you heard from Maeve?"

"I found a note from her yesterday and another today. I didn't know if she'd be able to get out with the rain and all, but she did. In the first one, she was just telling me she got hired on. It's the second one you need to see." She reached into her skirt pocket and pulled out a folded piece of paper.

Frank took it and unfolded it to see Maeve's careful, schoolgirl hand. As he read, he felt as if the blood was draining from his head. He swore under his breath, then remembered he wasn't alone. "Sorry," he muttered.

Allie didn't seem offended. "That's something, a child so young saying a thing like that."

"Someone must've told her," Frank said.

"I can't think why they would. Maybe she just overheard it. People don't realize how much children understand. Do you think it's true?"

Frank felt the anger like a white-hot coal in his chest. He wanted to crumple the paper and tear it to shreds. "Like she says, it would explain how they knew somebody had taken advantage of Christina," he admitted reluctantly.

"Could Dr. Brandt have done it?"

"You mean raped a helpless girl?" he asked bitterly.

"Yes," she said gently.

Frank didn't want to even think about the question. "I don't know. I never met the man," he hedged.

"You must know something about him, though," she pressed.

304

"I know what his wife thought of him . . . still thinks of him," he corrected. "She'd never believe it."

"Women can be easy to fool. We see what we want to see when we're in love." She sounded like she spoke from experience. "But don't forget the letter someone wrote to Mr. Decker about him." The letter that had accused Tom Brandt of seducing young women.

"If this is true"—Frank held up Maeve's note—"then it was probably Mr. Alberton who wrote that letter."

"Unless Christina isn't the only one he raped."

The blood that had drained from Frank's head now rushed back with a roar like a freight train. Dear God in heaven, this couldn't be happening. "We don't know that he raped anybody."

"Maeve said she's afraid of doctors," Allie reminded him.

"*I'm* afraid of doctors," Frank snapped. "It's not because one raped me."

He could see from her expression that she understood his need to deny the facts Maeve had uncovered. He hated her for that.

"You don't have to tell her," Allie said.

"Tell who?" he tried.

"Mrs. Brandt. You don't have to tell her any of this."

"I know I don't," he said in despair. "One look at my face, and she'll just know."

• • •

AFTER MAEVE AND IRIS HAD FINISHED THEIR supper, Maeve rang for a maid to come and take away their dishes. As the girl placed the dishes on the tray, Maeve casually asked, "How many are on the staff here?"

The girl looked up in surprise, then glanced anxiously at Iris, who was playing contentedly with one of her dolls. None of the maids wanted to linger in the nursery a moment longer than necessary. "I'm sure I don't know," the girl said and went back to her work.

"I know all the house staff," Maeve said, undeterred. "But how many work outside?" She rose from where she'd been sitting and moved to stand in front of the door, silently telling the girl she wouldn't be able to escape until she'd answered.

The girl sighed. "There's the gardener and his helper, and three boys in the stable."

"Are any of them around my age?" Maeve asked with just the right amount of inappropriate interest.

The maid frowned. "Mrs. Alberton don't allow us to have suitors."

"Who said anything about suitors? I just asked how old they were," Maeve reminded her, leaning back against the door and folding her arms in silent determination.

"The gardener is old," the maid said in defeat. "He's probably forty. The others . . . Joe and Toby. The other two are too young."

"Which one does Kerry like?" Maeve asked.

The girl's eyes widened in surprise. "She don't like none of them," she insisted, and picked up her tray. She headed toward the door with her head down, daring Maeve to move or be trampled.

"Then which one likes her?" Maeve asked, not budging an inch.

The maid looked up, and this time Maeve saw fear on her face.

Maeve straightened. "I won't tell her you said," she promised. "I just don't want to make her mad. Which one likes her?"

The maid glanced over her shoulder to see if Iris was listening. She appeared to be engrossed in her play. The girl took a step closer to Maeve and spoke in barely a whisper. "They both do."

FRANK WASN'T SURE WHY HE HAD GONE FROM Grand Central Station to Bank Street. He should have gone home. He should have avoided Sarah at all costs. Still, he'd found himself in front of her house, but when he knocked, no one had answered. He'd gone back down the front steps and stood staring up at the town house to see if any lights were burning, but the place was dark.

"She's on a delivery," a familiar voice called.

Frank wasn't surprised to see Mrs. Ellsworth standing on her front porch. He couldn't remember ever escaping Mrs. Ellsworth's notice when he'd visited Sarah's house. "Is Catherine with you?"

"No, Mrs. Decker took Catherine to stay with her."

*"Mrs. Decker?"* he repeated in surprise.

"Yes, she dotes on the child," Mrs. Ellsworth said. "Have you eaten? I've got some cold roast beef and a bit of apple pie. Come on in."

Frank had never refused Mrs. Ellsworth's apple pie. She was already in her kitchen by the time he made his way up her front stoop and into her house.

"Make yourself at home," she called.

By the time he'd hung up his hat and found her, she had set him a place at the kitchen table and poured him some coffee. He sat down gratefully. "Where's Nelson this evening?" he asked about her son.

She gave him a secretive grin. "He's escorting a young lady to the theater. A very nice young lady," she added. "They met at church." Nelson had made at least one disastrous mistake in his choice of female companions in the past, Frank knew.

"I'm glad to hear it," Frank said.

Mrs. Ellsworth made him a thick sandwich and set it before him. Only then did he realize he was starved. He devoured the food greedily, murmuring his appreciation. She waited until he'd finished his first piece of pie before asking her question.

"What's wrong?" she asked, setting another piece of pie before him.

"I went up to Yonkers this afternoon to check on Maeve."

"Is she all right?" she asked in concern.

"She's fine, or at least she hasn't asked for help. She's sent a couple messages to Allie."

"How do they do that?" she asked with interest. Frank figured her life had never involved the transmittal of secret messages.

"Allie found a place near the house where Maeve can hide a note. Then Allie checks the place every day."

"So if she needed help, she'd let Allie know."

Frank nodded. "And if there's an emergency, they arranged a way for her to signal for help."

"Oh, my," Mrs. Ellsworth exclaimed, her eyes shining. "How exciting."

Frank didn't think that Maeve having an emergency would be the least bit exciting, but he didn't say so.

"So if Maeve isn't in danger, why do you look like you lost your best friend?" she asked.

Frank ran a hand over his face. "You have to promise not to tell Sarah."

"Oh, dear," she said in dismay. "Of course. I'd never hurt her, not for anything in the world. Did you find out something?"

"Nothing for certain," Frank said. "But Maeve found out that the little girl she's taking care of is the child of Christina Alberton."

"She's the girl who went crazy when her brother died, isn't she?"

"That's right."

"But how could she have a child? Who could have fathered it?"

"The girl who takes care of Christina told Maeve that a . . . a doctor did it," he admitted reluctantly.

"A doctor!"

"Yes. The family allowed him to examine her alone, and then later they found out she was with child. She told them it was the doctor who attacked her."

Mrs. Ellsworth was staring at him in horror. "Did the girl tell Maeve it was Dr. Brandt?"

"No. Maeve couldn't ask outright without giving herself away, and the girl might not even know the doctor's name."

"But it couldn't have been him, could it?" The question sounded more like a plea for reassurance.

"How well did you know him?"

"Not real well," she admitted. "He wasn't home much, and when he was, they kept to themselves, the way couples do. Do *you* think it was him?"

"I have no idea, but somebody thought so," Frank reminded her. "That's why he's dead."

Mrs. Ellsworth shook her head. "I won't believe it. It's impossible."

"Why is it impossible?"

"There are lots of reasons a man might attack a woman," she said, thinking out loud. "None of them makes it right, of course, but if a woman makes a man mad, for instance, or if she's no better than she should be, he might excuse himself that she had it coming. This is different, though. This Christina couldn't have done anything a man could use for an excuse. She was young and innocent and not in her right mind. A man who would take advantage of a girl like that, he's not even a human being."

That was it. That's what had been bothering Frank all afternoon, ever since he'd read Maeve's note. "You think you'd have known if Brandt was that evil," he guessed.

She nodded. "I get feelings about people. For instance, I never had much use for the police until I met you."

Frank might have felt flattered in other circumstances. "But you said yourself, you didn't know him that well."

"But Mrs. Brandt did," she argued. "Surely, he couldn't have fooled her. She would have known if he was that evil."

"Would she?" he asked. He remembered Allie's argument that a woman in love often didn't see a man for what he really was, and he'd seen far too many women throw themselves away on unworthy men. Men who abused them. Men who cheated and lied and beat them. Yet still the women remained loyal and blind to all their faults.

Mrs. Ellsworth reached across the table and laid her hand on Frank's arm. "Oh, Mr. Malloy, if this is true, she can't ever find out."

"No," he agreed. "She can't."

• • •

IRIS WAS SOUND ASLEEP AFTER OFFERING ONLY a token resistance to being put to bed. Maeve wondered how long she could keep up this good behavior before something set her off into another tantrum. She reminded herself this wasn't really her concern, since she'd only be here a few more days at the most, but she couldn't help worrying about what would become of the child in a house where her very existence reminded them of her mother's shame.

Maeve had just sat down at the small table to compose another note to Allie about her conversation with the Albertons when the nursery door opened and Kerry appeared. She didn't look happy.

"Is the brat asleep?" she asked.

"Her name is Iris," Maeve reminded her, wondering what Kerry called Christina when no one else was around. Maeve quickly turned over the paper she'd been writing on and stood up.

"Writing a love letter?" Kerry taunted.

"It's to my aunt Allie," Maeve said.

"You think you're something special because you can write," she guessed.

"I was lucky I got to go to school."

"Well, I wasn't lucky," Kerry said, making no effort to hide her bitter anger. "I never got to go to school. I had to work from the time I could walk."

Maeve had had enough. "Did you come in here just to make me feel sorry for you, or did you want something?"

Kerry straightened in an effort to regain some dignity. "I came to tell you to mind your own business."

"About what?" she bluffed, thinking the maid had told her about Maeve's questions.

This seemed to confuse Kerry for a moment, but she recovered quickly. "I don't want you sneaking into our rooms like you did today."

"We didn't sneak in."

She pressed her lips together in silent fury and two red spots formed on her cheeks. "I don't want you just coming in anytime you feel like it. You upset Christina."

"She didn't look upset. She looked happy when Iris gave her the flowers."

"She got upset later," she said, and Maeve could see she was lying. What she didn't understand was why Kerry needed to lie.

"That's too bad," Maeve said without sympathy. "If you just tell me when you're meeting one of the stable boys, I'll be glad to stay out of your way."

"What do you mean?" she demanded, but the flush crawling up her neck betrayed her.

"Which one is it you like? Just tell me, and I'll leave him alone."

"I don't know what you're talking about," she tried. "I don't even know the boys in the stable. How could I?"

"I don't guess it would be too hard. I figure they'd come sniffing around a pretty girl like you all on their own."

"You sound like you know from experience," Kerry said in an attempt to turn the tables.

"I know better than to lift my skirt for a stable boy, if that's what you mean," Maeve countered.

This infuriated her. "I don't lift my skirt for a stable boy or anybody else, and if you say anything different, I'll get you thrown out of here without a reference."

Maeve raised her hands in mock surrender. "I don't care if you do or not. I'm just telling you not to come in here all mad at me for catching you. If I wanted to get you in trouble, I would've told Mrs. Alberton already."

This mollified her a little. "I'm not fooling around with those boys," she said, still a little defensive. "I wouldn't settle for a stable boy either. They'd like me to, though, so they keep coming around."

"Can't blame them for that, I guess. If it bothers you, though, why don't you tell Mrs. Alberton? She'd put a stop to it."

Kerry frowned, not liking the suggestion, although Maeve couldn't understand why. Unless she just liked the attention. But that was silly. If the Albertons even caught her flirting with the boys, she'd be turned out. "I can take care of myself," she finally said. "Like I said, just mind your own business and let me mind mine."

"Fine," Maeve said. "Next time we'll knock before we come in."

314

"I don't want you coming in at all."

"Mrs. Alberton said she thought it would be a good idea for Iris to visit Christina," Maeve said. She wasn't really lying. Mrs. Alberton hadn't contradicted her when she'd suggested it, so Maeve took that for approval.

"I don't believe you," Kerry cried.

"Ask her yourself," Maeve challenged, knowing her own confidence would practically guarantee Kerry would do no such thing.

Kerry set her jaw stubbornly. "If Christina gets upset, it'll be your fault."

"What happens when she gets upset?" Maeve asked, truly curious.

"She . . . she screams and cries and carries on something awful."

"Do you have to hold her down?" Maeve asked, remembering how frightened Iris had become when Maeve held her down during one of her tantrums. She'd seen someone holding Christina down and hurting her. If Kerry hurt Christina . . .

"No," Kerry snapped. "She just curls up in a ball and rocks back and forth, making the worst racket you ever heard. That usually sets Iris off, too, and then the both of them are howling. It's enough to drive a body to distraction."

"I guess that's why the Albertons sleep on the other side of the house."

"That and because they don't want to see either of them. Who would?"

"Christina is still their daughter," Maeve said. "And Iris is their granddaughter."

Kerry's jaw dropped. "Who told you that?"

"Iris," Maeve said, watching Kerry's reaction carefully. "Didn't you know?"

"Of course I know! I was here when . . . when it happened."

"When the doctor attacked her, you mean," Maeve said. "That's how you knew what he'd done, because she got a baby from it."

Kerry studied Maeve for a long moment as if taking her measure in a new way. "That's right," she said finally.

"Why didn't you tell me the whole story?"

"Wasn't none of your business," Kerry said, assuming her usual haughtiness.

"I don't know why not, if I'm Iris's nursemaid."

"Then it wasn't my place to tell," Kerry argued.

"Who told Iris, then?"

Kerry had no answer for that. She just pressed her lips together again and refused to reply.

Maeve decided to try a different tactic. She moved closer to Kerry and lowered her voice conspiratorially. "That was a terrible thing, what the doctor did. I guess Mr. Alberton was pretty mad."

"Never saw anybody madder," Kerry confirmed with renewed confidence.

"What did he do to the doctor? Did he get the law on him?"

"He wanted to, but they couldn't prove he was the one what done it."

Maeve feigned shock. "Didn't he do anything at all to him, then?"

Kerry pretended she didn't want to say, but Maeve could see she was dying to tell.

"What is it?" Maeve coaxed. "Tell me!"

"I heard him say he'd make sure the doctor never did such a thing again."

"How did he do that?" Maeve asked, horrified.

Kerry shrugged one shoulder. "I never found out."

"Do you know what his name was? The doctor, I mean."

Kerry smiled with smug superiority. "Of course I do."

"What was it, then?" Maeve challenged.

"Brandt."

# 14

SARAH TRUDGED HOME THE NEXT MORNING, bone-weary but happy to have delivered a healthy baby boy into the world. The streets were peaceful on this Sabbath morning while people took advantage of a day of rest from work. She'd been thinking only about stripping off the clothes she'd been wearing for over twenty-four hours and falling into her own familiar bed until she climbed her front steps and unlocked her door and stepped into the empty house. For years she'd never thought a thing about coming home to an empty house, but now the silence was deafening.

Funny that she'd never noticed how different a house felt when it was truly empty and not just full of sleeping people who weren't making any noise. The stillness made her heart ache. She missed Catherine and Maeve with a longing that was physical pain. Even knowing Catherine was perfectly safe and probably very happy at her mother's house didn't ease the longing to see her. And Maeve . . . Was she all right?

Angry now, Sarah slammed the door and locked it securely behind her. How could Malloy put a young girl like Maeve in danger like this? And for what? To ease Sarah's mind? To punish a killer? What good would that do now? Nothing would bring Tom back and chances were that even if Malloy identified the killer, he wouldn't be able to punish him. And now Malloy was hinting that she might find out things about Tom she didn't want to know. No good could come of this, she was sure. Why had she ever given Malloy permission to start in the first place?

She walked into her office and plunked her heavy medical bag down onto the desk. Tom's medical bag. Tom's desk. Forcing that thought from her mind, she opened the bag and began to unpack it. She hadn't gotten far when someone knocked on her front door.

Sarah swore under her breath. She didn't want company, and she certainly didn't want another delivery until she'd had a chance to rest. But when she turned, she saw a familiar figure silhouetted on the frosted glass. With a weary sigh, she went to open the door.

Mrs. Ellsworth stood on the front stoop, looking apologetic. "I know you're tired, and I won't even come inside. I just wanted to tell you that Mr. Malloy came by last night to let you know he'd checked on Maeve and she's doing fine."

"Is she? What did he say?" she asked eagerly. "Please, come in. We can't talk on the doorstep."

"Only for a minute," Mrs. Ellsworth protested, crossing the threshold with obvious reluctance. "You were out all night."

"I managed to sleep for a while," Sarah said. "What did he say about Maeve? Tell me everything."

"That Pinkerton woman is keeping in touch with her," Mrs. Ellsworth said. "They have a system so Maeve can secretly leave her notes every day."

"How do they do that?"

"She hides them someplace outside the house, and the woman checks the spot every day."

"Has she found out anything yet?"

"Nothing . . . nothing useful," Mrs. Ellsworth hedged.

Sarah frowned. How very unlike Mrs. Ellsworth to withhold anything. Usually, she was only too

319

happy to share every scrap of information she knew on every subject. "What did she learn that *wasn't* useful, then?" Sarah asked.

Mrs. Ellsworth bit her lip. "Like I said, nothing really. Mr. Malloy can tell you better than I. I'll go now so you can get some rest and—"

"No, you don't," Sarah said. "You aren't leaving here until you tell me what Malloy said."

"It's so sad," the old woman said, wringing her hands in distress. "I don't like to talk about it."

Sarah just stared at her, implacable.

Finally, Mrs. Ellsworth said, "The child, the one Maeve is taking care of, she's . . . The poor crazy girl is her mother."

For a moment Sarah couldn't grasp the significance of it. "She's . . . Christina Alberton has a child?"

"Yes, the poor thing. But like I said, it's sad but it didn't help much. And Maeve is safe, and the Pinkerton woman, what's her name?"

"Allie," Sarah supplied automatically.

"That's right, Allie. She's keeping a close watch. They even have a signal in case Maeve is in danger. And Allie checks their secret hiding place every day to get messages from her. I'll be going now. Try to get some rest, dear. I'm sure there's no hurry for you to fetch Catherine home. Your mother must be happy to have her."

Mrs. Ellsworth was halfway to the door before Sarah had figured it out.

"Christina Alberton has a child," she said.

Mrs. Ellsworth stopped and turned back warily. Her face had lost all color.

"Who fathered the child?" Sarah asked. Her mouth felt very dry.

"We don't know, dear," Mrs. Ellsworth said gently. "It could have been anyone."

It *could* have been anyone, but only one man had been accused of seducing his young female patients. Sarah pictured Tom's face, seeing him as clearly as if he'd been standing in front of her. *No, he couldn't have done such a thing!* Sarah's knees suddenly gave way and the next thing she knew, she was on the floor. Mrs. Ellsworth had rushed to her and was helping her up into a chair.

"Are you all right, dear? When did you eat last? Just sit here and I'll get you some tea. We'll fix you right up. Don't worry about a thing."

Sarah could hardly hear her for the roaring in her head. This couldn't be true; it just couldn't. Tom could never have done such a thing, could he? Not the man she'd known. Not the man she'd loved.

*Please, God, don't let it be true*, she prayed, even though she knew it was far too late for God to change anything at all.

FRANK HAD WAITED UNTIL HE SAW THEM returning from church. Oscar Werner and his sister, Johanna Rossmann, were dressed in their Sunday best. Werner would want to put on a good front. A

321

man whose daughter was a madwoman would want people to see that he and his remaining family were still respectable and proper and completely sane. Frank felt a small stab of regret for Mrs. Rossmann's plight. Bad luck had left her widowed and dependent on her brother's charity. What would become of her if her brother turned out to be a murderer?

Frank gave them a few minutes to take off their hats and coats and get comfortably inside, but not long enough for them to be seated at the Sunday dinner their cook would have prepared for them before he pounded on their front door.

The maid who answered remembered him from his earlier visits. "Nobody is home," she tried almost desperately, but Frank pushed past her into the front hallway.

"Tell Mr. Werner I'm here to see him." He handed her his card.

She didn't want to take it. Her face was white.

"Who's there, Annie?" a man's voice called, and Werner stepped into the hallway from the room Frank knew was the parlor.

"Detective Sergeant Frank Malloy from the New York City Police," Frank told him.

Mrs. Rossmann had reached the doorway by then, and she gasped when she saw him. "What are you doing here?" she demanded. "Haven't you done enough?"

"I need to ask Mr. Werner some questions."

"You know this man?" Werner demanded of his sister.

"He . . . he's been here before," Mrs. Rossmann admitted.

"Because of Ordella?"

"No," she said, still staring at Frank with pure hatred.

"I'll be happy to explain it to you," Frank offered. "In private," he added with a meaningful glance at the wide-eyed maid.

Mr. Werner hastily ushered Frank and Mrs. Rossmann into the parlor and closed the door behind them. "What is this all about?" Mr. Werner demanded the moment the door was shut.

"He thinks you're a murderer," Mrs. Rossmann said furiously.

"What?" Werner asked in outrage.

"Mrs. Rossmann, you should leave," Frank said.

"I'm not going anywhere," she replied.

"Johanna, be quiet," her brother snapped in frustration. "What are you doing here?" he demanded of Frank.

"I'm investigating a murder," Frank said.

"Whose?" Werner asked and then had a sudden, horrifying thought. "Not Mrs. Leiter? Or Mrs. Yates?"

Frank figured the Yates woman must be the minister's unlucky wife. "No. Dr. Brandt."

"Who?" Werner asked in genuine surprise.

Frank wondered if a killer could possibly forget

the name of his victim. "Dr. Tom Brandt. He came to see your daughter after the incident with Dr. Leiter."

"The one who upset her so much," Mrs. Rossmann reminded him bitterly.

Now Werner remembered. His face flooded with color and his anger evaporated. "He . . . Are you saying someone killed him?"

"You know perfectly well someone did, Mr. Werner," Frank tried.

"No, I don't! How could I?"

"Because you were there when it happened, Mr. Werner."

"No, he wasn't!" Mrs. Rossmann cried. "He couldn't have been!"

"What are you talking about?" Werner asked. "I don't know anything about this."

"Yes, you do," Frank insisted. "You hired a boy to fetch Dr. Brandt. He can identify you."

"No, he can't!"

"Why not?" Frank challenged.

"Because . . ." He stopped, searching for a reason. "Because I wasn't there!"

"He especially remembered your walking stick, Mr. Werner," Frank said. "The one with the big silver head."

"I don't own a walking stick," Werner insisted.

"Not now," Frank agreed. "You probably threw it in the river after you beat poor Dr. Brandt's head in with it."

"I didn't throw it in the river!"

"What did you do with it, then?" Frank asked.

Werner stared at him in surprise. "I didn't do *anything* with it! I never owned a stick like that, and you can't prove that I did!"

"We'll see about that."

"You won't see about anything," Werner said, fighting to regain control of the situation. "Get out of my house."

"And if I don't?"

"I'll have your job," Werner threatened. "You can't come into a respectable man's home and accuse him of murder! Now get out."

Frank could have forced the issue, but he thought Werner might be as good as his word. With Roosevelt leaving office any day, he couldn't afford to take the chance. He took one last shot. "Remember the boy, Mr. Werner. He knows what you look like."

*"Get out!"* he shouted.

Frank decided he would. Werner was too angry to be guilty. He was wasting his time here. And if Werner wasn't guilty, that meant Alberton probably was, and that meant Maeve might be in danger.

But when he stepped into the hallway, he saw the maid hovering there in the middle of the floor. From the look on her face, she'd heard everything, and then her wide-eyed gaze darted away from his and toward the staircase that led to the second floor. Frank half expected to see someone standing there, but no one was. He looked back at the maid, but she was still staring at something on the stairs. He walked closer, and this time when he looked up the stairs, he saw it. One of the family portraits that lined the walls. This one was of a middle-aged man who looked a lot like Oscar Werner.

And he was holding a walking stick with a large silver head.

MAEVE HAD EXPECTED TO ACCOMPANY THE Albertons to church that morning to help mind Iris, but to her surprise, the family didn't take the child with them. Not this Sunday and not ever.

"They don't want anybody to know about her," Cook explained in a whisper when Maeve expressed her amazement after they'd left.

Iris was eating a cookie at the kitchen table, oblivious to their discussion.

"But aren't they worried about her immortal soul?" Maeve asked. In her experience, church-going folks worried about this all the time, especially for their children.

"I don't suppose they are," Cook said, shaking her head. "I guess they expect her to end up like poor Miss Christina, so there's no use in even trying."

"If they keep her locked up all the time, she just might," Maeve said in disgust.

"What are you saying?" Iris asked between bites of her cookie.

"Nothing for your ears," Maeve said. "Finish your cookie, and we'll go out for a walk."

"It's going to rain again," Cook predicted with a disapproving frown.

"We'll come back if it does," Maeve said. She was desperate to get out so she could leave her newest message. Allie's eyes would pop right out of her head when she read it.

Maeve had hardly slept all night for trying to figure out how Kerry could be wrong. Except Kerry wasn't wrong. Christina had a baby, and Iris was the living proof. That meant some man had gotten her with child, and how many men had spent any time at all with her, much less time alone with her in her bedroom the way Dr. Brandt had?

The very thought made Maeve sick, and she couldn't help wondering if Mrs. Brandt would ever want to set eyes on her again. Maeve didn't think she'd want someone around who reminded her of such a terrible thing. She absently fingered the folded note in her pocket and wished fervently that she'd never gotten involved in any of this. Why had she thought it would be exciting? Why had she thought it would help Mrs. Brandt?

"I'm finished," Iris announced, brushing the crumbs from her hands. She scrambled down from her chair and presented herself ready to go.

"What do you say to Cook?" Maeve prompted.

"Thank you for the cookie," Iris replied obediently.

Cook had provided the cookie as a reward for Iris's recent good behavior, and now she seemed genuinely shocked to see it continuing. "You're welcome, child," she said faintly.

"Come along, then," Maeve said, taking her hand. They stopped by the back door to put a bonnet and jacket on Iris, then made their way out and through the garden.

The rosebushes were leafing out and tiny buds had begun to form on the tips of the tender new shoots. Too bad Maeve would be gone before they bloomed. She imagined the garden would be beautiful.

Iris ran most of the way to the creek, with Maeve following along behind. Iris had spotted a trace of color near the bank and gone straight to it, determined to pick some more flowers. Maeve went straight for the rock. It was the work of an instant to lift the rock and hide her note beneath it. Then she went to where Iris was pulling up a bunch of wildflowers by their roots and bringing great clods of moist earth with them.

"Careful!" Maeve cried. "We can't take all that mud inside with us!"

"Why not?" Iris asked.

"Because Cook will skin us alive, that's why! Here, break the stems off like I showed you before."

They didn't have time to pick more than a few before they felt the first raindrops. Iris was delighted and turned her small face up to see if she could catch some of the drops in her mouth. Maeve had to practically drag her along back to the house. Mrs. Brandt would have been angry if she'd taken Catherine out in the rain. Maeve only wished someone cared as much about Iris.

They were hurrying through the back garden when something, some motion, caught Maeve's eye. She looked up at the back of the house to see what it was.

"What are you looking at?" Iris wanted to know. She had stopped to stare up, too.

"I don't know. I thought I saw something moving."

"It's that boy," Iris said wisely.

"What boy?" Maeve asked in surprise.

"The boy who comes. He's bad," she informed Maeve solemnly.

"How do you know?"

"He makes Kerry laugh."

That didn't make any sense to Maeve. "How do you know he's bad, then?"

"I just do," Iris said confidently and skipped off toward the house.

Maeve looked up again, just in time to see the curtain covering the French doors to Christina's room flutter, as if someone had been taking a peek out to see what they were doing.

Maeve hurried to catch up with Iris. "Is there a way to get up on the balcony from the outside?" she asked, pointing.

"Yes," Iris said.

Maeve had to fight her frustration with the child. "Do you know how to do it?"

"There's a secret door," Iris said as if she was surprised Maeve wouldn't know such a simple fact.

"Where is it?" Maeve asked. The rain was starting to fall in earnest now.

Iris looked up at her with eyes shining with excitement from her secret. "Here it is." She took Maeve's hand and led her to the back of the house, where a large wooden column supported the end of the balcony.

At first, Maeve didn't see a thing, but then Iris pointed with a tiny finger to the almost-invisible latch. One touch opened a curved door that formed half of the column. Inside was a wrought iron spiral staircase leading upward.

And on the metal treads were muddy footprints.

"IT ISN'T TRUE."

"Of course it isn't true," Mrs. Ellsworth assured Sarah for at least the tenth time.

"I would have known if Tom was that kind of man."

"Of course you would," Mrs. Ellsworth agreed. Each time she agreed, Sarah was more certain she didn't agree at all.

They were sitting in Sarah's kitchen, where Mrs. Ellsworth had fixed a meal that Sarah couldn't possibly eat. Her stomach was so knotted, she didn't think she'd ever be able to swallow food again.

"Malloy warned me," Sarah remembered. "I should have listened."

"You're just upset right now," Mrs. Ellsworth reminded her. "And tired. Everything will look better when you've had some rest."

Sarah thought she could sleep for a hundred years and never see any improvement in her situation. "I want Maeve to come back home."

"Of course you do," Mrs. Ellsworth said. She was humoring her, and Sarah was in no mood to be humored.

"No, I mean it. I want her to come home today. And I want Malloy to fire that Pinkerton woman, and I want him to stop trying to find out who killed Tom. I want *all* of this to stop right now."

Mrs. Ellsworth just stared back at her helplessly. "You should try to eat something, dear."

Sarah wanted to scream, but she held her temper. "I can't."

"At least drink some tea," she urged.

Sarah lifted the cup to her lips, but the fragrance made her stomach roil, and she put the cup down again. "I have to see Maeve."

"What on earth for?"

"I need to find out exactly what she heard about Tom."

Now Mrs. Ellsworth looked frightened. "You can't just go up and knock on their front door and ask for her."

"Why not?"

She had to think for a moment. "Well, because they might know who you are," she tried.

"What if they do?"

Mrs. Ellsworth reached across the table and laid a hand on Sarah's arm. "Mr. Alberton could be Dr. Brandt's killer," she said reasonably. "If he figures out who you are and that Maeve is working for you, heaven knows what he might do."

"But Malloy knows everything," Sarah pointed out.

"Mr. Alberton doesn't know that," she reminded Sarah. "He might think if he gets rid of you and Maeve, he'll be all right."

"He'd never get away with it!"

"But you and Maeve would still be dead!" Mrs. Ellsworth said in exasperation. "Mrs. Brandt, please don't do anything until you've talked to Mr. Malloy."

The last thing Sarah wanted to do was talk to Malloy. Arguing with Mrs. Ellsworth was pointless, too. She would have to placate her. "You're right," she said, surprising her neighbor with her sudden shift in mood. "I'm too exhausted to even think clearly right now. I'll try to get some sleep and then find Malloy and talk things over with him."

Mrs. Ellsworth sighed with relief. "That's a wonderful plan. Can I do anything for you before I leave?"

"No, thanks, you've been a good friend, Mrs. Ellsworth. Run along now and don't worry about me. I'll be fine."

She didn't look as if she quite trusted Sarah's change of heart, but she did allow herself to be escorted out the back door. Sarah watched until she was safely inside her own house. She'd have to be clever to elude her neighbor's well-meaning observation, but the old woman would be expecting Sarah to go to bed, so she might not be watching very closely. Sarah could sneak out the back way, too. Mrs. Ellsworth wouldn't be expecting that.

MAEVE DEBATED CLIMBING UP THE SECRET staircase, but that wouldn't tell her anything she didn't already know. It obviously led up to the second-floor balcony and came out at another door that had been cleverly concealed in the same wooden column. Probably whoever had built the house had thought an outside staircase would be unsightly or maybe an invitation to intruders. Whatever the reason, only those who lived here would know about the staircase and be able to come and go at will. Very convenient for Kerry's secret admirers.

Iris got tired of waiting for Maeve to do something, and she slipped into the stairwell and started up the steps.

"Come here, Iris," Maeve said sharply.

For a second, she thought Iris might defy her and race up the steps, but after a second warning, the child reluctantly came back down.

333

"Don't you want to see where they go?" she asked, disappointed.

"I know where they go. Who uses them?" she asked as casually as she could, closing the door and making sure it latched.

"The bad boy," Iris said. "I'm not supposed to tell."

"I won't tell anybody that you did," Maeve promised. So much for Kerry's claim that she didn't fool around with the stable boys. Maeve supposed that if she was stuck out here in the country taking care of a crazy woman all the time, she might be tempted to do something equally stupid for a boy who made her laugh, as Iris had said. "Let's go inside where it's dry."

Iris went along without protest, and after Maeve removed her jacket and hat, she ran ahead up the inside stairs and down the hallway to the nursery. Maeve followed more slowly, glancing at the door to Christina's rooms as she did. She briefly considered going in, but she'd promised Kerry she wouldn't enter without knocking first. Kerry would be humiliated at being caught with her lover, too, and she was the kind to take revenge. Maeve could accuse her to Mrs. Alberton, of course, but if it came down to Maeve's word against Kerry's, they'd probably believe Kerry. No, catching Kerry in the act wouldn't help Maeve at all, but knowing she was there to be caught might prove useful. Maeve decided to tuck her knowledge away for the future.

Maeve and Iris passed the rest of the morning playing with Iris's dollhouse. It wasn't as nice as Catherine's because Iris had broken a lot of the furniture during past temper tantrums, but Iris didn't seem to care if the rooms were sparsely furnished. The doll family who lived in the house was somewhat the worse for wear as well, with some figures missing arms and even heads. Iris didn't seem to mind that either. In fact, only one of the figures was completely whole, and she was lying on a bed in one of the upstairs bedrooms. Iris hadn't touched her, though.

"Who's this?" Maeve asked finally, reaching for the figure.

"Don't!" Iris cried in alarm.

Maeve withdrew her hand at once.

"You can't play with her," Iris said.

"Why not?" Maeve asked.

"She's crazy," Iris informed her solemnly. "She has to be quiet."

"Like Christina," Maeve guessed.

Iris nodded.

As if on cue, Christina began to wail. The sound sent chills up Maeve's back, and Iris crawled over and silently asked to be taken in Maeve's arms for comfort. Maeve was only too happy to do so.

They sat there on the floor for what seemed a long time, until Christina's wails stopped, or at least grew quiet enough that they could no longer hear them.

"He makes noise," Iris said into the silence.

"Who does?"

"The bad boy. He must make noise. That's why she doesn't like him."

The logic was childish, but Maeve thought she followed it. Apparently, Christina got upset when Kerry had her male visitor. Iris knew Christina needed quiet, so she assumed the boy made noise that upset her. "Does she do that every time the boy visits Kerry?"

"She does it a lot," was Iris's reply.

SARAH HAD BEEN IN TOO MUCH OF A HURRY TO remember to take an umbrella with her. Luckily, her cape provided some protection against the rain that had started soon after she left the house. Not many cabs operated on Sunday, so she had to walk to Grand Central Station. Luckily, she remembered the town where the Albertons lived, and the ticket agent was able to tell her where to get off. She had to wait awhile at the station, since the trains didn't run as frequently on Sunday. The ride wasn't terribly long, but the swaying of the car lulled her into a light doze. The conductor had to awaken her for her stop. She thanked him profusely and slipped a dime into his hand in gratitude.

Once at the station, she realized she had no idea where to go from there. What had Allie said when she'd been telling Maeve their plans? Oh, yes, she'd be staying at a boardinghouse. The stationmaster seemed to know exactly whom she was trying to find and pointed her in the right direction. The rain was coming down steadily now, and even though it was only midafternoon, the sky was charcoal gray.

Sarah was thoroughly miserable by the time she found the right house. She must have looked equally miserable, because the woman who answered the door fairly turned up her nose at the sight of her.

"I don't have any rooms to let," she said.

"I don't need a room. I'm looking for someone, for Allie Shea."

"Don't tell me you're her *sister*," the woman scoffed.

"No, just a . . . a friend," Sarah said uncertainly. Had Allie told the woman to expect a visit from her sister? "I have to see her. It's very important."

The woman looked her over again, apparently worried about Sarah dripping on her floors. "I guess you'd better come in, then," she offered grudgingly. "She ain't here, though. Off on one of her jaunts."

Sarah slipped off her cape and politely shook the worst of the wet off of it, then stepped inside. "Jaunts?" she echoed.

"On that bicycle of hers. In the rain," she added contemptuously. Plainly, Allie's behavior did not fit the landlady's notions of propriety. "Put your things there," she added, pointing to a row of pegs on the hallway wall. "You can wait in the parlor."

*Bicycle?* Sarah thought as she hung up her cape. Well, she supposed that made sense. The Albertons' house was out in the country, so Allie would need a way to get to and from it every day for Maeve's messages.

The landlady had disappeared down the hall, so Sarah entered the parlor and found two women sitting near the stove. One was knitting, and the other was reading by the light of a lamp. They both looked up curiously as she entered. "You're looking for Mrs. Shea, are you?" the knitting one inquired.

"Yes, I am," Sarah replied.

"She'll be back soon," the woman informed her with authority. "She never stays out long."

"Unless she's got herself killed on that contraption of hers," the reading woman remarked sourly.

Having no other choice, Sarah sat down to wait.

Because it was Sunday, the other servants had the afternoon off, so Maeve had to fetch her and Iris's noon meal. When she took the tray back down to the kitchen, she was surprised to find the cook sitting with her feet up, reading a cast-off newspaper. As far as she could see, no preparations had been made for serving the Albertons their Sunday dinner.

"Are Mr. and Mrs. Alberton back from church yet?" she asked the cook.

The woman looked up in surprise. "They're

having dinner at somebody's house today," she said. "They won't get home until suppertime."

Maeve felt the hairs on the back of her neck prickle. This could be her chance to search Mr. Alberton's rooms for the silver-headed cane. Allie had warned her against taking foolish risks, but she wouldn't be taking any risk at all. She could put Iris down for her nap, then sneak over to the other side of the house. The rest of the servants would be off for the afternoon and Kerry would have no reason to be over there, so with the Albertons gone, she would have no fear of discovery.

She left the tray and hurried back up to the nursery. Iris was just where she'd left her, back playing with her dollhouse. She was so intent, she didn't even hear Maeve come in. Maeve stopped to listen, surprised to hear the child was actually speaking to the dolls.

"Ha-ha-ha-ha-ha," Iris was saying, pretending to laugh, but it wasn't a happy laugh. To Maeve, it sounded almost mean. Who had Iris heard laughing like that?

"No, no, don't hurt me," Iris said in a whiny voice.

Maeve knew that voice only too well, and it sent a chill up her spine. She must have made a sound, because Iris looked around and saw her. She sprang up, scattering the dollhouse furniture.

"What were you doing?" Maeve asked and knew instantly she'd made a mistake. Iris had sensed her alarm and now she was frightened.

"Nothing," the child said. "I wasn't doing nothing." She backed away and then darted into her bedroom and slammed the door shut. Maeve would have to coax her out, and even then, she probably wouldn't answer any questions.

Maeve looked down at the dollhouse. The room where Iris had scattered the furniture, the room where she'd been playing, was the dollhouse room where she'd told Maeve not to play, the room where Christina had to lie quietly. The Christina figure now lay on the floor. Maeve picked her up and examined her. Unlike all the other figures, she was in perfect condition. Iris had protected her even when she'd torn limbs off all the other dolls.

But someone else hadn't protected the real Christina, and Iris knew it. That was Christina's voice she had been imitating, begging someone not to hurt her. And the laughter could only have been Kerry's.

Not only did Kerry entertain the stable boys but she mistreated Christina, too. And now Maeve knew it.

# 15

THE INSTANT FRANK SAW THE PORTRAIT, THE maid scurried away, leaving him alone in the hall. He stepped over even closer to the stairs so he could see the painting clearly. The man did resemble Oscar Werner, but the style of his clothing told Frank it was probably a portrait of Werner's father. The man held the cane in both hands, and the silver head was plainly visible. The engraving in the silver seemed to be a crest of some kind.

Frank turned back to face the now-closed parlor door. "Mr. Werner," he called loudly enough to be heard.

An instant later, the door flew open. Werner appeared, glaring at Frank. "I told you to get out," he reminded Frank.

"I thought you said you didn't own a cane," Frank said with a meaningful glance up the staircase.

"What are you talking about?" Werner fairly exploded from the room, pushing Frank aside as he passed on his way to see what Frank had indicated.

Mrs. Rossmann had followed Werner into the hallway, but stopped just outside the door, watching Frank warily.

"What the . . . ?" Werner exclaimed, looking up as if he'd never seen the portrait that had probably hung in his stairwell for decades.

"What is it, Oscar?" Mrs. Rossmann asked in alarm.

"It's the cane your brother said he never owned," Frank replied.

Werner whirled to face him. "That belonged to my late father."

"Did you bury him with it?" Frank asked mildly.

"No, of course not," Werner snapped.

"You mean the cane in the painting?" Mrs. Rossmann asked, her eyes wide.

"Do you think I used a cane from a painting to kill a man?" Werner scoffed.

"No, I think you killed him with the cane that's in the painting, though," Frank said.

"That's ridiculous!" Mrs. Rossmann insisted.

"Utterly ridiculous," Werner confirmed angrily. "I haven't seen that cane in ages. I don't even know where it is."

"Dr. Brandt was killed *ages* ago," Frank reminded him. "Four years ago, in fact. What did you do with the cane when you were finished with it?"

"I didn't do anything with it!" Werner cried. "I haven't even seen it since my father died eleven years ago."

"That's too bad," Frank said without a trace of regret. "I guess I'll have to get some police officers in here to search your house for it. They'll probably make a mess of it, and they're not always real careful. Things could get broken," he added with a meaningful look at Mrs. Rossmann, who looked as if she might cheerfully strangle Frank.

"I can find it for you," she said through gritted teeth.

"Don't be silly, Johanna," her brother protested. "You aren't going to do any such thing. Get out of here, Malloy, and if you come back, I'll have the mayor on the telephone before you get through the door."

Frank figured he was bluffing. Nobody would call the mayor on a Sunday. Nobody could *find* the mayor on a Sunday. He didn't bother to point that out, though. He just took his hat from the hall coatrack and made his exit without another word.

There was a police call box on the corner. He figured he could easily round up half a dozen patrolmen who were bored.

SARAH WAS TOO DISTRACTED TO MAKE conversation with the two women, which was just as well because they proceeded to ignore her completely. She sat and fidgeted and stared out the window and paced the floor for at least half an hour before she finally heard an awful sound from the front of the house.

"That's Mrs. Shea," the knitting lady announced. "With her bicycle."

Sarah hurried out to the front door to find Allie Shea. She wore a hideous rain slicker and was wrestling an enormous bicycle up the porch steps. It seemed bigger than she was and twice as heavy.

"Let me help you," Sarah exclaimed, rushing to her aid.

Allie looked up in surprise. "Mrs. Brandt, what on earth are you doing here?"

"I have to talk to Maeve," Sarah said, moving to the opposite side of the bicycle and taking hold of it. The monstrous thing was even heavier than it looked. How on earth did the woman manage it by herself?

"Who's Maeve?"

Sarah looked up to see that the two ladies from the parlor had followed her out to watch Allie's struggles and had apparently chosen to eavesdrop as well.

"No one you'd know," Allie said cheerfully. "Should you be outside in this weather? You could catch a chill."

This sent the two women back into the shelter of the house, although they continued to watch the bicycle's progress through the long windows that ran on either side of the front door.

"Wait until we're alone," Allie whispered in warning.

Sarah bit back her questions while they struggled with the machine. Once they had it on the porch, Allie wheeled it around to the side of the house and leaned it up against the wall.

"I've got to get a rag and dry it off or it'll rust," she said with an apologetic smile. She started inside, but one of the ladies helpfully handed a rag out to her. Apparently, they were familiar with her routine.

Sarah waited impatiently as she watched Allie carefully rubbing the moisture from the bicycle's frame. Only then did she notice the mud spatters on Allie's boots and the hem of her dress, which was visible below the slicker. The wheels of the bicycle were coated with mud and the fenders were covered with splashes of it.

"Curse this rain," Allie said cheerfully. "When I made these arrangements, I was picturing long, pleasant rides in the country air."

Sarah felt an urge to apologize and knew that was crazy. She hadn't caused the rain. She hadn't even sent Allie and Maeve out to this godforsaken place. She glanced at the nearby window and saw the two ladies still watching them closely. "I'm sure they think you're out of your mind to be riding a bicycle in this weather."

"They're right," Allie confirmed. When she'd finished with her task, she stood back to examine her handiwork, then turned to Sarah. "Let's get someplace warm and dry, shall we?"

Sarah gladly followed her back inside. By the time Allie had hung up her slicker and removed her muddy boots, the other two ladies had resumed what must be their usual positions in the parlor and were apparently oblivious to Allie's activities. Allie led Sarah down the hall to the kitchen, where she prepared a pot of tea for the two of them, then carried it upstairs, with Sarah at her heels.

Allie's room was tiny and tucked under the eaves, making it impossible to stand upright in spots, but she had a small table with cups and spoons and a bowl of sugar on it. While the tea steeped, Allie lit the wall jets in a futile effort to cut the gloom of the rainy afternoon. The room only had one chair, so

Sarah sat on it while Allie perched on the side of the narrow bed.

"Pour the tea, will you?" Allie asked, still chafing some warmth back into her fingers.

Sarah did as instructed, and when they had both been served, Allie turned her bright gaze on Sarah again.

"So, what brings you all the way out here on this ugly day, Mrs. Brandt?"

"Like I said, I want to talk to Maeve."

"About what?" she asked innocently.

Sarah sighed, impatient with her playacting. "Malloy told Mrs. Ellsworth what Maeve found out about Christina."

"And I guess Mrs. Ellsworth told you," she said.

"Not intentionally," Sarah admitted. "She isn't a very good liar, though. I knew something was wrong the moment I saw her."

"Poor thing," Allie said sympathetically. "I'll have to give her some pointers."

Sarah shot her a murderous glare that affected her not at all. She just smiled back benignly. "And what would you be wanting from Maeve that I can't tell you?"

Sarah felt the rage welling up in her. "I . . . I just need to hear what that girl told her, in her own words."

"I can *show* you her own words if you like," Allie offered.

"You mean the notes she left?"

"That's right."

"Yes, I want to see them," Sarah decided.

"Are you sure?"

"Of course I'm sure!"

"Are you? What she found out is a pretty bad thing to hear about your husband, Mrs. Brandt."

"Do you think I don't know that?" Sarah asked in outrage.

"I think you might not want to see the words written down, all plain like that. Better if I just tell you about it."

"It doesn't matter what she found out anyway," Sarah said, trying for a bravado she didn't really feel. "None of it is true!"

"Maybe not," Allie said, taking a sip of her tea.

"What do you mean, maybe not?" Sarah asked in surprise.

"I mean, maybe it's true and maybe it isn't. If you don't know for sure, you can always make yourself believe it's not."

"I know it's not!" she insisted.

"Then why did you come all the way out here in the rain?"

Sarah's head began to ache. She closed her eyes, but that didn't help. "I have to know for sure," she said finally.

"No, you don't," Allie said, her voice still as calm and even as if they were discussing the weather. "You can get back on the train and forget you were ever here."

"It's too late for that."

"No, it isn't. You'd be surprised how easy it is once you set your mind to it. Just pretend you never heard anything bad about your husband. Forget everything else and just remember him like you knew him."

Sarah stared at her in amazement. How could she even suggest such a thing? And then she realized what Allie was doing and why she was doing it. Her hands started to shake, and her cup rattled in its saucer. She carefully set it on the table so she wouldn't break it when she found out what Allie was hiding from her. "You've heard something new, haven't you?" she said, her voice hoarse with the tears that were already building in her throat.

Allie wanted to lie. Sarah could see that, but Allie didn't bother. Instead she set her cup and saucer on the bed, reached into her pocket, and pulled out some folded pieces of paper. As Sarah felt the blood roaring in her ears, she watched as Allie carefully unfolded them.

"This one is first," she said, handing it across to Sarah, who took it with trembling fingers. "Doesn't say much, just that she got hired."

Sarah skimmed the familiar handwriting and finished with a sense of relief. Nothing alarming here. When she looked up, Allie handed her the second note without comment. Sarah found it difficult to breathe as she read the words Maeve had written so neatly. Her heart pounded in her chest as she read the awful story of how Christina had been abused. She took a minute to swallow down the lump in her throat and looked up. "There's no proof it was my husband, and he would never have done a thing like that."

Allie didn't even blink. She handed Sarah the last sheet and said, "She left this one today."

Sarah had to force her eyes to focus because her brain didn't want to comprehend the squiggles of ink that stretched across the page. She had to stare at it for a long time before the words began to make sense, and even then they didn't make sense, not really, not at all, because they were lies, terrible lies, terrible ugly lies that she would never believe, not in a million years, no matter who told them.

"Mrs. Brandt?"

Someone was calling her name, someone very far away, and then the note disappeared, snatched away by some unseen hand, and someone was kneeling in front of her, chafing her wrists and saying her name, over and over.

"Don't faint," Allie begged. "That's it. Look at me. Keep looking at me. Take a deep breath."

Sarah thought that an odd request, but when she obeyed it, she realized she'd been holding her breath or at least that she'd stopped breathing for some reason.

"That's it. Take another breath."

Sarah did, even though the pain in her chest was so great she thought there couldn't possibly be room for air in there, too. Allie picked up Sarah's cup and pressed it to her lips, forcing her to take a sip. She almost choked, but Allie kept pouring it until she swallowed it down. Then she coughed a bit, and the world came back into focus again. Sarah wanted to cry or scream or punch something. Instead, she jumped to her feet, startling Allie and nearly knocking her over from where she was kneeling in front of her.

"I need to see Maeve."

"That won't change anything."

"I still need to see her."

"If we go to the house, we'll have to take her away with us. She won't be safe there anymore after that," Allie warned.

"I don't *want* her there anymore. And I don't care if I never find out who killed Tom, if that's what you're worried about."

"Because of what Maeve heard about him?"

"No!" Sarah nearly shouted. "Because I don't want her in danger anymore. I can't stand to lose anyone else."

Allie pushed herself up to her feet. "She's not in any danger. They don't know who she is or why she's there."

"But what if they find out?" Sarah argued. "If this is true"—she indicated the notes that now lay scattered on the floor—"or even if the Albertons just *believe* it's true, he's probably the killer."

"If she's in danger, she'll give me a signal."

350

"A signal you can see from here?" Sarah scoffed.

"I check the house several times a day."

"And what if she can't send you a signal?"

"She's a smart girl," Allie reminded her. "She won't take any chances."

"I need to know she's all right."

"I can leave a note in our spot. She might get a chance to check it this evening, and she could reply to you. Would that satisfy you?"

No, it wouldn't, but Sarah knew if she pressed Allie, she wouldn't go at all. "Yes, it would. Let's do it right now."

"*You* can't go," Allie said.

"Why not?"

"All I have is my bicycle, unless you were going to run alongside of me to keep up." She glanced meaningfully out the window, where rain was still streaking down.

Sarah glared at her in frustration, but she reminded herself to be calm. Once they reached the Alberton house, Sarah could break away from Allie and find Maeve. She would just have to be careful not to let Allie guess her true intent until then. "I need to see for myself. Can we hire a wagon somewhere?"

"I don't know. It's Sunday . . . but I can try," she added quickly when Sarah would have protested. "Let's go down to the station. That's the most likely place to start, and I can send a telegram from there, too."

"Who are you going to telegraph?"

"The Agency," Allie said.

"What for?"

"To tell them you're here," Allie said. "Someone should know you're here in case something happens to us."

"Do you think something will happen to us?" Sarah asked in amazement.

"No, but I never take chances."

"What are you doing?" she asked when Allie knelt down beside her bed.

"I'm writing a note to Maeve," she said, pulling a writing box out from under the bed. In a matter of minutes, she'd scribbled a note that she didn't let Sarah read and stuffed it into her pocket. "Come on," she said, opening her bedroom door and not waiting to see if Sarah followed.

THIS TIME WHEN MALLOY POUNDED ON THE Werners' front door, Oscar Werner himself opened it. He had probably intended to throw Frank down the front steps, but the sight of the five strapping policemen behind him stopped him cold.

"Come on, boys," Frank said, pushing past Werner before he could collect his wits. The cops were streaming in after him, but the last one wasn't across the threshold before Johanna Rossmann was screaming at them to stop.

"Call them off, Malloy! I found it!" she was shouting.

Malloy called a halt to the invasion and looked up to where she stood on the landing, just in front of the portrait of her dead father and his cane.

"What do you mean, you found it?" Malloy asked in the sudden silence.

"I found the cane you're looking for, the one in the painting. Come up to the attic and I'll show you."

"Johanna, what are you doing?" Werner cried. "He's trying to prove I killed a man with it!"

"Don't worry, Oscar. I can prove you didn't," Mrs. Rossmann said, drawing herself up to her full height and staring down imperiously at Frank and his henchmen.

"How can you do that?" Werner demanded.

"Come up and see. Call off your dogs, Mr. Malloy," she said. "We have nothing to hide."

IRIS DIDN'T WANT TO TAKE A NAP. AS IF SHE sensed Maeve's desperation to be rid of her, she stubbornly refused to settle down until Maeve was forced to lie down on the bed beside her and wait in tortured agony for the child to finally, after what seemed like hours, grudgingly fall asleep.

She'd spent that time trying to figure out what she should do about stopping Kerry's abuse of Christina. She could write Allie a note and sneak out to hide it, hoping Allie hadn't already been by to pick up her message today. But even if she had, there really was no hurry. She'd be back tomorrow, and one more day wouldn't make that much difference. Allie would get her note sooner or later, and she would know what to do. Allie would take care of everything.

Yes, Allie had told her not to take foolish chances, and that was the most sensible thing to do. She could write her note to Allie with the information about Kerry abusing Christina, then search Mr. Alberton's room. That probably wouldn't take long. If she found anything, she'd add it to the note, then sneak out to hide it and be back before Iris woke up from her nap and long before the Albertons got home from their visit.

Writing the note took only a few minutes. She stuck it into her pocket, checked to make sure Iris was still sleeping soundly, then slipped quietly out into the hall. She wasn't exactly sure how to get to the Albertons' part of the house from here, but after only two false turns, she realized she needed to go downstairs and back up again. Someone had put up a wall to separate the two halves of the upstairs so the adults didn't have to see or hear the children.

But the wall hid Kerry's sins from them as well, Maeve thought bitterly as she crept quietly up the stairs to the Albertons' hallway.

The first door she opened led to a very feminine room, probably belonging to Mrs. Alberton. She doubted Mr. Alberton would hide a murder weapon in his wife's bedroom, so she continued on to the next door. It led to a more masculine room, and Maeve slipped inside.

The room smelled of pipe tobacco and leather. For a second the smells took Maeve back to one of the many rented rooms where she had lived in her childhood, sitting at her grandfather's feet while he puffed on his pipe and explained to her once again how to spot a mark. Shaking off the memory, she concentrated on remembering how Allie had told her to search a room to make sure she didn't miss anything. She started to her left, where a tall chest of drawers sat. One by one, she opened the drawers and quickly felt for the shape of anything hidden underneath the neatly folded clothes that might be a walking stick. After that came the door to a dressing room, where she quickly looked behind the door and under the furniture and in the cupboards there. Then she went back into the bedroom and examined the bed, sliding her hands beneath the mattress to see if anything felt out of place, although she couldn't imagine Mr. Alberton sleeping with a lumpy cane beneath his mattress for four years. Then the windows, which looked out over the front of the house. She searched behind the draperies and checked the window wells for anything hidden there. She'd reached his sitting area, where a pipe stand held his smoking materials, when she thought she heard a noise.

She froze, holding her breath as she listened intently. Probably it was just the large house settling or an acorn bouncing off the roof somewhere. Cook had said the Albertons wouldn't be home until suppertime. But then she heard it again. A door had opened and now it closed. Then she heard someone moving around in the next room, in Mrs. Alberton's bedroom. The sound was unmistakable because the door that connected Mr. and Mrs. Albertons' bedrooms was ajar. Why hadn't she noticed that before? Why hadn't she closed the door? Dear heaven, if Mrs. Alberton was home and had come upstairs, was her husband going to walk into his room at any second?

FRANK TOLD ONE COP TO COME WITH HIM UP to the Werners' attic and the rest to stay right there. They followed Mrs. Rossmann up the stairs with Werner close on their heels.

The attic in the Werners' house was a dreary place, cluttered with decades' worth of cast-off clothing and furnishings. Several large trunks sat beneath the eaves, covered with a thick coating of dust.

"This is insane," Werner protested as they reached the top of the steps. No one paid the slightest attention to his protests.

Mrs. Rossmann led them over to one of the trunks that stood open and partially emptied. What appeared to be a stack of old clothing sat on the floor in front of it. "These are my father's things," Mrs. Rossmann said. "The cane is in there, and it wasn't used to kill anyone. Look for yourself."

Frank couldn't imagine how she could be so certain. He looked down into the trunk and saw a long object wrapped in yellowed newspaper. He reached down and picked it up. The newspaper was as fragile as dried leaves and crumbled where he clutched it. He looked at the heavy end of the stick and saw what appeared to be badly tarnished silver through the folds of paper.

"The cane has been in that trunk for eleven years," Mrs. Rossmann said.

Frank gave her a pitying look. "There's no way to prove that," he said.

"Yes, there is," she informed him. "It's been wrapped in that paper since it was put in there. See the way the paper is molded to it? And you can't unwrap it without destroying the paper."

"Yes, but—"

"It's newspaper, Mr. Malloy. Look at it," she said triumphantly. "It's *dated*."

Frank turned to face the feeble light coming through a dusty dormer window, and he could easily read the date: April 11, 1886. Almost exactly eleven years ago.

Frank knew when he was beaten. He looked over to where Werner stood, still angry at his sister for helping the police. "Good job, Mrs. Rossmann. You've cleared your brother of a murder charge."

Fighting panic, Maeve darted as silently as she could to the hallway door. She pressed her ear to it, listening intently, but she heard nothing outside of it. Risking everything, she turned the

357

knob carefully and let the door open just a crack, just enough for her to peer out. She almost collapsed from the relief of seeing no one in the hall. She might have only a few seconds. Mr. Alberton could be coming right behind his wife. She couldn't go back the way she had come for fear of running into him. She'd never be able to explain why she was in this part of the house. She saw a door on the other side of the hall, so taking a deep breath for courage, she sidled out of the bedroom, darted across the hall, and was through the other door in no more than a second.

Not a moment too soon either, because just an instant after she'd closed the door, she heard footsteps coming down the hallway. They came closer and closer, and just when Maeve thought her heart would burst in her chest, she heard Mr. Alberton's bedroom door open and then close behind him.

She let out her breath in a whoosh, then turned to look around and see where she had escaped to. This room was furnished as a bedroom as well, but she could easily see it wasn't in use. No personal items lay on the dresser and no clothes hung in the wardrobe. She could probably hide in here until the Albertons went back downstairs, but she'd still have to risk going down the front staircase and getting caught. And Iris might wake up and call for her before they decided to go back downstairs, and then what would happen? Luckily, this room faced the rear of the house and opened onto the balcony that ran past Christina's rooms. Maeve could slip out and make her way to the secret staircase. Then she could go down to the creek, leave her note for Allie, then come back again, just as she'd planned. If she left the balcony door to this room unlocked, she could also sneak back down this way to finish searching Mr. Alberton's room when the next opportunity presented itself.

She took an extra minute to let her heart rate return to normal and then, after checking to see that the balcony was empty—no marauding stable boys paying an afternoon call on Kerry—she slipped out and started down the balcony. She fought the urge to run. No use calling attention to herself if anyone happened to be around. By the time she reached the door to Christina's rooms, she was feeling rather confident again. Allie would be proud of the way she had handled that crisis. She was just passing Christina's bedroom window when she heard a sound that froze her blood.

"Ha-ha-ha-ha-ha."

The laughter Iris had been imitating. Kerry's laughter. Only this was so much worse, so much meaner and so wicked. Almost against her will, Maeve moved closer to the window, the window that was heavily draped because sunlight disturbed Christina. No one would see Maeve standing there. And when she pressed her ear against the glass, she heard the other voice, Christina's voice, pleading desperately.

"Please, don't hurt me."

Rage was like a freight train roaring in her head. Maeve didn't hesitate a moment. She turned and raced back to the door and threw it open.

"Ha-ha-ha-ha-ha," came from the bedroom.

Maeve wanted to commit murder. She raced across the room to Christina's bedroom door and pushed it open, ready to tear Kerry limb from limb, but what she saw stopped her dead.

Kerry stood at the foot of the bed, her evil laughter dying away. Christina lay on the bed, just as she had in Iris's dollhouse, but a man was on top of her, holding her down just the way Maeve had held Iris down when she'd thrown her tantrum, holding her hands and her legs so she couldn't struggle, and Christina was pleading just as Iris had.

"Please don't hurt me!"

The man had looked up in surprise, as shocked as Maeve, or nearly so, and for a moment, no one moved or even breathed.

Kerry recovered first. "What are you doing in here? I told you never to come in here!" she screamed, but Maeve wasn't afraid of her. She wasn't afraid of anything anymore. She saw everything clearly now and knew exactly what she had to do. Kerry was coming after her, so she ran out, through the main room, across the hall, and into the nursery, pulling the doors shut behind her to slow Kerry down. Into her own bedroom and she slammed the door. Her meager belongings hung in the wardrobe. She needed only a moment to find what she wanted, then another to open the window and put it in place.

She could hear Kerry in the nursery now. She pulled open her door and stepped out to face her.

"I'm going to kill you!" Kerry cried.

"THIS IS A WILD-GOOSE CHASE," ALLIE INSISTED as they watched the stationmaster hitching up his gig. He'd agreed to allow them to rent it, providing they returned it in time for him to get home for supper.

"You don't have to go," Sarah reminded her.

"And leave you alone to do God knows what?"

Sarah looked at her, wondering how she'd known what Sarah had planned. She was as poor a liar as Mrs. Ellsworth. Maybe she should ask Allie for some pointers. But not right now.

"You sure you want to do this?" the stationmaster asked, looking up doubtfully at the leaden sky. The gig was little more than a seat between two wheels and would provide them no shelter at all from the elements.

"Oh, yes," Allie assured him cheerfully. "The rain's almost stopped now anyway, and Mrs. Brandt has to get to her patient, don't you?"

Allie had told him Sarah was a midwife and had to get to a delivery. Sarah supposed half-lies were easier to tell. She'd have to try that in the future.

361

"Yes," she said obligingly. "But Mrs. Shea will have your gig back in no time."

Sarah climbed up and Allie followed, her rubber slicker making rude noises. Settling onto the seat beside her, Sarah gladly allowed Allie to pick up the reins and slap the reluctant horse into motion.

The rain really wasn't letting up, and it stung their faces as they drove. Sarah bit back her complaints, but Allie glanced over to gauge her misery.

"Remember, this was your idea."

"How far is it?"

"Not more than two miles," she said.

Sarah managed not to groan. "And you ride your bicycle all that way?" she asked in amazement.

"You get used to it. I like to ride in the country. Not so much danger of getting run over, like in the city."

"The Albertons' son was killed riding a bicycle."

Allie just gave her a look.

Once the horse got going, he was in even more of a hurry than they were and set a brisk pace. After only half an eternity, Sarah could see a large house in the distance. "Is that it?"

"Yes," Allie said.

The rain had darkened the sky and now the sun was setting, too, somewhere behind the clouds, but still Sarah could see something odd about the house. As they drew closer, she began to make sense of what had been just a slight movement before. "Look, someone left a window open and a curtain is blowing out."

Allie's head jerked up, and she looked where Sarah was pointing.

"Dear God in heaven," Allie breathed and slapped the reins with an urgency she hadn't shown before.

"What is it?" Sarah asked in alarm as they jerked backward from the sudden increase in speed.

"That's no curtain. That's the red scarf I gave Maeve. It's her signal that she needs help."

# 16

"KILL ME?" MAEVE MOCKED. "GO AHEAD AND try."

When Kerry saw how calm she was, her fury turned to fear.

"You can't tell anyone!" she cried.

"Quiet," Maeve said. "You'll wake Iris."

Kerry anxiously glanced over her shoulder at the door to Iris's bedroom, as if she expected the child to come bounding out. "You can't tell anyone," she repeated in an urgent whisper.

"Why not?" Maeve asked.

"Kerry?" a masculine voice called.

Kerry swore in a very unladylike fashion and hurried back to the hallway, with Maeve following close behind. The man—he was a boy, really, now that Maeve had a good look at him—stood in the doorway to Christina's rooms, adjusting his suspenders. Maeve wondered idly if he was Joe or Toby.

"Get out of here, you idiot!" Kerry said in a furious whisper, racing across the hallway and pushing him back inside the room.

"But I didn't finish," he protested.

"What do I care? Get back to your horse shit!"

"I want my money back, then," he insisted, resisting her efforts to push him backward toward the balcony door.

Kerry glanced over her shoulder to see if Maeve had heard, and Maeve smiled to let her know that she had. "We'll settle up later," Kerry told him. "Now get out before you get in trouble."

The boy looked up at Maeve and for the first time he seemed to realize she might be some sort of threat to him. "I'll be back, though," he told Kerry, and then hastily made his escape, leaving the door hanging open.

"Is the doctor gone?"

Maeve's eyes widened at Christina's plaintive question coming from the other room, and she ignored Kerry's shouted warning and hurried into Christina's bedroom. Christina had pulled her nightdress down and curled up into a protective ball in the middle of the bed. Her eyes were large and terrified.

"Is he gone?" she asked Maeve.

"Yes, he's gone," Maeve assured her.

"Leave her alone," Kerry tried desperately, standing in the doorway. "You'll just upset her."

Maeve continued to ignore her. She reached down and gently stroked Christina's tousled hair. "Who was that man, Christina?"

"He's the doctor."

*The doctor.*

Maeve turned back to face Kerry. "He pays you to let him use her like that?"

"It doesn't hurt her," Kerry insisted.

"It *does* hurt me," Christina said, and Maeve managed not to wince.

"She don't know what she's saying. She's crazy," Kerry reminded her. "He pays me and so does the other one, but I'll . . . I'll split it with you now. Nobody has to know but us."

Behind her, Maeve heard Christina crying softly, but she steeled herself against the rage she felt. "I'm just trying to figure this out," she said. "How long have you been doing this?"

"What does that matter?" Kerry's voice was shrill with panic. "I'm telling you, we can split the money from now on. Do you want to be stuck here for the rest of your life? All you have to do is keep your mouth shut!"

"Why did you tell her he was a doctor?" Maeve asked, genuinely confused.

Kerry sighed in exasperation. "I had to figure out something when her belly started to swell up, didn't I?"

"You mean you've been doing this since back then, before Iris was born?"

"How do you think Iris *got* born?"

"You were selling her to stable boys that long ago?" Maeve asked, trying to make her horror sound like plain old amazement.

"Stable boys and their friends," Kerry snapped. "What does it matter?"

"But you said it was a doctor," Maeve reminded her.

Kerry threw her hands up in frustration. "When they found out about the baby, I had to tell them *something*, and then I remembered that doctor had been to see her, so I said he must've done it."

"And they believed you?"

"Of course they believed me!"

Maeve had never been so angry in her life, but it wasn't like any other anger she'd ever experienced. It burned like a white-hot flame in her chest, and she felt amazingly calm and powerful, as if she could even stop time if she wanted to. She started walking toward where Kerry stood in the doorway.

Kerry watched her in surprise and instinctively stepped back when Maeve gave no indication she would hesitate to knock her over if she needed to. "What are you doing?" Kerry asked in renewed panic as Maeve passed her and headed for the hall door. "Where are you going?"

"I'm going to tell them," Maeve said simply.

"Tell who? Wait! Don't go! You can have more

366

money! Is that what you want? You can have *all* of it!" Kerry cried. "Stop!"

But Maeve didn't stop. She'd almost reached the doorway to the hall when Kerry gave a strangled cry and charged. She struck Maeve in the back and sent her sprawling.

The shock immobilized her for a second, just long enough for Kerry to roll her over, climb on her chest, and put her hands around Maeve's throat. Maeve looked up into Kerry's eyes and saw true madness.

"FASTER!" SARAH CRIED. "CAN'T YOU GO ANY faster?"

"Not in this mud," Allie shouted back. "The horse might slip and break a leg." Her gloved hands clenched the reins as the horse's flying hooves threw clods of mud back on them.

Sarah strained to see the house, which didn't seem to be getting any closer. She could see the red scarf clearly now, fluttering in the wet wind.

"If she was able to put it out, she can't be in too much danger," Allie argued.

Sarah was still praying as hard as she could. Why had the Albertons built their house so far off the road? she wondered wildly as Allie managed to turn the horse into the drive. It would take them forever to reach the front door! She wanted to jump out and run. Surely, she could go faster than this! But she forced herself to hang on, knowing that was

367

just an illusion, and the horse would be the fastest way to get them there. Allie sawed on the reins as they finally, after an eternity, reached the house. Sarah was on the ground in an instant, pounding on the front door before Allie could tie off the reins.

Then Allie was beside her, pounding, too.

"Where are they?" Sarah demanded. "Why don't they answer?"

Allie stepped back and looked up at the house, as if trying to figure out an alternate entry point. Then she reached out for the doorknob and tried it. To their amazement, it turned and the door swung open.

Allie muttered something that sounded like, "Country people," but Sarah was already inside, calling for Maeve.

A middle-aged woman who was obviously a kitchen servant was coming down the entry hall toward them. "Hey, there, what're you doing, busting in like that! Wait, you're getting mud all over the floor!"

"Where's Maeve?" Sarah demanded.

"Who wants to know?" the woman asked, outraged.

"I'm her aunt," Allie said, managing to sound reasonable. "There's been an emergency, and we have to fetch her right away."

"Well, why didn't you say so?" the woman said in disgust, convincing Sarah she really did need some pointers in lying from Allie. "I'll get her for you."

And then they heard the scream.

• • •

MAEVE HESITATED ONLY AN INSTANT BEFORE reaching up and raking her nails across Kerry's face. Kerry screamed and loosed her grip just enough that Maeve was able to throw her off. Kerry got a fistful of her hair, though, and then they were rolling across the floor, kicking and clawing. Maeve came around on top just as they crashed into the piecrust table, and the edge caught her on the forehead, knocking her to the floor. In a flash, Kerry was on her again, choking her, and this time she'd braced her knees on Maeve's arms, so she couldn't fight back. Maeve was bucking and struggling frantically, but she couldn't dislodge Kerry, who was staring down at her with naked hatred as she choked the life from her. Black spots were dancing before Maeve's eyes, which was why she wasn't sure exactly what happened next. She heard a crash, and water and flowers and broken glass came raining down on her, and Kerry's hands were no longer around her throat. Sucking in great gasps of precious air, Maeve shoved Kerry's weight off her and sat up. Kerry was moaning and reaching for a large red gash on her temple. Christina stood over them both.

"I had to make her stop hurting you," she told Maeve.

Maeve realized she was covered with the wildflowers Iris had given Christina yesterday. Was it only yesterday? Christina had smashed the glass that held them over Kerry's head. Then Maeve heard someone calling her name in a very familiar voice.

Sᴀʀᴀʜ ꜱᴀᴡ ᴛʜᴇ ᴏᴘᴇɴ ᴅᴏᴏʀ ᴅᴏᴡɴ ᴛʜᴇ ʟᴏɴɢ hallway, so she headed toward it, with Allie and the other woman close behind her. What she saw when she got there stopped her, and Allie nearly knocked her over.

"What is it?" Allie demanded, pushing Sarah unceremoniously out of the way so she could see. Maeve and another girl were on the floor and a third girl, clad only in a nightdress, stood over them. "Maeve, are you all right?"

Sarah and Allie rushed over to help Maeve to her feet. She was rubbing her forehead and looked slightly dazed.

"Watch out for the glass," the girl in the night-dress said. "I had to hit Kerry on the head."

The other girl still lay on the floor, moaning softly, and blood was running down the side of her face from a gash on her temple. What looked like bunches of wildflowers were scattered all over both girls.

"You're all wet," Allie observed to Maeve. She and Sarah were helping Maeve shake the shards of broken glass from her clothes.

Then Sarah realized the girl in the nightdress was barefoot. "Be careful, dear, or you'll cut your feet," she said, leaving Maeve to Allie's care. She led the girl away from the broken glass

370

and sat her down on a chair. "Are you all right?"

She looked up at Sarah with eyes so sad, Sarah thought her heart might break. That's when she realized who the girl was.

"Are you Christina?"

The girl seemed pleased that Sarah knew her name. "Yes, I am. I'm Christina Alberton. Have we met?"

"She tried to kill me," Maeve said, surprising them all.

Sarah looked up in alarm, but Maeve was glaring down at the girl on the floor.

"She *did* try to kill her," Christina confirmed. "Kerry had her hands around Maeve's neck. That's why I hit her with the glass. She'll be mad at me now."

"It doesn't matter if she is," Maeve said gently, coming over to Christina and laying a comforting hand on her shoulder. "You don't have to be afraid of her anymore. She's leaving here, and she'll never be back."

Allie was helping Kerry sit up when they heard a commotion out in the hallway. Then a middle-aged man burst into the room. "What's going on here?" He looked around, trying to make sense of what he saw. "Who are you people and what are you doing here?"

"She tried to kill me, Mr. Alberton," the girl Christina had called Kerry cried suddenly, pointing at Maeve. "She attacked me for no reason!"

"Liar!" Maeve cried, but Sarah took her arm to restrain her when she would have gone after Kerry again.

"She is a liar, Father," Christina said calmly, rising from where Sarah had seated her and looking oddly dignified in the midst of this startling scene. "She was the one who attacked Maeve."

"Why would she do a thing like that?" Mr. Alberton asked, obviously at a loss to understand any of this.

Just then a small, well-dressed woman rushed into the room, followed by the servant who had met them downstairs. They were both panting. The woman who must be Mrs. Alberton took in the amazing scene in one quick glance and said, "Good heavens, Kerry, you're bleeding!"

Kerry cried out, putting a hand to her head, but Allie grabbed her hand and sat her down before she could get hysterical. "It's nothing but a scratch," she insisted.

"Will someone tell me what's going on?" Mr. Alberton said. "And who are you, madam?" he asked Allie.

"I'm Allie Shea of the Pinkerton Detective Agency," Allie said, drawing gasps from Kerry and the Albertons.

"And so am I," Maeve said, exaggerating slightly. "And I found out something terrible this afternoon, Mr. Alberton. I found out Kerry has been selling your daughter to the stable boys."

"You lying bitch!" Kerry screamed, jumping up from her chair, but Allie caught her easily and slammed her back down again.

"Go on, Maeve," Allie said, pinching Kerry's shoulder in a way that made her reluctant to try moving again.

"What do you mean, selling her to the stable boys?" Mr. Alberton asked.

"They sneak up here on the secret staircase, and they use her like a whore," Maeve said baldly, this time drawing gasps from everyone. "They pay Kerry for letting them do it. I know because she offered to let me have half the money if I didn't tell you."

"Kerry, that can't be true," Mrs. Alberton cried, aghast.

"She's lying!" Kerry insisted slightly less forcefully than before, since Allie still had her by the shoulder.

"That's not all." Maeve continued as if Kerry hadn't spoken. "She's been doing it for years, since she first started taking care of Christina. I know she told you it was a doctor who got Christina with child, but it wasn't. Kerry made that up so you wouldn't find out what she was doing."

This time Sarah gasped, covering her mouth to hold back the emotions flooding through her—relief and dismay and horror over the evil Kerry's lies had caused.

"She said they were doctors," Christina said

softly. "She said that was my treatment, to make me better."

Mrs. Alberton made a strangled sound and looked very much as if she might faint. The servant who had come upstairs with her took her arm, led her over to a chair, and helped her sit down.

But Sarah was watching Mr. Alberton's face. All the blood had drained out of it, leaving him pale and stunned. "You told me it was the doctor," he said, staring at Kerry as if he'd never seen her before. "We trusted you. You said it was the doctor!" he nearly shouted, as feverish spots bloomed in his cheeks.

"Which doctor did she tell you it was?" Allie asked. "Dr. Brandt?"

Alberton's whole body jerked, as if she had struck him. "How did you know?" he asked wildly.

"Because someone killed Dr. Brandt shortly after that."

"He only wrote a letter," Mrs. Alberton said quickly, defensively. "He wrote a letter to someone about what that doctor had done to Christina. That's all he did."

"Is it, Mr. Alberton?" Allie asked, sounding amazingly like Malloy. "Is that all you did? You just wrote a letter to Felix Decker and then forgot all about the doctor who had ruined your daughter?"

"Yes, that's all," Alberton confirmed, his voice strained. "That's all I did!"

Sarah was surprised to her hear own voice

responding. "I don't think so, Mr. Alberton," she said, fairly trembling with rage. "I think you wanted revenge. I think you tricked him into meeting you and then you killed him!"

Alberton stared at her in horrified silence, his lips moving but no sound coming out.

"You *killed* him?" Kerry asked in amazement.

He turned to her almost in relief. "I killed him because of *you*!" he cried in anguish. "You lying bitch!"

Kerry sprang to her feet and, wrenching free of Allie's grip, bolted for the still-open door to the balcony. Before anyone could react, Alberton ran after her.

"Father!" Christina cried.

Allie was the first one after him, with Sarah not far behind. For a second, Sarah couldn't imagine where Kerry was going, since the balcony simply ended at a brick wall. Then she saw part of the wooden column swing out, and she remembered what Maeve had said about a secret staircase. Kerry ducked inside, but the moment she'd lost opening the door had been a moment too long. Alberton lunged for her, and they both disappeared into the stairwell. Just as Allie reached the door, they heard a horrible scream and then an awful, muffled thud.

When Sarah reached the door, Allie was scrambling down the spiral staircase, her shoes making a clanging sound on the metal as she ran. Sarah stopped at the top to peer over. Alberton and Kerry had gone over the railing and down into the stair-well. Instinct told her to follow Allie down and try to help, but she didn't move. She didn't want to help either of these people who had killed Tom. She wanted them both to die.

SITTING IN FELIX DECKER'S PARLOR, MALLOY felt as out of place as a whore in church. Or maybe it wasn't being in the Deckers' house at all. Maybe he just felt awkward because he had no idea how to act with Sarah after what had happened.

"How are you feeling?" he asked her. She was sit-ting across from him on a sofa that probably cost as much as he made in a year.

"I'm trying not to feel at all," she confessed. "Did Allie tell you I went up there to bring Maeve home? I didn't want to find out who had killed Tom any-more. I just wanted everything back the way it was before."

"I shouldn't have—"

"Oh, Malloy, don't blame yourself!" She stopped him impatiently. "I wanted it. It's not your fault I changed my mind."

They sat in silence for a few seconds, and then she asked, "What's happened to them?"

She didn't have to explain whom she meant. "Mrs. Alberton didn't want to bring charges against Kerry," he said, taking the easiest one first. "She didn't want any more scandal, and Christina could never have given evidence against her anyway."

"Has Kerry gotten any better?"

"No, she still can't move her legs, and the doctors say she never will."

"What will become of her?"

"They're sending her to Blackwell's Island," he said, naming the island that housed an assortment of refuges for the dregs of society nobody wanted around.

"There's some justice in that, I suppose," she mused.

"Probably more than if she hadn't been injured and was just sent to jail," Frank said.

"What do you mean?"

"A crippled girl who can't fight for herself? She'll never get enough to eat, and if she gets sick, nobody will care. She'll suffer worse than Christina did, and she probably won't last long out there."

He watched the emotions play across Sarah's beautiful face, and his own heart ached with her pain. "It's all right," he said.

"What is?"

"To hate her. To want to see her suffer. I wish I still believed. I'd like to think of her burning in hell."

Her eyes filled with tears, but she angrily blinked them away. "She hurt so many people."

And drove Alberton to murder an innocent man, he thought. "Alberton won't go to trial."

"He won't?" she asked in surprise.

"I brought charges against him," he quickly

explained, "and he's in the Tombs, but . . . he isn't going to live long enough."

"Why not? I didn't think he was that badly hurt."

"He wasn't, but . . . I guess he couldn't live with the guilt of what he'd done. He stopped eating and . . . I got a message today that he has pneumonia." They both knew that was a death sentence.

Sarah sighed. "Somehow, I don't hate him as much as I hate Kerry. He killed Tom, but . . . I guess I can understand why he would want to murder the man he thought had done that to his helpless child. If someone did that to Catherine . . ."

"I know," he said. "I know."

Frank glanced around the richly appointed room with its velvet draperies and gold-leaf picture frames, and remembered a long-ago conversation he'd had with Sarah's father. Felix Decker had wanted to find Tom Brandt's killer because he thought the truth would bring Sarah back home. He had been right. "You said you wanted everything back the way it was before, and now it is," he said.

"What do you mean?"

He shrugged his broad shoulders. "You're back here with your family. You're home."

"Is that what you think?" she asked in surprise.

"It's the truth." She'd been living at her parents' home for over a week now.

"No, it's not," she assured him. "I'm only . . . I needed some time to recover after what happened,

Malloy. To come to terms with Tom's death once and for all and to mourn him all over again. And I didn't want to go home without Maeve to look after Catherine." Maeve had stayed behind at the Alberton house for a while to make sure Christina and the little girl were all right and that they got someone competent to look after them both.

"Mrs. Ellsworth would have helped out."

"I know, but I didn't want to impose on her, and ... and I have to admit, I've enjoyed being here and letting my mother spoil me a bit. Catherine enjoys it, too, but as soon as Maeve comes back, I'm going home. To my real home."

"Are you sure?" he asked uncertainly.

"Of course I'm sure."

Frank felt relief wash over him like a wave. When he looked at her again, she was smiling that smile she wore when she knew something he didn't. "What?" he asked.

"What if I'd told you I'd decided to stay here? What would you have done?"

"What do you mean?" he hedged.

"Would you have tried to convince me not to?" she asked with a playful grin. "Would you have broken in one night and carried me off to rescue me?"

He gave her one of his glares, which never seemed to affect her the way they affected everyone else in the world. "If I carried you off, it wouldn't be to rescue you."

"Oh, really?" she asked in mock surprise. "And what, pray tell, *would* it be for?"

"You don't want to know," he assured her.

"Oh, Malloy," she said, shaking her head. "I most certainly *do* want to know, so why don't you come over here and tell me?"

# Author's Note

I HOPE YOU ENJOYED THIS BOOK AND ARE AS happy as I am to finally have Tom Brandt's murder solved! I'd like to offer special thanks to author/clinical psychologist Mary Kennedy for helping me identify the correct diagnosis for the disorder that Tom Brandt was investigating. I first introduced it in *Murder on Lenox Hill* with Miss Edna White. The disorder I have called "Old Maid's Disease" was first referenced in ancient times in the works of Hippocrates, Erasistratus, Plutarch, and Galen. In 1623, it was described in a treatise by Jacques Ferrand called *De la maladie d'amour ou mélancholie érotique.* Through the years, it has been called old maid's psychosis, erotic paranoia, and erotic self-referent delusions, and is currently called erotomania or de Clerambault's syndrome. Individuals suffering from this disorder often engage in the behavior we now call "stalking." In this book, I have used the four characters who exhibit erotomania to illustrate several different manifestations of the disorder. Edna White and Amelia Goodwin are delusional stalkers who frequently have had little or no contact with their victims and actually believe they are having a relationship with their victims even though they might never even have met. Ordella Werner is a love-obsessed stalker, the type who becomes obsessed with a person with whom she has had no close personal relationship and develops a completely fantasized relationship with the victim. When affection is not returned, the stalker often reacts with threats, intimidation, and even violence. Christina Alberton is said to be suffering from dementia praecox, which is what we now know as schizophrenia. While some schizophrenics also exhibit erotomania, Christina's erotomanic symptoms were fabricated by her caregiver, as you now know.

In the course of writing this book, I had occasion to research stalkers and their unfortunate victims. I learned that many states have passed tougher laws to enable them to prosecute stalkers before they actually become violent, but not all states have followed suit. A law that does not allow law enforcement officials to take action until a stalker becomes violent is grossly inadequate, since in most cases, the stalker's first act of violence ever is to kill or attempt to kill his or her victim. If you or someone you know is being stalked, please do not take it lightly or hope that ignoring it will make the stalker stop. To find out how to protect yourself, contact the National Center for Victims of Crime at www.ncvc.org/src or 1-800-FYI-CALL.

Please let me know how you liked this book by contacting me through my website at www.victoriathompson.com.